I LOVE A GOOD PARTY

By
JONATHAN
REISLER

Copyright @ Jonathan Reisler 2024

Cover Design: Jonathan Reisler

Contact: stickyaka@gmail.com

All rights reserved. No part of this publication may be reproduced, stored in a retrieval system or transmitted in any form or by means, electronic or mechanical, including photocopying, recording, scanning or otherwise (except in the case of brief quotations embodied in critical articles or reviews) without the written permission of the author or publisher.

All characters appearing in this work are fictitious. Any resemblance to real persons, living or dead, is purely coincidental.

Chapter One

"On a clear day, how it will astound you, that the glow of your feelings outshines every star, you feel part of every mountain, sea and shore, you can hear, from far and near, a world you've never heard before."

—*Alan Jay Lerner/Lane Burton*

"You're going to New York City! You're going to New York City! Oh my God. David! It says *MLI, 2 World Trade Center, 80th floor*!" gushed Jane, his sister. "I am speechless. Oh my God...you did it, Dave! Mom! Mom!"

.

.

.

.

.

VVVVRRRROOOOMMM!!!
SSSSMMMMMAAASSSSHHH!!!!!!

Zzzzt! Zzzzt! Zzzzt! Zzzzt! Zzzzt! Zzzzt!

A BlackBerry cell phone, its shiny glass face now cracked, had been set on *vibrate*.

It landed next to David's twitching body after the second plane hit. The phone buzzed, like a chainsaw, incessantly. It woke David up, but only for a few precious seconds.

Just moments before the impact, David was finishing up a phone call and running frantically into the MLI boardroom for a one-on-one meeting with Ellery, his boss and mentor, to discuss what had just happened to Tower 1. No one knew what to do next. Then, life as he knew it, as we knew it, was changed forever.

"GET THE HELL OUT OF THERE NOW!!" screamed a voice on the other end of the line.

It was too late.

David was dying. His chest had been pierced by a huge glass dagger, a chunk of the shattered boardroom window. He bled profusely. He choked, then gurgled.

"What happened?" asked *the world*.

It didn't really matter. Everyone was dead. Everything was dead. For all intents and purposes, David was dead, as well.

"Can you hear me?? Can anybody hear me, man?? Jesus. Are you people even alive?? Can you walk?? Get the fuck outta there!!! Now!!! Go to the stairwell…"

The line went dead. Immediately thereafter, the second tower collapsed.

Those poor, damned souls, those trapped in the World Trade Center towers when the planes hit them, all went to hell, or at the very least, the closest thing to it that existed on Earth. Every living thing on our dear Mother Earth has the essence of creation in it but on the morning of 9/11, there ceased to be living things in Manhattan, for time itself had stopped.

On display? The inequities of the ant hill. What people did for one another just to get out of the towers alive before the last grain of sand fell was heroic, godly even. Quashed that day? Any hope for mankind to further blossom. Revealed? How terror affects our own sense of mortality. People were reduced to crawling corpses, corpses looking for any way they could to escape the inferno. Some of them jumped.

A kind soul carried out what was left of David Stevens from the rubble of 2 World Trade Center. It was an act of pure love for one's fellow man. David was somewhere in between life and death, so he never got the name of the angel who saved him.

Good and evil displayed themselves to everyone who lived through the morning of September the 11th, 2001. This was not God's work, it was just proof that if there was a God, he didn't care much for the folks on Wall Street.

Somebody up there loved David Stevens, or *Dave*, as his friends called him. He died in the back of an ambulance that day, but his problems only began afterwards, when they resuscitated him.

Chapter Two

"Girl, you think you've had loving, girl you think you've had fun, girl you ain't a seen nothin' 'til I come along, I'm a daddy, I'm a daddy, I'm a daddy, yeah, I'm a daddy, daddy, I'm daddy rolling stone."

—*Pete Townshend*

"This one's a live one!!!!"

"Get him in!!! STAT!!!"

David Stevens began his career on Wall Street as a newly-minted associate in mergers and acquisitions during the summer of 2001. He didn't work there very long. He had a promising career ahead of him according to Ellery McTier, COO and senior partner at McTier and Longley Investments, *MLI*, the No. 1 firm in town.

Ellery recruited David right out of U of Penn-Wharton. David was a top-five candidate according to the faculty; not No. 1, but *top-five*, for certain. Top-fives were most notable. They were the ones who worked their asses off to get there. You wanted a top-fiver. Nothing came easy for them, they didn't cost a lot to start, they were reliable, loyal and unassuming. The best of all for Ellery? Small towns. Most top-fivers came from a suburb or a satellite, never a big show, never a big city, and if they did, they came from poor neighborhoods. It was consistent in every one of their profiles. David came from West Mifflin, a small town not too far from Pittsburgh.

"Can't miss."

Joining the MLI firm that summer was David's greatest achievement. He fulfilled a promise he made to his ex-Marine, Vietnam-veteran father that he would graduate from Wharton and never return to West Mifflin; David lived up to his word by landing the job in New York.

"Only coming back to bring presents for birthdays and holidays," David told his mother, "That was the deal."

David earned this damn-good opportunity. He busted his tail off as a bartender, delivery man, playing poker and selling pot to pay for his tuition at Wharton. His family could never afford it and he wasn't going to be able to live a proper life shouldered with debt, fiscal or emotional. He knew his father was looking down from the heavens, smiling. Cancer denied the man the chance to see his son in that nice, clean, Brooks Brothers suit and tie, let alone the black, well-polished Rockport shoes. *"Shiny boots,"* his dad called them.

The final time David saw his mentor Ellery McTier was when he opened his only functioning eye and found Ellery laying next to him, decapitated, the rest of his body smoldering in flames, blood flowing out of shards of broken glass that had lodged themselves into his lifeless limbs and torso.

The final time David saw the McTier and Longley Investments offices was when he looked up from a stretcher, unable to breathe, his ribs all but crushed, and saw the office, and the rest of the World Trade Center towers, laying in ruins.

David was chucked into the back of an ambulance with several other charred and mangled victims. As it fled from the scene, one of the victims to David's immediate right gasped and died. David looked out the window but he couldn't see anything. The ambulance itself had been engulfed by a monster of dust and debris, flying paper and screaming people, a harbinger of what would become our world today.

Then, with one long, final exhale, *David* died.

Beep. Next Message.

"Good morning, *Steel-town*. It's *Shawna*. You know that. Ha! Some of the girls are going out for drinks tonight, and Cathy asked me if *you* would like to join. She wasn't really subtle about it. I think she likes you, dude. Why wouldn't she? I like you, dude. I think I better make that clear to her. Anyhoo, if you want to join in, send me an email at lunchtime and we'll, uh, hook it up! Love you. You fed Chuckles, right?"

Beep. Next message.

"Dave! Dude, that game last night was off the charts! We got so stoned we barely saw it finish. Giants suck. Can't even beat Brian Griese? That's so fucked up. Glad I listened to you. Made a shitload of coin off your new bud Billy from downstairs in asset management. He's really not too cool. Almost backed out of the bet! Anyhow man, free lunch on me. Free, free, free! See you at the office for a bong hit, knucklehead. It's Lester. Pffft!"

Beep. Next message.

"Yoooo! Dave, man! It's Bill. My freakin' head. Your friendly co-worker Lester? That dude is a beast. Remind me never to watch football with him. Yo, that weed we smoked? Made me hallucinate, bro. He was, like, *"c'mon, Billy, you're such a lightweight."* Hey, I'm no Rastafarian, y'know? I've been puking my brains out all morning. I am so sick right now. Not going to work today. No way. Ellery and 2 World Trade can do without me this fine Tuesday morning. Please pity me. You want to come by after work? Shit! It's barely 6 a.m. Jesus Christ! I'm going back to sleep..."

Beep. Next Message.

"David. David, oh lord. David, call me. It's mother. I'm watching the news. Dear Lord, please call me. I need to know you are alright. It's mother. I will try you again."

Beep. Next message.

"David. It's mother. Please, David. Please call me. I love you son, I'm so worried. Are you okay? Please call. If you can, please call."

Beep. Next Message.

"Click. All our networks are busy at this time. If you'd like to make a call, please hang up and try again. This is a recording. Please hang up now. If you'd like to make a call, please hang up and try again. This is a recording. Please hang up now...."

Chapter Three

"Everybody that's on my block, they're tired of me, that ain't no shock, and I ain't got no idols, I ain't got much taste, I'm shiftless when I'm idle, I got time to waste."
—Paul Westerberg

"You know he wants to, but who knows if he's, like, *sane*?" said Lorena.

There was a pause.

"I've tried for months," replied Billy impatiently, "his therapist says he'll snap back sooner or later and he'll say *yes*. I'll call you back, babe. He just called me on my cellphone."

Dave overheard their conversation through his receiver. He knew it was time. Billy was well-intentioned, but Billy also reminded Dave of the past, when things looked promising.

Time passes. People change. Circumstances change.

Dave's reasons for wanting to work on Wall Street in the first place died with his father, but the future Dave had envisioned for himself in the investment world once he got there and began work at MLI died with Ellery McTier, the COO of MLI, a man who truly believed in Dave's potential.

In the *perfect,* as he and Shawna, the girl Dave fell madly in love with, would refer to it, Dave would soon become a partner at McTier and Longley, they'd get married, Cathy would serve as Shawna's maid of honor and Lester would be

Dave's best man. Shawna planned on having twin daughters, living in Scarsdale, and sooner or later, in the *perfect*, Dave would scratch the door of his Volvo on a tricycle the twins left at the entrance to their driveway. That was how Shawna described their future together, and that became Dave's life when he spent endless months in a coma after 9/11. Scarsdale, the Volvo, the tricycle, Shawna. His world was just that, an imaginary one, the *perfect,* nothing more, nothing less, until they brought him out of it.

The recurring *perfect.*

It never changed.

It was as real as anything.

Dave told every therapist who saw him, over and over again, how vivid the dream was, how haunting, how he couldn't shake it at night, how he didn't want to fall asleep because he didn't want to go to that world, and once he was in it, how he didn't want to wake up.

Of course, they understood.

Therapy wasn't going to cure him entirely; losing Shawna was more painful and more difficult a puzzle to solve than any of his other injuries.

Head trauma. That's what they called it. Easy diagnosis.

He discussed his nightmares, menageries of frightening images from his last glance back at Ellery and the dead, their severed bodies wasting away among the dust, debris, and ashes. They prescribed stuff, because they told Dave that his condition was just temporary.

His slightly-damaged vision could see small scars from healed wounds on his arms, legs, chest, but the real damage, the damage to Dave's soul remained hidden from view and would remain that way. It was impossible for him to articulate those feelings, to the therapists, to anyone. Dave was a very broken man.

Like all those who lived to tell a tale from that cauldron of evil forever known as 2 World Trade Center, Dave Stevens' emptiness and multiple personal losses were emotional baggage that would never go away. No therapy, drugs, alcohol, or other vices could ease his sorrow.

Time. Dave just needed time.

"Improvement comes with time, Mr. Stevens."

Therapists always preached patience.

The rest of 2001 didn't exist for Dave; he lived in the *perfect*. He was only brought out his coma in early January of the following year.

The entire year 2002 was spent recovering; it challenged Dave physically, but more so, spiritually. He remained in his uptown apartment for the most part, constantly visited by a parade of doctors and therapists, but by the summer of 2003, all that remained of his wounds were a few chipped teeth and some scarring on his chest and forehead. Beyond a fresh prescription to correct his vision and a new pair of glasses, the doctors' jobs were complete. They were able to put Humpty Dumpty back together again. Dave had no excuse to put his life on hold any longer.

Everyone Dave knew and loved in New York City died in 2 World Trade Center on 9/11, everyone that is, except Billy. Billy was an acquaintance and co-worker of Dave's; they weren't really what one would call *friends*. Billy was hungover and missed work at MLI that morning. Lucky him.

Billy spent a lot of his spare time visiting Dave and accompanying him on his numerous appointments and small surgeries in the wake of the tragedy, but it was rather obvious Billy did so mostly out of the guilt he felt for having slept through the whole disaster.

Dave was insolvent. He hadn't worked a day since the beginning of the end of his beginning, so to speak. Whatever money he'd earned at MLI went towards student loans, the move from Philly to New York, furniture, rent. Insurance settlements from the tragedy languished in the grey zone of 9/11 lawsuits, so Dave had virtually nothing to fall back on and nothing coming in. He was unproductive. It was *"go-time,"* his father's ghost whispered.

Dave lived in a one-bedroom apartment uptown. His refrigerator, at all times, was barren, his pet cat was sneaky and annoying, always hungry, and his next-door neighbor, although quite loveable, was very, very intrusive. He had Billy's friendship, but Dave didn't socialize with him, or anyone for that matter, very much. His entire social life vanished on 9/11.

He was lonely.

"*Sorry Dave.* Yeah. I had to take the other line. I hope you don't you mind that I kept you waiting," said Billy.

"Yeah, okay. So, what's the deal?" Dave replied.

Billy was in shock. Dave was finally ready for his first real night on the town since the tragedy. The shattered glass was open to the idea of crazy glue.

"What? Hey, yeah man! That's it! That's the spirit! Dave, my man! So, listen up..." Billy could not contain his excitement. "I met this crazy chick. Her name is Lorena. She's a lot like *Shawna*..."

Billy paused. That might have blown the whole deal right then and there. It was an accident. Talking about Shawna was a nuclear bomb. The therapist told Billy to refrain from mentioning her *specifically*.

"Sounds wild, go on...," Dave replied.

That was a close one. Billy got lucky.

"Lorena works at this bar on B Street. I was waiting there for a client who never showed up and well, you know, Lorena is feeling bad for me..."

"*Billy?*" said Dave, impatiently.

"Okay. Okay. Well, we're sipping back a few Rolling Rocks. You know me, can't deal with Bourbon. She just comes right out and asks me if I want to have sex with her once her shift is over. Wow! Could not have been easier. I'm figuring she must have a set of balls under that belt, but no, no, it's all good. I lounge around until she gets off at 3 a.m., and wouldn't you know it? She changes her mind about the sex and just wants to walk around and shoot the shit with me until the sun comes up. My luck. I meet a *nice girl.* She's really cool, though, and she knows a lot of people, man. *A lot.*"

Billy kept things interesting for Dave, his thoughts were convoluted, he had twice as many questions as he did answers, and he never had a concrete plan of his own, but at least he met someone and he had a social life, one that Dave sorely lacked.

"Hey, that sounds really sweet. You charmed your way out of sex, William. I'm really proud of you."

Dave made a joke. That was huge. Before the world changed, Dave wasn't exactly the class clown to begin with, a joke was rare. This one had a lot of significance.

"Funny, Dave. Oh. I get your point. Yeah. Well, we're walking around in Midtown and she says she finds me attractive. Does that mean *relationship* attractive?"

Billy's scattered thinking was one of many reasons why he never received a promotion at McTier. Billy had a tendency to lie and take advantage of situations. He used Dave as a barometer all the time because Dave was smarter and much more intuitive.

"Are you going to see her again?" asked Dave.

"Yes! That's it! Of course, I remember now. She said she wanted to get together on Monday, after work," said Billy, "something about a party."

"You mean, at 3:00 a.m.?"

"No. No. No. She's not working Monday night. I'm working on Monday."

"That you are, William, but during the day."

Dave had loosened his proverbial tie.

"Yes! When I'm done, I'm supposed to swing by this art gallery or something. I have the address. She's bringing a friend, *I might add*. Free drinks. It'll be chill... Are you up for it? I'm sorry, Dave. Too much, too soon?"

Dave left Billy hanging for a moment. There was always a degree of uncertainty when it came to Dave's personal issues. Billy could never predict whether Dave was well enough to go out or not. It was a day-to-day decision, and up to that point, Dave had always declined. Billy didn't want to push too hard.

"Just drinks? I thought you said we're going to a *party*?" replied Dave, enthusiastically.

"Yes, I did say that, didn't I? Sure. Sure, I mean, if you're ready, man."

"As ready as I will ever be," replied Dave.

Billy was amped up.

"Man, that's great, Dave Stevens! Friggin' great to hear. So, here is the dilly-o. Lorena's girlfriend's name is Patricia. *But don't call her that*. She only answers to *Trish*. Lorena will, of course, introduce her as Patricia, but you are to introduce yourself and say 'Hi, *Trish*, pleased to meet you.' That's it. The girl is peculiar. Then again, so is Lorena. Trish. Repeat after me."

"Trish."

"Good! Dave, you do that, only that, and you save us 15 minutes of having to listen to the Trish/Patricia story. She told it to me. You'll learn all about why she hates her mother, the whole 9 yards. It will really weird you out."

"Okay. Copy that. *Trish* it is." Dave replied.

"Super, man." Billy continued. "Now, this chick Trish has another girlfriend named Zulu."

"*Zulu*?"

"Yes, that's what she said. *Zulu*. Trish told Lorena that her girlfriend Zulu works or has or owns this art gallery on Lafayette. Something like that."

"Lorena's friend Trish's girlfriend Zulu? Owns an art gallery? Am I getting it right?" asked Dave.

"Exactly!" said Billy. "I only met Trish, like, once. I've never met Zulu. I don't know who she is. Anyhow, Monday nights, they have these open mic things; painters, poets, rappers, these *pseudo-vernissages*. Cool New York people. Mostly freaking wealthy, art-buying folk. They hang out, check out paintings, drink free champagne, eat caviar, designer cupcakes, and hook up, I guess."

"Pseudo. Vernissage. Those are big words for you, William. That's not *short the mortgages*. That's *Soho-speak*."

"There's a catch," said Billy.

"What's the catch?" asked Dave with bated breath.

"The catch is, you need an invitation to get in, or at least, you have to know someone who is invited who can get you through the door. High security guest list. RSVP. So, my man, we have the three magic degrees of separation: me to Lorena, Lorena to Trish, Trish to Zulu! It's Zulu's place. We are in with the in-crowd, homie! Front of the line, yo. So? You're in??"

The recovery process had been a brutal one for Dave. Physical and psychological therapy, minor memory loss, the long road back to *almost-normal*; it was torture, cruelty thrust upon him by an uncaring universe that mercilessly took Dave Stevens' first and only swing at bat away from him. Very little time was spent on re-building self-confidence and social graces; it was all about moving Dave's arms and legs properly, sweating him out until his muscles regained their strength. The Nurse Jones and Dr. Steins of the world never helped Dave with his soul. He was just a slab of meat that needed tenderizing, that was their only job.

In the days that followed September the 11th, the Joneses and the Steins had a lot of work to do, maybe too much.

Sometimes it got too personal.

They broke down, but they kept on tenderizing.

There was a long pause.

Billy grew antsy. Dave always said *yes*, then *no,* politely, but this time things seemed different.

"Yeah. *Zulu*. Sounds crazy. I'm in. Call me when you're coming to pick me up. I'll be ready by the time you get here. I can't wait!" Dave replied.

When you have nothing to lose and everything to gain, it is easy to grow impatient.

Nearly two years after he died on 9/11, Dave Stevens had finally grown very, very impatient.

Chapter Four

"I said I'm travelin' on the one after nine oh nine, I got my bag, run to the station, railman says 'you've got the wrong location,' I got my bag, run right home, then I find, I've got the number wrong."

—*Lennon and McCartney*

His therapist told Dave to accept his recurring nightmares.

"Live with them, and take your meds," this one particular therapist recommended. "Send out your CV. Look for work." Dave's case wasn't a mild one by any means but it was manageable. He didn't want to take the meds even though the therapist suggested that they were *"en vogue,"* and okay to take. "OxyContin just got FDA-approved a few years ago. It's a miracle drug. Perfect for you."

His dad said pot, opium and heroin never solved any of the Marines' problems when he was a killing machine back in Vietnam, nor afterwards, when they all came home from the war. Dave wanted nothing to do with any of it either, and like his father, he never took a pill or a puff, but he occasionally sold a little weed back in the old days and often found himself at the bottom of an empty bottle when he got down on himself.

Dave didn't lose his sense of purpose though, which spoke volumes about his strength of character. Equating his own toughness with that of his late Third Battalion Marine father's, Dave surmised that if his dad could get through 'Nam, he could get through 9/11. Dad killed and dismembered men, women and children; one indelible memory of a headless Ellery McTier laying by his side wasn't going to destroy Dave. It wasn't permitted. Dave's father had a long shadow.

Dave sensed he had aged. There was no delaying his return to a structured life. He was now in his mid-20s, the world had moved on without him. Not much for playing the victim, Dave was hired, in part, because Ellery McTier sensed his pureness, his *good energy*. Dave still had plenty of it to pass around.

"You looking at me? You looking at me?" joked Dave, as he stood in front of his mirror and did his best Robert DeNiro impression.

He laid out his collection of neckties on his bed. Some were bought back home on a shopping trip to Pittsburgh with his mother and sister just before he left for New York, others he bought with Shawna on Broadway. The ties were supposed to be lucky. Paisley, plaid, solid satin, striped, all varying in width, he held each one up to his optical-white, buttoned-down collared shirt, but had difficulty deciding which one to choose for the impending soiree.

Dave hadn't dressed up for a night out in years. It was 85 degrees in the city, and he wasn't the slightest bit aware of what to wear for a *pseudo-vernissage*, as Billy put it. He didn't do a lot of *vernissage*-ing in Pittsburgh or Philly. Dave couldn't tell the difference between a Disney and a Renoir, to be honest.

In the past, Dave let his work do all the talking. Finance talk. Buzz words. Smart investing. He was able to describe what *"living the dream in a McMansion"* looked like to a client with ease, but when it came to making the right impression, Dave knew looking the part always made the difference, so he only purchased nice, expensive suits. His wardrobe, however, was now dated, his pockets empty, and he had more baggage going around in his head than the Newark airport carousels.

It took more than rehabilitation for Dave to muster up the strength to begin any sort of job interviewing process, it took courage. He couldn't follow his own train of thought, let alone securities market data and trends. A couple of years out of the game was a long time. Having barely scratched the surface at McTier and Longley, by 2003, Dave was no longer a first-round, highly-touted draft choice that financial institutions were desperately seeking to hire. He wasn't *a wizard* nor was he *fresh*. A few months' worth of experience at MLI wasn't worth a drop of rainwater in a bucket. Dave interned while at Wharton, but he never cut his chops in New York; the fact that he owned a wealth of promise meant very little to the new players on the field.

The interview process shattered Dave's confidence and crushed his dreams. Out of the wreckage of 9/11, Wall Street looked to recover, to make sense of what had happened, but the war on terror had become the new drain, an endless pit, and while Dave was looking ahead to the healing process, no one wanted a reminder of the good old days. As far as the market was concerned, the good old days were laid to rest on barges destined for scrap yards in New Jersey. There were fresher, untainted, undamaged *top-fivers* to choose from, none of whom had the pall of dead former competitors following them in their shadows.

Most of his interviews were predictable, all similar in nature. More often than not, Dave was saddled with some assistant HR person who would "advise if anything came up," and who would suggest he "email me every once in a while, to keep in touch." On one occasion, a divisional manager with no decision-making ability promised to "pass the folder directly upstairs." The interviews were all unsuccessful, Dave was either unceremoniously dismissed or given a pity parade if the subject of 9/11 came up.

At Saxon and Gold, Dave interviewed with Sharon. A *fresh* pick and the daughter of Norton Saxon, the senior partner no less. Sharon had just graduated from Yale and was given an undefined role in the family business. Being a Saxon, she insidiously pulled rank around the office, blazing quite a reputation as a ball-buster. Her father Norton was a well-respected senior member of the New York financial community and he knew Ellery McTier very well. He considered Ellery one of his fiercest, but friendliest, competitors. The Saxon family traced their ancestry back to the original settlers of New Amsterdam. Their fortune was *old money*, and it was huge.

Sharon may have been a recent graduate, but her claws had been sharpened by years of tutelage in the family business. All Dave really had to offer was his now-antiquated Wharton grades, a promise, and his near-death experience. Sharon was an Arts major at Yale, so she had a flair for the dramatic; she only minored in finance. Her *Papa* Norton scheduled the interview with Dave but rudely excused himself, sending a half-hearted apology through his less-than-charming daughter.

Sharon made her presence felt immediately, walking around the Saxon and Gold boardroom like a runway model before settling into a chair, whipping back her hair, and placing her well-manicured nails on the desk. She then opened their already-tense meeting with an unsettling, phony giggle.

"Ha! So, I'm, like, *a little nervous*. Papa, I mean, *Norton*, um, *sincerely* apologizes for missing this meeting. He knew about your, um, career misfortune? You were, like, in the South Tower when it collapsed? Or did you just get out like everybody else and *then* it collapsed?" Sharon wasn't just being insensitive, she had bad intentions.

"2 World Trade Center. Our offices were there. Can we talk about my internship and resumé? Ellery McTier recruited me when I was at Wharton a year before I graduated and..."

Sharon bluntly interrupted him.

"Like, who is Ellery McTier? Is that a cable show or something? I've heard of them. They're lawyers who sue over Meso-pneumonia Filomena or something like that…"

"No. Ellery McTier owned a brokerage firm. He knew your father well," Dave explained.

"Lots of people know my *Papa*," Sharon nastily replied.

Dave looked down at his Rockports, the *shiny boots*, collected his thoughts, and reminded himself that he was back at the beginning, Square One, interviewing. He tried humility.

"Ellery McTier is, *was* rather, a very famous investment banker and brokerage firm owner. He was your father's biggest competitor, but he only had kind words to say about your father, from what I recall." said Dave, softly.

"And you don't recall much, I guess. So where is he now, Ellery? If he was so great, why are you looking for a job? Oh, right. That. Hmmm…"

Sharon was prickly and intentionally snide. She wanted to see Dave snap, she baited him, and as expected, she got what she came for. Dave leaned over the desk, got up into her grill, and lost his shit.

VVVVRRRRRROOOOMMM!!!!
SSSSMMAASSSSSHHHH!!!!!!

"Ellery McTier could put your fucking father Norton Horton Morton in his back fucking pocket, you stupid ass!!!"

Dave bit her like a venomous rattlesnake, blowing his load. He then wilted away like a dying daisy and sat back down. It was the end of the line, at least for this opportunity.

"Whoa, dude! A little testy. I think this little talk is over," said Sharon, now in a state of disarray herself. "Sorry for, like, *your loss*. Are you okay? Or do I have to call security?"

Dave's sudden outburst shattered Sharon. Weary and frightened by Dave's short fuse, she quickly realized that she was out of her league. She lacked maturity and decency; taunting Dave was the most abusive thing she could have done. She got spooked, but she had it coming.

"Hey look, I'm sorry. I haven't worked in a while. Things are still fresh, as you can imagine. Maybe you can't. I just got a clean bill of health for my wounds. My bad memories are hard to handle, but I'm not crazy," Dave insisted, trying his best to diffuse their heated exchange.

"There are programs for disorders like that, you know. You're handicapped, mentally, I mean, right? You take the right medication, go to group therapy, you'll recover in no time. You can come back and interview again. Yeah. You can. Groups. Those are good. Like, I have a lot of sympathy for people who go to groups, you know, to talk. You do that, okay Steve? I know we have a quota we have to fill for people like you, Steve."

"That's Dave. Dave Stevens."

"Yes, oops! My bad. So sorry, Dave. Dave. Right."

Sharon wasn't done by a long shot. She doubled down with feigned empathy.

"So, my *Papa*, you know, he could have been at a meeting with someone like you at Eleanor McBride, or whomever you worked for, if he hadn't been in the Bahamas golfing that day. He couldn't get home for, like, four days after the attacks, so he can totally relate to what you went through. The inconvenience. So sad. So sad. Good on you, man. Good on you."

Sharon escorted Dave back to the Saxon and Gold lobby and took one final swipe at him just to be cruel.

"I will totally consider you for a *call back,* Steve. You deserve that. Earned it. For us all, man. On the front lines of 9/11, sir. You are, like, an American hero, alright?"

Hero. His dad was a hero.

Dave fared no better with the rest of his late mentor Ellery's friends and former colleagues. After a whirlwind week of meetings, endless discussions and empty promises, career change seemed inevitable. Fail.

He was granted an interview at Waxman, Swimmer and Calais. It was Dave's last chance for a job on Wall Street and he knew it.

Waxman, Swimmer and Calais were the new top dogs in town. After 9/11, they emerged as a powerhouse simply because they were one of the last firms standing. Their offices were situated adjacent to the Trade Center, and luckily, WSC escaped unscathed; nobody who worked there died. They swooped in and serviced the understaffed, and suddenly, heavily-unrepresented market. Making fortunes and gaining a huge share of the securities trade in the aftermath of a very unsettling and unusual time, WSC wasn't hiring anyone. Their bases were covered.

Dave knew the WSC interview would be a disaster, his back-breaker. There would be no return to the past for *David* Stevens. Their COO, Babe Waxman, despised Ellery McTier and was happy to see him gone.

"Hmmmm," he grumbled as he lit his Briarwood pipe. "What would Ellery McTier want with a highly-touted, intelligent, young man from Wharton?"

"Well Mr. Waxman…"

"Call me *Babe*…"

"Yes, well, Babe, you know Mr. McTier was building the future of the market. He had me looking at offshore possibilities, mergers primarily. My assigned client portfolio was 90 percent Chinese when I started. Ellery said that everyone knew who these specific clients were, the ones he assigned to me, and that most of you, I mean, the other firms, were jealous we managed them."

Waxman took that as a slight, words echoed from a grave. Ellery McTier was respected, but in truth, he was hated as well, by many people. Dave wasn't around when those old feuds began, and he was unaware that Ellery was Babe's greatest nemesis, the enemy. This was not going to be a friendly-fire interview like the one Dave had with Sharon Saxon. Things got ugly immediately.

"What's so great about you, David Stevens?" demanded Waxman. He wanted to put a swift end to their meeting.

"Well, sir. I really grinded in Philly. You saw my transcripts. Those grades didn't come easy. Ellery trusted me because I may have been young, new, but I knew what I was doing and I didn't have bad habits. It is the Chinese century, right? I handled his top clients the very first day I started there."

Waxman was unimpressed. He hated McTier. He seethed even more because he felt granting Dave an interview was a waste of his time. Under duress due to professional courtesy, an obligation, an unwritten law amongst Wall Street COOs that sickened Waxman, he showed respect to McTier's legacy, Dave, and then he stepped on him like gum under his shoe.

"Yes. Ellery was a hell of a liar. Do you think I'd want one of McTier's show dogs shitting on *my files*? Mr. Stevens, I want you to know that I called you in today for this interview against my better instincts. I gave you my time because I'm generous. Most valuable thing I have is my time. The only thing left of McTier and Longley is you. All of Ellery's plum clients that were left without representation are now spoken for, indeed. Look out the window. The rest of Ellery's dreams are ash and debris decaying in that pit outside this office. My wife asked that I show you mercy and see you today. I did that. She even insisted that I just sing *Kumbaya*, give you a hug *and* a job because you're a survivor. She's probably right. She's very altruistic. I should be more sensitive, philanthropic even, but you know what? We're all survivors. I didn't much like Ellery when he was alive. Can't see how I'd have any use for his orphan now that he's dead," said Waxman.

"I didn't lose my ability to be great, sir. I was highly recruited. McTier gave me an opportunity, but he knew it was earned. I can do this job better than anyone in your firm, sir. Let me prove it to you!" begged Dave.

"Calm down. Calm down. I've heard that one a thousand times, usually when I'm firing people, not looking to hire them," said Waxman. "Look son, I understand your anxiety. You've been out of the game a while. You only got your feet wet. I know you are smart kid, a top-fiver alright, but you're broken, young man. I suggest you consider getting away from this line of work, maybe leave New York altogether. After what you've been through? Let me see, you're Pittsburgh-raised, right?"

"Suburbs," Dave replied. Coming from the suburbs meant something to Ellery, but it didn't seem to have much impact with Babe.

Waxman glanced over Dave's resumé one more time. He lifted his head and took a long, deep, final look into Dave's eyes. Waxman set the resumé down on his desk, reached for a matchstick, lit his pipe, drew from his smokestack, and blew a foul-smelling, sweet tobacco cloud in Dave's direction.

"West Mifflin. Suburb outside of Pittsburgh. Steel town. Sounds exciting. Why not go back there? Become a bank manager or account executive. Small city. Fresh start. Less excitement. If you stay around here too long, a kid like you, you'll only stumble your way into some shit you'll wish you hadn't. Your destiny died on you, Mr. Stevens. Don't push your luck. This advice is free, son. The last freebie you're going to get if you stay in New York, that much I can promise you. Suzanne will see you out," said Waxman as he pointed towards the WSC lobby. "Take a bottle of wine. They're at reception. Chinese rice wine. Ugh. Definitely not Northern California. New Chinese clients. They give the shit away. They are free, though. I guess one more freebie before you leave. Good luck, Stevens. Maybe you'll find better than this. If you don't, come back. I might have something for you, downstairs, to start."

Babe Waxman crushed Dave Stevens like a bug. The dozen or so rejection letters and phone calls Dave received were easy to swallow but Babe Waxman's free advice was not. Perhaps he did Dave a favor by telling him the truth, but it didn't mean his methods were kind or sound. Ellery McTier had something that Babe Waxman would never have, even in death, and Waxman knew it as much as Dave did.

Dave needed the job, a victory, something, but Waxman left him decimated. Dave spent the weeks that followed the WSC interview locked up in his apartment, leaving only on occasion to buy peach Snapple, chicken with rice, and cat food at the bodega across the way.

Dave was fading again and his mother worried, but she could never muster up enough cash to visit him, nor could his sister Jane. Jane had enough on her hands taking care of her children. Marrying a drunk and abusive husband in the first place never helped her situation, but she had few men of quality to choose from in West Mifflin. A trip to visit her brother Dave in New York City was just a Wheel of Fortune, once-in-a-lifetime vacation.

Honk! Honk! Honk!

Dave gazed out the window of his 158th Street and Riverside apartment. Billy was double-parked out front, his hazard lights were flashing. "Black tie?" Dave thought aloud, "Billy said we're going to an art gallery. I guess it calls for a black tie. Dress for the occasion, Dave Stevens. Play the part."

Chapter Five

*"Yeah, yeah, she's the one, yeah, yeah she's the one,
when I see her on the street, you know she makes my life
complete, and you know I told you so, she's the one, she's the
one."*
—*Joey Ramone/John Cummings/Douglas Colvin*

So many faces.

"Maybe this wasn't such a great idea after all."

Billy meant well. He and Dave hadn't gone out much together before that evil Tuesday morning. Billy worked downstairs in the pen. Dave swam in different circles. Now the tables had turned. Dave needed Billy more than ever. Billy was compassionate but he always had an ulterior motive; that night, he needed a wing-man.

Coercing Dave out of his comfort zone was cathartic for Billy for he, too, felt an overwhelming sense of loss and guilt. He didn't make it to work at the World Trade Center that day, but most, if not all of his colleagues and intimate friends did. The vast majority of them perished. Everybody Billy worked with at McTier and Longley was gone, except for Dave, obviously. Billy may have escaped unscathed, but he was still horrified.

Their common friend, Shawna, was the tie that bound them. It was she who befriended Dave at McTier and Longley. If not for her, Billy and Dave would have never crossed paths.

"You feeling okay, bud? I mean, you're out and about, bro! Fresh air. Fresh. Fresh. It's amazing I pulled you out, don't you think?" said Billy, seeking Dave's approval. He didn't want to be blamed if Dave had a breakdown. Billy's self-serving behavior was, at times, grotesque.

"Oh, yeah, yeah. Great idea. This is great. Been years now, living in the city, I don't think I've ever really been out, can you believe that?" Dave replied. "The first few weeks I was at McTier, I spent every other night either buying furniture with Shawna, working late, or going over to Lester's place which was only a couple of blocks away from MLI. I can't say I remember much from those nights at Lester's. Yeah, Lester..."

The men were silent. They had an eerie moment of reflection. Normally, Billy was not one to be at a loss for words, but this moment was unique. Dave hadn't talked about the old days in a while. Billy managed to lighten up the situation.

"Can't believe I'm laughing about this, bro, but Lester's pad saved my life. If anyone says smoking too much weed is harmful, well, I'm living proof to the contrary!" declared Billy with a smile.

He nudged Dave and cut the tension in the air. Dave was finally out of his comfort zone, the prodding helped.

"Lester Roots. Aptly named he was; when I needed to chill, to breathe, to understand this monster of a city, Roots was always there, smoking a bone, laughing. I used to freak out a lot at the beginning. Pittsburgh isn't New York. He was there for me, man. Yeah. Lester was a great guy."

Billy ended the nostalgic discussion quickly and tried to focus Dave's thoughts on the moment at hand.

"You're going to like Lorena. She knows a lot of cool people. Connected. You never know. She just might introduce you to your future wife, or boss, or both," said Billy.

Dave looked out the window of Billy's rickety jalopy. Every face he saw represented someone new, something undiscovered, a different taste, a unique perspective. Every streetlight, every block, every stop they made along the way broke down his reservations about moving on with his life.

David Stevens was born on Valentine's Day, 1978 at about 9 a.m.. He died on September 11th, 2001, at 10:03 a.m. He was resurrected four minutes later, then he died again, and again. He did not resume living in earnest until Billy, his handler, a stranger, took him out on the town that night.

"Thanks for doing this with me, man. I really appreciate it," said Billy. "Three's a crowd. I didn't want to be saddled with Trish."

"Oh. No problem," replied Dave, lost in own his thoughts, lost in the streetlights.

"I really think I have a chance with Lorena. She was so open when we first started to talk. I feel like I know her so well already."

"A few drinks in you, and you'll become a better judge of character, William. I hope you even recognize her when we get there, buddy," said Dave. "Slow your roll, give yourself a little time. One date, man? Maybe she's not all she's cracked up to be."

"Oh, she is, Davey-boy. Oh, she might be it. *The one*. I've never met anyone so hot and candid in my entire life. This girl has absolutely nothing to hide," insisted Billy.

"I can't wait to meet her. If she's anything like Shawna, as you say, then I'll find her company very, very interesting."

So many faces. So many lights. His heart bounced back from the defibrillator, but his soul still danced with Shawna and still laughed with Lester. Dave was left rudderless, without real friendships or love, and stung by the loss of his mentor, Ellery McTier, the only man, other than his own father, that Dave respected and admired to any great degree. Dave was still quite fragile for sure, but at least now, he was willing to hit the reset button.

"All right, my friend of a friend, Lafayette and Reed Street. Here we are. Find some parking and party time it will be. You sure-sure you are okay with this?" asked Billy, expecting to get the green light from his new sidekick.

Rehab? Done. Dave beat death and learned how to live with horror. He now embraced life, but he was penniless, so free booze, free food, free conversation and unpredictable opportunities sounded great. They were just what the doctor ordered.

Dave adjusted his tux and tie. "Oh, I'm okay with all this. Oh yeah. I am so okay with this!"

Chapter Six

"Dizzy in the head and I'm feeling bad, the things you've said have got me real mad, I'm gettin' funny dreams again and again, I know what it means, but..."

—Peter Townshend

"2-0-4, 2-0-6, 2-0-8...and, boom! 212! Here we are! And there's Lorena and Trish, waiting right out front," said Billy gleefully.

"Trish is the one with the lime hair and the cigarette, right?" asked Dave, desperately.

"Nope. That's my girl, Lorena. Your dream date is that bookish blonde with the glasses, Patricia. Should be an interesting way for you to get your game back on, Rocky Balboa. That chick has more issues than *Time* magazine... Good luck with that! She's quite the femme fatale," replied Billy.

"You've got to be kidding," said Dave, glumly.

Billy paused, stared at his dashboard light, and considered everything that had gotten them to this point. He was part elated and part frustrated. Dave didn't have to do this for him, or anybody, for that matter.

"Look, Dave. Nothing's perfect. Make the best of it."

"I will. I will. I'll try. I'm good."

Billy rolled down his window and shouted at their dates. He wasn't very smooth or low-key. Dave felt a little embarrassed to be in the car with him. Dave found loud people unpleasant under normal circumstances, but not this time, not this night. Billy could blow his horn all he wanted; Dave had finally arrived. The last time Dave felt any true sense of calm was when he heard the late Ellery McTier say *"Welcome aboard son, you have no idea how happy we are to have you here."*

"*Hola, chicas*! Don't run in there without us. I've got Mr. Stevens sitting next to me here. We'll just be a second!"

Hola chicas was music to Dave's ears, going out on a double date with Lorena and Trish was a step forward. Dave was just happy to be anywhere outside of his own head.

"Going to pull up ... right ... here," said Billy, as he parked his vintage, rusty, cream-colored BMW convertible. He cranked his park brake, one that desperately needed lubrication. "...and away we go! Good spot, same block."

Billy was pleased with his prime parking location. He jumped out of the car, walked around to the passenger side where Dave sat silently contemplating, and he opened the door.

"You know, we don't have to do this. So, you coming?" said Billy, with his usual disregard for Dave's feelings.

"Yeah, I'm coming."

Dave got out of the car and shook his head from side to side, releasing cobwebs from his mind, body and soul.

As the men walked towards their destiny, a rather nondescript building, Lorena, Billy's lady-in-waiting, came running up the block and swan-dove into Billy's waiting arms.

"Wheeee! You are so much cuter than I remembered, little Pillsbury dough man!" screamed Lorena. She giggled like a toddler.

Lorena was attractive, if not a tad daring. Anyone with a sense of humor and style would have found her quite alluring. As for Billy, he thought she was *the coolest girl* he'd ever met. Dave wasn't into Washington Square/Bohemian-types, but he was pretty certain Lorena was more interesting than Trish.

"Oh, you must be Dave. He's not wishy-washy, Billy! Why would you say that? Look!" said Lorena. "Billy and I are going to stay behind a second and *catch up*, isn't that right, Billy? You guys go on ahead. Dave, this is Patricia. Trish, this is Dave."

"Hi. I'm Dave. Dave Stevens. Nice to meet you, Lorena… and you must be *Patricia*." Dave ignored Billy's warning and soon realized the mistake he'd made.

"Oh. Hello," she replied coldly, "It's *Trish*. Not *Patricia*. *Trish*. Patricia is my mother's name. People called her Tippy, or PP. I hate that name. People call me Trish. When I was in high school, they called me TP, as in toilet paper. I didn't like that either. That's why it's Trish."

Dave took in an earful, but Trish's tale wasn't done.

"I studied at Cornell. Minor in Native American studies and Paleontology. They called me '*Teepee*' when I was there. I liked that. That had a different connotation; teepees, as in shelters. It was okay to call me Teepee there. I work at the NMAI now. Makes sense. You know it? The NMAI??"

"NMAI?" asked Dave.

"Yes. The NMAI," she replied, "The National Museum of the American Indian. Bowling Green. You must have walked by it a million times. Lorena told me you worked not too far from there before..." She paused. "You should come by sometime. You'll learn something."

Trish was slightly condescending and dry, like a cheap martini. Dave wanted to ease in. *Trish* was a lot to swallow in one sip.

"Yeah, okay. I get it. I was a business grad. History? Arts? Can't make much bread there, but it's important, I guess. So, um, *Trish*, your work at the museum, it must be the reason why we're here tonight, huh?" Dave's curiosity was piqued.

"You are not brain-dead after all," said Trish. "Lorena said you were sad, ugly, pathetic and brain-dead, but you are none of that, huh? I think I'm going to like you."

"You're actually attractive," replied Dave. "Billy said you were plain, thick, you know, a bit of a dim bulb. Now that we've met, it isn't your fault, really now, is it?"

They broke the ice.

Dave offered his arm to Trish. She latched on and guided him towards an unmarked door that led to the gallery's entrance. Lost in the moment, which was, in fact, a nice change for him, Dave took a deep breath and closed his eyes, shutting down the pain he'd become so accustomed to for years. He let go the anger he felt from being blackballed and belittled by the likes of Babe Waxman and his ilk, if only for a little while. He was on a date, a meet-up, to expand his horizons on a new playing field. Trish was the perfect foil. She was unassuming, perky, plain, and intriguing. Dave was having a *time*.

A large crowd of punk rockers waited on a queue outside the gallery. Trish took Dave to the front of the line.

Whomp! Whomp! Whomp! Whomp!

She pounded fiercely on the front door, hard enough for the sounds of her strikes to echo. A panel on the door slid open, a pair of waiting eyes behind it replied.

"Can I help you?"

"*Teepee. Party of 4*," said Trish.

She smiled at Dave. He was noticeably uncomfortable.

"Relax, Dave. *We're in.*"

Trish looked over Dave's shoulder, put her fingers in her mouth and whistled loudly.

"Come on, you lovebirds! Button up and get moving!" she shouted. Billy and Lorena, both happily disheveled, ran to the door and arrived just in time to enter.

"Teepee? Party of 4?" asked Dave.

"Oh yeah, yeah. You can't just walk in," said Trish, "you've got to be on the guest list. If you aren't invited, you'll wait here all night, but you won't get in! Plain and simple. Gotta be on the list, or know someone who is, handsome. That's me!"

"You're pretty connected huh?" replied Dave, "Bloody impressed."

"Oh, Dave, I get invited to these silly things all the time," said Trish as she tugged him into the awaiting festivities. "I get so many emails and invitations; I can go to a party every single night of the week if I want. I go out a lot! I meet different people. I can be anyone I want to be. Don't get out much, do you, Dave?"

"No, not like this!" he replied, his pulse racing as they drew closer to the entrance.

"I may seem a bit meek, Dave, but I love to dance! I love to lose my shit!" screamed Trish as she frolicked into a throng of party people.

Thump! Thump! Thump! Thump! Thump! Ptoo! Ptoo!

The place was jammed.

Dave watched Trish play up the room, instantly becoming the center of attention on the dance floor. She was royalty to these people, this rabble, her subjects. She knew everybody. They fed off her energy.

If Dave thought he had a hope of keeping her close to his vest that evening, he was mistaken. Billy sold him on a conventional date with a petite nerd, but Trish was nothing less than a major-league social butterfly. Only moments before, she was a prodding caterpillar.

Dave had forgotten his butterfly-catching net back at McTier and Longley. He felt uneasy, *awkward.* He was still short on the little guts it took to dive into the pile of cool people and nice clothes. *How are you* and *what is your name* didn't come out of his mouth easily when it wasn't sincere.

Thump! Thump! Thump! Thump! Thump! Ptoo! Ptoo!

The music.

Thump! Thump! Thump! Thump! Thump! Ptoo! Ptoo!

Thump! Thump! Thump! Thump! Thump! Ptoo! Ptoo!

The gallery was not much more than an optical-white painted, cavernous loft space lit with strobe lights. There was a July Christmas tree adorned with obscenely sexual ornaments placed in the center of the room. Every bar station was swarmed with patrons lined up tenfold, all of them waiting for Cosmopolitans, the house specialty.

There were only five paintings on display at the gallery, but they were all huge, each measuring 10 feet by 20 feet in length, massive enough to cover all the walls in their entirety, from ground to ceiling. The works featured striking subject matter, mostly bruised and beaten cherubim and seraphim.

Out of thin air appeared an army of mostly-naked servers clad only in knee-high, white leather combat boots, sparkling masks and tiny wings. They offered a wide variety of tasty and interesting finger food: sliders, spring rolls, sushi, oysters, pigs in blankets, spicy Thai shrimps on sticks and more.

Soon afterwards, another legion of servers appeared, naked as well, but they were painted red from head to toe and had horns on their heads. They served drugs. One devil had pre-rolled joints, the others offered assorted mystery pills and lines of cocaine to snort.

Thump! Thump! Thump! Thump! Thump! Ptoo! Ptoo!

Thump! Thump! Thump! Thump! Thump! Ptoo! Ptoo!

Dave's heart fluttered from sheer excitement. He drifted aimlessly for a while, eventually locating Billy and Lorena hidden in a corner, making out. Trish, on the other hand was in the midst of being hoisted on a chair, barely able to keep her glasses on her nose.

Suddenly, in a crowd of hundreds, Dave felt very alone and unwell.

"Not having a good time?" whispered a deep voice into his ear.

Dave felt a stranger's warm breath rolling down the back of his neck. He nervously turned around. A giant man wearing a crystalline minidress with clear, Lucite high-heeled shoes, a matching ruby-colored paillette handbag, and a large, white afro wig on his head, was sitting behind him, shaking his mane like a hungry lion. Dave was startled by his/her presence, but he had hoped to meet someone unusual, and unusual, in this case, was an understatement.

"Oh, no, no. I'm fine. Just a little... I don't know."

"Sad? Lonely?"

"I haven't been out in a while. My name is Dave. Dave Stevens," he said, offering his hand.

The giant came around and sat down next to him, joining Dave at the thigh.

"Oh, my my! I just like you from *hello, Dave...* I am Zulu. I am the artist. This is *my event*. I will not have unhappy guests here! Who let you in?"

"Hey, my friend mentioned you. Can't forget *Zulu*. She just didn't say you were a ..."

"A guy?" asked Zulu.

"*You*. She didn't say you were you." replied Dave, with a smile. "I came with a girl named Patricia. I don't know her last name. Short, blonde. People call her *Trish*. Do you know her? She's the one sitting on the chair they're carrying around the dance floor at the moment."

"Oh, that little Indian squaw, Teepee? She is a wild one!" said Zulu. "Two-faced bitch! She brought you and dumped you the minute she walked through the door, huh? Her M.O. Typical. But I guess you knew that, right?"

Dave nodded and said little. He didn't want Zulu to know he was new to this sort of *vernissage thing*. Zulu smelled fresh meat, not often did he come into contact with newbies.

"Alright, then. You with Teepee? You with Zulu, baby. You just have a good time, deary. I'm here if you, um, say, *need* anything. Zulu caressed Dave's face and smiled. "I'll remember you, Dave. *We cool. We cool.*"

Zulu then faded away like a ghost, passing by the Christmas tree as he left. The tree was shorter than Zulu, and less imposing.

"Hmmm. Yes. *We cool.* Cool." It had been some time since Dave felt cool.

Dave spent the rest of the night largely ignored, just another face in a faceless crowd. Billy came around eventually and asked Dave if he needed a ride home. Dave graciously declined, allowing his friend and his new gal pal Lorena to leave on their own journey. Being the third wheel wasn't the plan. Trish was Billy's plan for Dave. That wheel was flat. It didn't work out.

The gallery was a long way's away from Dave's apartment, the entire length of the island of Manhattan, more or less. He didn't have money for a taxi nor did he have any food at home to eat, but he now had *options*.

"What have I been missing? Free! That's what! Drugs? Booze? Naaahhh...Food! *Free food!*"

Trish had long forgotten about Dave. Left alone, he felt as if he didn't belong there. Wanting desperately to leave but hungry, Dave sat quietly, like a jaguar in the reeds, and waited to pounce on any server that made rounds with hors d'oeuvres and finger-food trays. Saying *please* and *thank you* as they came by, with great degrees of shame and humility, Dave lined his pockets with grub. He wrapped food in cocktail napkins and tucked it away, then he darted for the door like a thief in the night once he had all he could carry.

Dave hoped and prayed he'd be able to leave without anyone, especially Trish, noticing.

"I'll see you again, darling! Don't be shy!"

Frozen with fear, Dave realized the giant, Zulu, had been watching him. Zulu waved and laughed. Dave tried acting cool, but he tripped over the exit stairs and tumbled to the ground. He got up and clutched his jacket, making sure the finger food he took with him was still safely in his pockets. He was then rudely pushed aside by a pack of incoming nightcrawlers, further complicating his exit.

When Dave got out of the gallery, he took a deep breath of fresh air. The whole scene shook him up. It changed him. He'd never felt so desperate before, and it was exhilarating.

Like most shock, it had to be absorbed.

Chapter Seven

"So, in the mornin', please don't say you love me, because you know I'll only kick you out the door, yeah, I'll pay your cab fare home, you can even use my best cologne, just don't be here in the mornin' when I wake up, come on, honey."

—Rod Stewart and Ronnie Wood

Dave's long walk home was arduous enough to exhaust anyone; he marched on pure adrenaline.

Stuffing a tuxedo jacket with fried food didn't meet his dead, battle-scarred father's expectations. Dave lost his dignity and a bit of his sanity. All Dave's efforts to get better, to get back on his feet, on track, evaporated after one simple night on the town.

Billy's *help* wasn't particularly helpful. Trish dumped Dave the second they got to the gallery. Billy showed up with Dave but wasn't *there* for him that night.

Billy was jealous of Dave. Dave came in to MLI as an associate, Billy was just a *guy from downstairs*. Sure, they were mere acquaintances, but Billy felt an odd sense of responsibility when it came to Dave's well-being, one that would only be relieved once Dave made it full circle. After all, Billy came out of it whole, the least he could do was see Dave through to the end.

Dave, on the hand, was glad to pawn Billy off to Lorena. It took a burden off his shoulders. Just because they were the last two men left on the island, it didn't mean Dave had to share his fire with Billy.

Parched, his legs unable to take another step, his ankles swollen, his heels inflamed, Dave came home to a somewhat apocalyptic message waiting for him on his answering machine. It was from Billy and Lorena.

"Dave, my man, I hope you got in okay. I don't have time for this, man. Why'd you leave Trish by herself? Not cool. Really. What a dick move…hold on, babe."

"Hi, Dave!!! Dick move!! Will you come on, Billy?"

"Honey, c'mon. He's my friend…Anyhow, man, I thought I was helping you out here. You don't ditch a chick. What were you thinking? Catch you tomorrow."

Beep.

The entire situation went from *we cool* to *not cool*.

Deflating.

Depressing.

Dave removed his jacket and tossed it on his coat rack, but he forgot that he'd left the hors d'oeuvres in the jacket pockets. The hors d'oeuvres fell to the floor. He blew a gasket, picked up a spring roll, slammed it into his living room wall, fell to his knees, covered his eyes, and began to cry uncontrollably.

Then, he began to laugh and cry. He laid down on the ground next to a pile of greasy bean sprouts and shrimps and there, he fell asleep.

The sound of garbage trucks loading, beads of sweat on his brow from the piping-hot morning sunshine, and taps on his nose from the only unconditional friend he had in the city, his cat Chuckles, served as Dave's alarm clock the following morning.

Chuckles always sat on Dave's chest when he slept.
She was a gift from Shawna. Shawna gave Dave the pitch-black cat when he first moved into his apartment. Shawna lived nearby. Her place was a few blocks away, down by the water, with a nice view of the Hudson River.

Shawna knew the neighborhood well, having befriended a peculiar Thai lady named Miss K, the owner of the street corner bodega. Miss K owned an apartment building across the street from her shop and offered Shawna a place for rent when she'd been apartment hunting a few years back. The place was too small for Shawna, but she and the Thai lady remained friendly, and by chance, one early August afternoon, they ran into each again.

"You still looking for a place?"

"No, thank you so much. But I do have a friend who needs one…"

"Still available. My building. One-bedroom. Single professional, no kids, pets ok!"

It was meant to be.

"Just close your eyes and click your feet three times, Dave Stevens, and soon, you'll be home. There's no place like home."

Shawna moved Dave out of his hotel room and into the apartment a few days later. Chuckles was a housewarming gift, another kind gesture from a girl that Dave had only recently met at his new job at McTier and Longley.

They were destined for one another. Dave fell in love with Shawna instantly. Chuckles? Not as fast. Dave was too shy to express how he felt about Shawna at first because she was his co-worker, but she felt the same way. She kissed him in an elevator, and that was it. They were together, for what would have been forever. She called him the *newbie from Steel town* and he referred to her as his *Sacagawea in the city*.

Shawna was a local girl. She grew up in Harlem. The odds of her landing a job at MLI were as stark and long as Dave's were, but they both made it, so they had that in common. She started at MLI in 2000, almost exactly a year before Dave arrived. Shawna was a top-fiver as well, their profiles were similar. Shawna was already well on her way to the top of the firm by the time Dave got there; she was brilliant. Cupid's arrow intervened in her budding career. She and Dave were a match.

Without Shawna, Dave would have never met the Thai lady, got a roof over his head, a pot to cook in so to speak, or Chuckles; she set him up with everything he needed, her love included.

"Here, this is for you."
"I hate cats."

"Well, now you don't. Look at the little pussycat."

"It's black. Black cats are bad luck when you cross them."

"Oh, come on. I'm a black cat, a black panther! Look how cute she is! You'll cross her every day."

Shawna kissed Dave on the cheek. He looked back at her and blushed. The cat curled up on the floor, flipped over on her back and stretched. Dave sat down beside her to bond. The cat pawed his nose, then she scratched it, jumped, and darted out his kitchen window.

"Ouch!"

"See? She loves you!"

"Will she come back?"

"They always do as long as you feed them." Shawna gave Dave a can of cat food. "Always get her this stuff. I bought it across the street at the bodega. It's not the *cheap shit*."

"Why do I need this headache?"

"She'll make you chuckle when you are sad or lonely."

"Make me *chuckle*?? Chuckle?? Who says *chuckle* anymore?? I won't be sad or lonely, I've got you. I've got you, Shawna. You make me chuckle…"

Chuckles.

The irony was, there was nothing funny about Chuckles. Miss K thought she was a stray so she cared for her in Dave's absence as best as she could, but in truth, Chuckles belonged in the jungle or in a cage, not a two-room bachelor with a kitchenette. The cat ripped through everything: furniture, clothing, food. The brand-new, white, leather sofa bed that Dave bought for guests was Chuckles' first scratch post. She was not shy to speak her mind either, howling every night until Dave had her fixed. He was not about to give her up, though. Chuckles was all that was left of Shawna other than some silly pictures they took together in a photo booth at Chelsea Piers. He put those pictures up on his refrigerator and looked at them, and spoke to Shawna, every day.

"Fuck! Chuckles! What did you do?" Dave hollered.

Dave woke up on the floor next to his felled coatrack, his filthy tuxedo jacket, and remnants of food from the night before. Chuckles had eaten most it, but she made a huge mess of what was left.

"Meow! Meow!" Chuckles cried, selfishly caring little about the mess. She was hungry, as usual.

"I guess you like shrimp spring rolls, huh kitty? Maybe Trish will call me and we'll get some more soon."

Dave slept in his clothes. He did that often. During rehab, dressing and undressing was a difficult task. Some old habits were hard to change.

He opened up his email to find a message from Trish waiting in his inbox.

"David, David," it read, "my bad, so sad. Forgot to tell you I turn into liquid when I go to these things! So, you're cute. I'd like to see you again. Next time, I will pay more attention to you, but I won't promise, okay? Saturday night, there's a unique event going on. I can get us into a cocktail and Fight Club uptown if you want. I know it's a little odd and a bit scary, but I've been there before. You'll never see anything like it. You in? LMK. No rush. ;-) Trish"

Dave looked at Chuckles. She always pawed at his arm when she wanted food or attention. "Shall we go to the fights, Chuckles?" Dave thought aloud, for the cat's benefit, no doubt.

"Meow! Meow!"

"Yeah, thought so."

Trish wasn't striking, but she was attractive. A tightly-guarded person, she had a side of pretentiousness and unpredictability to her character. Trish seemed calm and reasonable but could flip the switch with ease.

"How did this little firecracker, an expert in North American Indian archaeology, get around to Fight Club?" Dave wondered. "What kind of people go to fight clubs? Fight clubs? They actually exist?"

Cleaning up after Chuckles was no easy task. Dave had spent the night sleeping restlessly, rolling about in the food that he'd left on the floor. Chuckles ate as much of it as she could, but the rest was left to rot. Some of it hardened and stuck, like cement, to Dave's shirt.

His apartment reeked of fried food and kitty litter smoldering in the Manhattan heat. Dave didn't feel like getting undressed, showering, or getting his life back together, quite the contrary. He saw no future beyond the five feet in front of him.

Babe Waxman opened Dave's eyes by telling him he was as useful as a one-gigabyte hard drive. At this point, it was easier to forget about the future, the one Dave had planned out so precisely. His personal finances were nondescript, in shambles. That was the irony.

At least he had Trish to latch onto; she put something out there for him. Everyone needs something to look forward to, right?

He began his reply to her.

 Tap, tap, tap, tap. "Hey, Trish!" He looked at Chuckles. "*Hey*, Trish, or *Hi*, Trish?" Chuckles stared quizzically at the computer screen.

"Hi, Trish. Fight Club? Sounds perfect. Can't wait to jump in there and make some money! I need me some money! I also have a wild side, you know. Will Lorena and Billy be joining us? Can't wait to fight!"
Click. Sent. Trish replied almost instantaneously.

"Oh. Tough guy. I like that. No. Just you and me. I want to get to know you better. I'll pick you up. I know you can't afford a cab. It's a date!"

Chapter Eight

"Give me back my wig, honey let your head go bald, give me back my wig, honey let your head go bald, you really had no business, honey, buyin' no wig at all ..."
—Theodore R. Taylor

"Death!" he thought, "If I have to fight to the death, I can do it, I've been there!"

He died once before. He felt indestructible.

His therapist warned him about that.

Dave had remarkably poor judgment for a man who was trying to put the pieces of his life back together. During the brief time Trish spent with him, she took Dave at face value. He wasn't exactly your typical combatant on a Saturday night fight card, but she may have underestimated how desperate he was for money and how fragile his state of mind had become since the tragedy. She never considered Dave would actually want to fight.

Uh-oh.

He spent the rest of the week holed up with boxes of soda crackers and peanut butter, cases of Corona, and pirated internet access. Five straight days of crash courses in jiu-jitsu, fight-club videos and martial arts movies fueled Dave's madness. He was bent on the opportunity to score and impress.

Crazy.

Soon enough, Saturday night came around and Trish picked Dave up for their date, but *Crazy Dave* had prepared himself for a *mission*. Nothing was going to stop him from cracking some eggs and making some desperately needed cash in the process, except maybe one thing, a little thing called *reality*.

"Hey, handsome, you look a little odd," noted Trish as she arrived.

There he stood, tough guy Dave Stevens, garbed in his tuxedo jacket, still malodorous from shrimp, a crinkled buttoned-down shirt, and heather-grey, U of Penn-Wharton sweatpants. He looked like a clown.

"Suited up for action!" Dave boldly replied.

"What, in heavens, do you mean?" Trish laughed, "You aren't suggesting you'll be fighting tonight, *are you*? For God's sake, Dave Stevens! Are you friggin' kidding me?"

"Yeah. I can do it. Men fight. My dad was in Vietnam. Why not?" said Dave, seemingly deflated, having spent the entire week committed to learning the ancient martial arts. He was serious, *Crazy Dave* was.

"Are you friggin' nuts? For one thing, you are my date, you don't just show up and pick a fight. These events are set up well in advance! I thought you figured that out. We're *guests*, David. Get it? *Guests*." she insisted.

"Guests? You mean we're on a *guest list*. That's it, huh? You know who's in charge, hosting this thing, don't you?" said Dave.

"*Maybe*," replied Trish, rather ambiguously, resigned to her potentially-blown cover, "but I stay under the radar, I don't want any attention, I'm just another party person. I suggest you do the same. I'm on the guest list because I don't make any waves. I blend in. That's why I get invited. I get an exclusive email with a list on it that tells me where all the free parties in the city are held every night. It's only sent to a few people. I am not going to jeopardize that by you acting like an idiot, understand?"

Dave backed down. "Yeah. I get it. I suppose I should go back in and get changed. Little embarrassed here. I'm used to going to, y'know, more conventional things, like quaint house parties. I went to a few before I got hurt. Conservative types. More my speed. Not exactly Fight Club. More, shall we say, *debating team*?"

"Well, come to think of it, you look weird and cool, like Eminem. You don't have to change out of those filthy sweats, you still look cute. Get in the car. Let's get inebriated!"

Trish sealed the deal.

The clouds lifted. Dave had *access*. Fight Club was the perfect stage for his real debut. Dave wanted to fight like his dad, but he was never called into service. Too young for the first Gulf War, Dave was still a casualty of America's wars. Pumped with excitement, fueled with karate-movie anger, Dave didn't feel insulted; whether he and Trish would ever date again after that evening was inconsequential. Who was she to him anyway? A stranger, he surmised, a stepping stone. They had an odd chemistry, but more the accidental kind.

Fighting for money? It sounded great to Dave, but after watching a week's worth of instructional videos, he didn't evolve into much of a gladiator and he knew it. He was relieved. It may have been foolish for Dave to dream of great knockout victories, but at least he now had the balls to dream.

Dave needed to feel the vibe of a woman, any woman for that matter. He had to finally break up with Shawna, so he decided to make a move on Trish, thinking they had a connection. They pulled up next to a loft on East 112th Street and 1st Avenue near Jefferson Park, a stone's throw away from FDR Drive and the East River. It was the perfect parking spot, given Dave's frame of mind. Dingy at sundown, crime-ridden, uptown, Dave knew the area well enough. The neighborhood suffered from hideous gun violence. All pretty random, too. It was a great place to feel edgy.

Dave leaned over and kissed Trish. She barely had the chance to turn off the motor.

"I'm, ah, okay..." She was pleasantly startled.

He kissed her again, only this time it was forced. Dave backed off. It was his first meaningful kiss in years, but it felt like he was cheating on Shawna, and Trish didn't seem all too receptive to his advances.

"Dave, gosh, it's our first date, solo, I mean. Why get all hot and heavy? I know what you've been through. We've all been through a lot. I like you. Just have a good time, okay? It's on me."

"I thought you said it was all free?"

Trish offered up something tangible, inviting and attractive. It certainly took the fight out of Dave. She defused a suicide bomber. Newbies at Fight Club were usually unable to pay their hospital bills at the end of the night. Dave focused on the moment more so now that his bravado had been tempered and his libido calmed to room temperature.

"*Access. I have access. What can I do with access?*" he pondered. Dave was confused and delighted, more so than he'd been in years.

As they made their way to the front door, Trish took full command of the situation. She didn't want her access jeopardized.

"Dave, don't say a word. Just stay behind me and follow my lead," she said curtly.

She knocked on the door gently. Trish knew the drill from venue to venue, being a seasoned party veteran. A tall, elegantly dressed, massive man greeted them. He wore a fitted charcoal-colored suit, a tonal navy shirt and a black satin tie. He was also barefoot.

"You forgot your socks," Trish said to the doorman.

Dave laughed.

Trish turned around and gave him an icy look. Dave was ignorant to the ways of access. No laughing. No talking. No joking. Nothing *odd*. Clearly, the remark about the doorman's socks was the code for preferred guests, those on the list. It allowed them entry. Dave learned something new.

"Enjoy the show. Have a lovely evening," said the doorman in his deep, murky voice.

He led Dave and Trish down a dark corridor and through a pair of black velvet curtains where they found themselves in a loud, smoke-filled, well-lit gymnasium cum dance bar. There were hundreds of people drinking, eating, dancing, laughing and fighting. Laser lights and a crystal disco ball hovered above an octagon that had been set up there for combat. The party was well under way. A micro-society all to its own, no one would ever have known about it if not, of course, for the top-secret guest list.

"This setup is really quite impressive!" shouted Dave.

"Everybody here got the email. It's the biggest party of the week!" Trish hollered back.

The music was excruciatingly loud. Every so often, the DJs would stop it to announce an impending fight in the octagon. The fights didn't last long.

"Do you want to dance?"

Trish was already in second gear, but she saw Dave's eyes were empty, and probably, his stomach as well.

"Oh! You sad little pup! You're hungry, aren't you? They have great grub here tonight!" she said.

"Famished. I am famished!" he shouted back, unashamed.

"Okay, you get a bite! I'll go say hello to a few friends. I'll come back!" she promised.

"Make sure you do this time around okay?" Dave insisted, knowing full well Trish's gloves had come off. He'd seen her flip before, she was a regular Dr. Jekyll and Madame Hyde.

Once again left alone to his own devices, Dave felt he had a purpose for being there. His intention was to get a feel for the circuit and learn what it took to get on the exclusive email list. Stepping up to the bar, Dave ordered a tall glass of whiskey on the rocks, the equivalent of four shot glasses, a quadruple. He swigged it back as if it was water, instantly polluting himself. He unraveled and became uninhibited, a different person entirely. Gone was the steady, reliable David.

It was a defining moment for Dave Stevens.

With a huge, freshly-filled glass of whiskey in his hand and an underground world at his disposal, a welcoming sight, Dave ran towards the tornado. He searched for Trish, but came to the realization that he could not care less where she had gone.

Dave spun around the room like a whirling dervish, bumping into people, pushing them around, angering them. Quite the annoyance in his inebriated state, Dave stumbled, luckily, into the *wrong,* but essentially *right*, party guest.

Thud!

"Watch where you are going, you little motherfucker!! If you ain't careful, I'll bust your stupid ass up in the cage! You'll be my lucky #4 tonight. I ain't had nearly enough blood in my mouth. Taste of blood. Mmm. Yeah, rrrrrrr…More blood."

The man towered over Dave and gazed down at him. Clad in a neon-colored Adidas tracksuit, gold Dior sunglasses, Air Jordans and a pair of 10-karat diamond earrings, he was on his way into the ring for a fight when the two men crossed paths.

"I know you! You're the little *hungry hippo* from my soiree! The little pocket stuffer!"

"Zulu!" replied an elated, but hammered, Dave.

"I see you're on the circuit now," said Zulu.

"Circuit? Circus? Circus shmerkis!" Dave could barely speak. "Oh, no. I am, uh…a bit drunk. Ha! I just came with Trish. She was nice enough to take me out."

"And you saw an opportunity to get food again, right?" Zulu replied.

"Free food?"

"Don't be so proud to tell the truth, hungry hippo. Most of the people here tonight are here for the same reason you are; not me, mind you. I'm filthy rich. I just want to beat motherfuckers up, so Fight Club is a thang for me. I'm in *that* mood, but don't you worry. I see you, baby. Do you know why I had the vernissage?" asked Zulu.

"Why?"

"Yes. Why?"

"Be-be-because you are an ar-ar-artist?" slurred Dave.

"No, douchebag, because I'm generous!"

"That. Because you're generous. Is that the code or something?" asked Dave, quite incoherently.

"Code? What fuckin' code, man? You trippin'?" replied Zulu. He paused for a moment. "Oh, you mean my list…"

"The list! Yes!" shouted Dave.

"What's your name again, hungry hippo?"

"Dave. Dave Stevens."

"No. Your real name," Zulu demanded.

"That's it. David Stevens. Generic? Yes. Real? Yes."

"Okay, Dave. Give me your email address. I like you. We'll have some fun together. You won't ever go hungry again, I promise." said Zulu.

"I, I'm, I'm not into guys, I just have to say that right away," confessed Dave, hoping not to jilt his new friend.

Zulu looked at his entourage, boy toys and muscle men among them, and let out a loud and hearty laugh. They all smiled adoringly at Dave, the drunk freshman. Dave said something really, really funny.

"Oh, I'm good, son," Zulu chuckled. "I'm not into starving little white boys. Those I keep as my *best friends*. *Amigos*!"

Dave tried sobering up but a half a bottle of whiskey made that difficult. He was relieved. He would not be thrown to the lions. He was too drunk to fuck or fight. That tough-guy in him vanished the moment he asked the bartender to make him a double-double.

Dave wore a stupid, uncomfortable smirk on his face. It matched his reservations about handing over his email address to a 6-foot, 8-inch transvestite, artist, octagon warrior and complete stranger. He wasn't worried because Zulu was any or all of those different people, but more so because only moments before, the guy wanted to smash his brains to sauce. Dave was certainly sober enough to know that Zulu was insane, but Zulu could grant him *full access* by emailing him the famous list, and that was Dave's ultimate goal.

Zulu handed Dave a blank business card and a diamond-laden pen that he drew from a tan-colored, leather fanny pack.

"Blank card. Blank slate. Write your e-mail address on it."

Dave wrote as legibly as he could, given his unsteadiness. He fumbled and dropped both the pen and the card to the floor before picking them up and handing the card back to Zulu. He placed the pen in his pocket, a knee-jerk reaction from his past life when he used to wrap up company board meetings. Dave always took the free pen.

"Uh, uh, uh! Pen, please!" Zulu insisted.

"Oh yeah, sorry," Dave mumbled, "what was I thinking? Hey, what's with the blank cards?"

"Maybe you should be mindful with your nose," said Zulu.

"You can trust me."

"Can I now?"

"Yes," Dave insisted.

"It's part of my system," replied Zulu. "I keep the cards in a tiny box tucked away in my safe. Accounting. You're going to be part of my exclusive club, Dave, just like your girl, Trish. The cards are my way of keeping tabs on my *friends*. It's best I know who's who."

Zulu gave Dave a bear hug and disappeared into the night. His exit with his entourage was grand. If it were at all possible for a man 6-feet, 8-inches tall, to just vanish, Zulu was able to pull it off.

Dave was justifiably nervous. He'd opened a line of communication with an odd, volatile, social beast, but on the other hand, he now believed he had the access he so desired. Dave still had no idea what it meant. High and dry, he found an empty couch, flopped down, closed his eyes and nodded off, only to be collected by Trish some hours later when the sun came up.

"Up and at 'em, tough guy!" shouted Trish, as she shook Dave to wake him. "Time to go! Guess you need to get in shape!"

Dave rubbed his eyes. He checked his pockets to make sure he had all his belongings, but his pockets had been emptied. Dave freaked out. "My wallet! My keys! Phone! They're gone, damnit!!"

Trish laughed heartily as she pulled Dave's things out of her handbag. "Oh, relax!" she said with a wicked smile. "I saw you crashed out like a meteor last night, so I held onto everything for you. No worries. Who would steal your empty wallet at one of these things anyway?"

"What time is it?"

"It's 7:30 a.m., Mr. Sunshine. I've got to be at the museum by 9, but if you want, we can stop off for some coffee. I still have a little time. Come on tiger, wakey-wakey!"

Trish offered her hand to help Dave get up off the couch he'd slept on all night.

"Boy, oh boy, you are some wild date, Dave Stevens," said Trish, a hint of disappointment in her voice.

"I'm sorry. One minute I'm standing around, talking to your friend Zulu, and the next? I'm all passed out."

"Did he ask you for your coordinates by any chance?" she asked.

"Yes. Why?" replied Dave.

"I guess he likes you!" she joked.

"Funny. No, seriously. Did he ask me for my e-mail because I'm going to get on that list, the one you're on?"

"Exactly!"

"Who is this guy, Trish?"

"Well, Zulu is a bit of an angel and a bit of a devil. He sees things, feels things. I told him what happened to you. He likes to make people happy. Zulu has an exclusive list of people he emails, like I told you. He sends them links, invites if you will, direct links online. The links get you in to all the best parties in the city, free parties, and all you have to do is click, enter your email address and confirm. Zulu's link puts your name on a preferred guest list. You choose any event you want to attend; they ask you your name at the door, and voila! It's a circuit, Dave. It's bigger than you think. Not just on weekends either. Come on big boy, dust yourself off, we'll talk about it over coffee. You have your shit together?"

Trish had more information to share. The diminutive dynamo acted suspiciously. She seemed well-intentioned, but her façade was less than convincing.

Dave blew his chance to fill his pockets with food. It was already morning, there was no sign of any octagon or party, the place had been cleaned out long before he woke up. There would be no Frisky Feast for him or Chuckles. He knew Trish would pay for the coffee and scones that morning, so Dave ordered himself an extra one for later when the waiter came around to take their order.

Chatting over lattes, Dave's curiosity got the best of him. He was desperate to learn more about the world of *free everything*. There had to be more to it all than just Zulu's list, there had to be other lists as well, so he asked Trish for some advice, but chose his words poorly in doing so.

"How do I become a full-time *freeloader* like you, Trish?"

Sometimes, words really do matter. Trish soured. Dave knew instantly that he'd crossed a line, but Trish was acutely aware that it was his hangover talking, and that he wasn't entirely off the mark. She didn't want to admit to anything, so she looked away briefly and collected her thoughts. She then responded to Dave in a fashion that addressed his question and put him in his place.

"Zulu and I have partied together countless times. The events he organizes benefit so many people. Maybe he wants you to learn something, about philanthropy, about society. I thought you might be the guy for me, Dave. Is that all you think I am? A freeloader? That's very low, Dave Stevens."

A cover achieved and her mission accomplished, Trish got up, reached into her pocketbook, pulled out a $20 bill, and handed it to Dave. "This should cover it, with tip. Don't take it, Dave. It's for the waiter," she insisted, "all of it."

"I wasn't going to..."

"You need a ride home, right? Sure, you weren't. Let me know if you hear from Zulu. A bit disappointing, Dave."

"Look, I'm sorry, I didn't want to upset you."
"It's all right. See you around," she said coldly. Trish was smart. She had Dave enamored with her and, now, he was also on the defensive. Dave had the wool pulled over his eyes, and all it cost Trish was a latte and a couple of scones.

"Can I get you anything else?" asked the waiter.

"How much was it?"

"Two coffees, two scones? $12, please."

"Yeah, no thanks, I'm good. Nothing else. Just wrap these up. I'll take them with me. Here's $20."

"Change?"

"Exact change. Every nickel, please..."

Chapter Nine

"And if the lights are all out, I'll follow your bus downtown, see who's hanging out, one way, or another, I'm gonna lose ya, I'm gonna give you the slip, a slip of the hip or another, I'm gonna lose ya, I'm gonna trick ya, I'll trick ya, one way, or another."

—*Deborah Harry/Clement A. Bozewski/Nigel Douglas Harrison*

Creak. Creak. Creak.

Dave dragged his feet like a Neanderthal as he soullessly walked up the stairs to his dingy second-floor apartment, still wasted from the excesses of Fight Club.

Shuffling his keys, he reached the top of the stairs and bumped into the banister, injuring his hip. He stumbled to his left, tripped over his own feet, his keys flew into the air and he tumbled into his front door. He picked the keys up and juggled them until he found the right one. As he pushed his door open, Dave was suddenly startled by a small but very familiar shriek from across the hall.

"*How your cat, Dave? Seriously, man!* Can't leave cat alone like that all the time. You bad person."

"DAMN!!!! GIGI!!!"

Miss K, or *Gigi* to those who knew her well, shook Dave's foundation, no matter the time of day. She got an absolute rise out of watching him freak out every time she snuck up on him.

Dave could not have asked for a better neighbor than Gigi. Diminutive, feisty, she immigrated from Thailand, arriving in Manhattan a couple of years before Dave got his job at MLI. The people in the neighborhood called her Miss K because her last name was quite difficult to pronounce, but more so because her upright, direct personality made her one to be respected.

Gigi had stars in her eyes and dreams of a Broadway career, so she left her wealthy family behind and moved to New York even though her sister and brother-in-law thought she was insane. Gigi's main obstacles were the English language for one, and the fact that she was essentially a country girl at heart, but she overcame everything. The city wasn't too big for her, nor the lights too bright, she just realized that acting wasn't all it was cracked up to be; her heart wasn't into it. All she really wanted was peace, quiet and a place to call her own, her *heaven*, as she referred to it.

It took only one single Broadway open-call audition for Gigi to realize she wasn't a very good actress. Her unsuccessful attempt at landing a role on stage soured her completely on the acting craft.

Gigi gave it up and reset her plan. With her savings, she bought a relatively large, but unloved, two-story property. She fixed it up and opened a quaint restaurant on the ground floor, bringing her Thai dishes and desserts to the locals in her neighborhood. She loved cooking. She named the restaurant *Heaven*. It was an instant success.

Her real dream, however, was to return once again to farm life. She missed her family farm back home in rural Thailand, especially her beloved chickens. She was lonely without her livestock, but she wasn't moving back, New York was now home, so she converted her roof into a farm, and how she did it was quite extraordinary.

Gigi's building slowly evolved into a well-kept zoo over time. Purportedly, she was the only person in Manhattan legally licensed to raise chickens and roosters in a multi-flat. She obtained the licenses by creating an enormous fuss at her local NYPD station after receiving a ticket from Animal Control. Gigi may have been tiny, but she was loud, argumentative and demanding. The cops surrendered to her. They personally escorted her to City Hall and back. The cops wanted to be 100 percent certain that Gigi was issued the right livestock licenses and permits because they never wanted to hear from her again. They circumvented every City and State bylaw on the books for her convenience. Animal Control never returned afterwards. If Gigi got on your back, you were finished.

Gigi's side of the building had more than enough ventilation to accommodate the coop, it was cool and comfortable, whereas Dave's side of the building was always hot and humid. Every morning, at the crack of dawn, the neighborhood woke up to the sound of Gigi's cock-a-doodle-doos. The chickens jumped in and out of her windows and crawled up the fire escapes to the roof. People came from all around to take pictures. It became a bit of a tourist stop until crime increased in the neighborhood, most notably at the bodega across the street.

Gigi's flat was across the hall from Dave's. It was the largest 8 1/2 apartment in the neighborhood. Dave's one-bedroom apartment was tiny in comparison. The building was a converted home, Gigi's restaurant occupied the ground floor; she and Dave lived upstairs. Essentially, it was Gigi's palace, Dave just camped out in the old parlor room.

Gigi loved making money and she was very shrewd, but she hated all the long hours and heavy workload. After a night of collecting eggs and crunching numbers, she sadly accepted that her restaurant had delicious food and brisk sales but they barely covered the cost of operation. Cooking was her passion, but it was not profitable enough. She required solid returns on her investments, so she closed the restaurant and pressured the owner of the corner bodega to sell the store to her.

The Dominican man who owned it showed little care for running it properly. After a series of hold-ups, he surrendered and sold to it Gigi for pennies on the dollar. She spent several months redecorating and restocking. She also installed a security system that seemed to remedy things. In no time at all, the bodega was printing money for her. She installed an ATM machine which served as a one-armed bandit. It had fees attached to every transaction. The bodega only accepted cash.

Soon enough, satisfied that the bodega could run on auto-pilot, Gigi cashed out a little by selling a minority share of the place, and all the responsibility of running it, to a middle-aged, soulless, listless, clammy Chinese man. He had a bad attitude, one that Gigi would not tolerate. To earn his share of the profits, he manned the cash register, stood guard, and ran the day-to-day operations.

Gigi warned her new partner that she'd monitor the cash register, that every penny would have to be accounted for, nothing was to be sold to anyone for less than the actual price, and no credit would be extended under any circumstances, not even a nickel. Gigi was done with heavy lifting. Her warnings guaranteed there would be no sticky fingers in their partnership. The Chinese man would be watched by her, on camera, 24/7.

He feared her. She was a keen investor.

Coming from an old, historic family of successful cockfighters in Thailand, Gigi brought riches with her on her journey, and they served her well. She knew she'd watched too many movies, that her lovely accent and poor thespian skills didn't cut the mustard and that the real world was far more interesting than her celluloid fantasies. Gigi K succeeded, her way. She found her own *heaven, like in the movies*.

With the bodega profits, she paid off the mortgage on the building she purchased, but she left the ground floor empty, minus the tables and chairs. Her intention was to re-open the restaurant someday; if she rented out the ground floor, that dream would die on her.

She kept her ownership of the building secret from Dave, preferring to stay low-key. No one needed to know her true worth. Gigi employed a collection service to pick up the rent money from Dave even though he was her one and only tenant. Dave didn't have a clue. Gigi invested in her own peace, spending her time cooking take-out food to sell at the bodega and raising her precious flock. Quietly, Miss K was the neighborhood's wealthiest resident.

"Dave, you. Dave Stevens. Look you. You such a mess. How life ever going to get better for you if you don't do anything to help yourself? Such a fool."

"Gigi. Geez, scared the shit out of me again, and again and again. When will you ever stop sneaking up on me?" said Dave, begging her to stop.

"If I don't sneak up on you, no one will. You all alone, and you be unhappy forever. You damned lucky you have a good friend like me, you dude goofy," she replied warmly.

"That's *goofy dude,* Gigi, *goofy dude.*"

Dave dropped his bag of scone remainders. They fell all over the entrance to his apartment. Gigi was incensed.

"What the hell happening here? What? This building a trash can now??" she wondered aloud. "Something is wrong with you, Dave Stevens? Why this food on the floor? Where did you get this food? At a coffee shop? You never bring coffee shop food home. You probably have no food. Cat must be so starving. Dave Stevens, I try, I really try…"

Gigi hovered over Dave. The first time she ever laid eyes on him was when the ambulance arrived. They carried him into his apartment a month after his surgeries. He was some *finance guy from across the hall that came by to see the place once with that nice girl, Shawna.* Dave moved in a week before 9/11. Gigi never actually met him before he got out of the hospital. Over the next year, she watched the health care specialists, therapists, and eventually Dave himself, come and go from the building. Once he was upward and mobile, Gigi latched on to Dave, first out of pity, but over time, because she saw that he was a genuine, decent man. They became good friends.

"Gigi, you are really an angel. You've got my back. I really appreciate it. I think Chuckles loves you more than Chuckles loves me, but then again, I don't think Chuckles loves anybody."

"You are 100 percent correct, Dave. Checkers only loves food. How do I know? Checkers at my place every day for shrimp, every day without fail. Do you know why, Dave? Cause you do not take care of Checkers very well."

"Chuckles."

"Chuckers."

"Cha. Kulls. Cha. Kulls. Chuckles."

"Cha. Kers. Cha. Kers. Chuckers."

"Kulls. Kulls. Cha-Kulls. Chuckles!" insisted Dave.

"Chuckers. Checkers. Ahhhh!" Gigi laughed, happily frustrated with her English skills. Dave had been teaching her English on the side, helping her annunciate her words. They bonded from those very lessons. "You such a mess, Dave, and bad cat father. I'll bring you some food. Shrimp today!"

Gigi knew Dave's recovery was going well. She prayed he'd eventually resume the career on Wall Street he had envisioned for himself. That way, peace would also return to her life. It was a soulful connection, he came to live under her roof, so for her, Buddha dictated this outcome. When Dave's life was in chaos, a life changed immeasurably due to 9/11, Gigi took it upon herself to keep her door slightly ajar at all times so that she could keep an eye on things. She didn't want Dave to think too much or fall into a pattern of isolation, sadness or deep depression. That's why she startled him often, to keep his blood flowing. She used her huge smile and positive energy to help rebuild Dave Stevens into a productive person. Her *heaven* had an order to things.

The only problem she ever posed was when she cooked for the bodega. The entire building smelled like her defunct Thai restaurant for days afterwards. Dave didn't mind the smell but it made Chuckles a little crazy. When Gigi's wok was in session, there was always a portion made for Dave. She bombarded him with large pots of all kinds of different Thai specialties. His favorite was her chicken and rice, but Chuckles was partial to her shrimp.

The second Chuckles got a whiff of Gigi's shrimp, she went nuts. She spun around in maniacal circles, then she jumped off the couch and onto the curtains. From there, she jumped onto a chair and then landed on Dave's kitchen counter, just to get her nose into that pot of shrimp. She waited on the kitchen counter patiently; she knew that shrimp was coming!

Whomp! Whomp! Whomp! Whomp!

Gigi always kicked at Dave's door, never shy to demand his immediate attention. She rarely used the door-knock.

"Here you go, Dave Stevens. Eat good food. Sleep early. Exercise. Do not drinking all the time, Dave Stevens. Not good for you to stay out all night. Like vampire. Who lives like this?" she said. She placed a pot of shrimp down on Dave's kitchen counter just as Chuckles anticipated she would.

"Gigi, why do you care about me? I am grateful, don't get me wrong. I'm not lonely, I have friends. Just knowing you are right across the hall helps a lot. I don't want to give you any trouble, not any more than I have already."

"Oh, Dave Stevens. Your life isn't so boring anymore. I'm starting to think you won't be around much in the days to come. I wish you would give me trouble. I am starting to miss you. My chickens give me more trouble than you." She opened the door to leave. Chuckles darted out and into the hallway, destined for Gigi's kitchen.

"Chuckles!"

"Oh, don't worry Dave. I know exactly where Chuckers is going. She chases chickens up on the roof but chickens are way too smart for your stupid cat. Chuckers goes down the stairs and back through the window into your kitchen, so she knows her way around okay. Keep your damn window open. Chuckers your cat, not mine. Don't worry man, Chuckers the least of your worries. If anything, you unbelievably lucky to have friends like me and Chuckers. We'll always save you from yourself!"

"Chuckles, Gigi. Cha-Kulls. Chuckles."

As she left, she glared at the scones on the floor in Dave's doorway.

"...and clean up this mess you made in my hallway," she demanded. "Neighbors like me, we don't like when tenants, I mean, neighbors, are sitting around, leaving all their food all over the floor! It's gross. Your apartment, too, Dave Stevens! Clean it up, for God's sake!"

Gigi K closed the door gently.

Dave took off his fetid tuxedo jacket and threw it on his couch. He sat down clumsily, only to realize he'd left Gigi's gift of sustenance on the counter.

"Maybe best to put the food in the fridge before I chill."

He got up, walked into his kitchen and opened the window just as Gigi had instructed. His apartment desperately needed some fresh air. He lifted the pot of shrimp off the counter and tried to open his refrigerator but struggled, the pot was heavy.

Suddenly, Chuckles made her return. She rocketed through the open window and jumped on Dave, causing the pot of shrimp to slip out of his hands. It fell with a mighty crash and splattered all over the kitchen floor. Shrimp flew onto the couch and onto his tuxedo jacket as well. Luckily, most of it remained in the pot after hitting the floor. They'd still have something to eat later, he and Chuckles, but there remained a terrible mess to clean up.

"Ahhh Fuck! God damn! Fuck! Fuck! Chuckles! I fuckin' hate you!"

Dave fell to his knees, covered his face, shook his head, and looked up at the ceiling, Thai shrimp sauce running down his cheeks. He lost it. He removed his shoes and socks, and danced in the pool of sauce. His laughter now bordering on insanity, Dave spoke in tongues and was on the precipice of a total nervous breakdown.

Meanwhile, Chuckles had a feast.

Dave drew a large steak knife from a drawer and turned it on himself. He placed its steely point on his sternum firmly and demanded a reckoning with the universe.

"I'm done with your signs, God. I don't see shit. I've had enough. Your signs are a joke. I'm here, but my life isn't. It was. Why did you take that? Why did you fuckin' leave me here? I'm not supposed to be here, damnit!!! I'm not supposed to be here…"

Dave trembled as he clutched the handle of the steak knife. He grit his teeth and began to push. The knife pierced his skin.

VVVVRRRROOOOMMM!!!
SSSSMMMMMAAASSSSHHH!!!!!!

Zzzzt! Zzzzt! Zzzzt! Zzzzt! Zzzzt! Zzzzt!

His phone.

Dave dropped the knife and ran to answer it, saucy hands et al. It was in his tuxedo jacket pocket.

"*Hello...?*"

"Hey, party king of Manhattan, it's your boy here! How have you been, buddy?"

Billy. The other one left. The sign.

Billy checked in, but he never wanted to hear good news from Dave. It was always going to be an ego thing. Billy liked having the upper hand on the guy from *upstairs,* he didn't want Dave to make *too much* progress. Billy won when Dave faltered. He could stick it to Dave and he liked it that way. Billy was unaware Dave's life had suddenly changed. Dave concealed it well.

"Hey, I've been okay, Billy. How have you been? How's Lorena? You guys really hit it off, I guess."

"You could say we are a *couple*," Billy replied proudly.

"You guys are a couple now? Wow. A couple. I don't think I know what being in a couple feels like anymore. Shawna was my forever girl, Billy."

Little did Billy know that Dave was contemplating ending it all.

"Dude, is that all you think about? Shawna? I know you loved her. You can't beat yourself up like that. You two weren't together all that long, to be honest. It's still fresh, but hey, you're movin' on, man. I hear you're doing pretty good yourself. Two dates, huh?" Billy's digs were never helpful.

"Yeah, I think I kind of blew it on our last one, though. I mean, we went out, we didn't really hang out very much, because, as you know, she tends to take off all the time, and this morning..."

Crisis averted.

"You got to the morning with Trish?"

Dave took a deep breath. "Yeah, not what you think. More like I passed out on a couch, she woke me up. We went for coffee afterwards. She told me to get my act together. I said some of the rudest shit a guy could say to a girl on a second date. I mean, if she never calls me back again, I certainly wouldn't be surprised. She's not girlfriend material, though. We may be friends or maybe frenemies. I think I'm done there."

"Well, I don't know, man. Lorena got some really good feedback about you from Trish. Seems she is *seriously* interested in you. Rather impressed!" said Billy.

"When was this?"

"Just a couple of minutes ago. Lorena and Trish were talking for like an hour. It's why I called you."

Dave found that odd. He'd just left Trish, and they left on, what he felt, were pretty bad terms. Why was she in such a rush to tell Lorena she liked Dave if, in fact, that really wasn't the case? Something didn't add up, so Dave played coy.

"That's cool. What did she say?"

"Lorena said, and I am paraphrasing dude, I had my ear to the wall, Trish thinks you're a cool guy and you have a good personality. She said you're low-key, she finds that hot."

"Hot?"

"Her words. Not mine."

Dave thought he'd struck out with Trish. The fact of the matter was that he'd slept all night long on a couch, he and Trish barely spoke before that, and when they spoke over coffee, the conversation was unpleasant.

"Wow. Cool. Listen Billy, can I call you back? I mean, I'm just finishing up breakfast here and I need to clean up."

"Did you actually cook for yourself?" asked Billy.

"Yes, sir. These days, good food, turning in early, getting exercise are my priorities," replied Dave, echoing Gigi's words; absolute lies and exaggerations.

"Alright, buddy. Anyhow, let me know what's going on over the next few weeks, my schedule is pretty open and I'm sure the girls wouldn't mind getting together, so let's do some fun stuff. I don't know, maybe go down to a bar, or a gallery?

Always something going on in the city, right, my man?" said Billy, unaware that Dave's playing field had changed.

"Cool, Billy. I mean, you're a *couple* now. You know the way things are with me being single, interviewing, all that. We'll try and get it together." Dave replied.

"Well, dude, I really didn't know you, you know, before, but now that I do know you, I know all this is not your fault. You were probably a big douche back in Pittsburgh, too..."

"Nice. From one to another, bro."

A phone call.

As best he could, Dave shook off the madness that nearly drove him to suicide. He cleaned up the mess and dedicated hours to making his place spotless. It had been some time since Dave Stevens' home had been that tidy. Of course, the smell of Thai shrimp would never surrender.

Dave showered afterwards, faced once again with inconsistent water pressure from a shower head that he'd asked to have repaired numerous times. Gigi's people ignored him. He asked Gigi if she had the same problem with the building's management and what could be done about it, but she blamed it on the *crappy landlord;* it was quite a ruse.

Naked as the day he was born, Dave was still physically fit and desirable. He closed his eyes and listened to the beat of every drop of water as they fell to the shower stall floor.

Tip tap, tap, tap, tap. Tap, tap, tap.

Entranced by the warm, soothing rhythm rattling his skull, Dave's mind drifted. Dead and alive, he was caught between everything worldly and a vast nothingness. How does one rehab a damned soul? How does one live a peaceful life after resurrection?

Everyone died.

Dave Stevens had the short straw.

Tip tap, tap, tap, tap, tap, tap, tap.

Drops fell on his forehead, cheeks, lips, chest. They always felt like fragments from the MLI boardroom window.

He closed the faucet.

Blop, blop, plop, plop, plop, plop, plop.

Dave remained in the stall and leaned against its cold wall until he was almost dry. Asleep on his feet, he daydreamed about Shawna. This was *their* time. He couldn't stop thinking about her.

He grabbed a crisp, freshly-cleaned, white towel and brought it to his face. He always used the same detergent; the brand that Shawna bought for him when he first moved in. The fragrance reminded him of her. She bought him everything he needed that first day: dishwashing liquid, sponges, a broom, a mop and pail, garbage bags, pots and pans, cups and saucers, plates, forks and knives, steak knives, even the steak knife he'd turned on himself.

Dave never yearned for anybody like he yearned for Shawna. He'd always miss her terribly. Shawna's absence created a deep hole in his life, her legend was too large for any other woman to match. Dave was distraught, resigned to the fact that she'd never return, but he never learned how to deal with these occasional episodes. He had few tears left for his old life, but rivers of tears left over for Shawna.

He missed her funeral.

They never found her body.

Dave stepped out of the bathroom and put on a comfortable robe. He sat down at his desk, booted up his computer, and opened up his email. A message from Zulu, as promised, was waiting for him. It shook Dave's foundation. He was scared to open it, scared shitless, in fact.

It would change his entire trajectory.

Subject: Zulu's Events Mandatory and not: Monday to Friday

To: Zulumail, davestevens <davestevenspa@com-cast.com>

1:59 a.m.

Children. Hop to it, get down and do it, fun for all if you need a rubber doll. I greet you, and seat you, for frolicking evil, be Knievel, and get your asses on my dance floor. Here's the city, from my big, old titty, you know who you are, and when you need to come. Stay in your shadows.

Love and lots, said Trixie.

Zulu.

https://www.zuluvent.fr/e/Mumbai-Beijing-Evening-of-delights00043000000120 crash:https://www.zuluvent.fr/-leap-wine-down-mandatory-brooklynyard-42846778890?aff=eand

https://www.zuluvent.fr/e/freedom fries-live-new-york-tickets+444885805688?utm_source=eb_email&utm_medium=email&utm_campaign=order_confirmation_email&utm_term=eventname&ref=eemailordconf-https://zuluvent.theseedrecordlaunch.spaces.nextous.qc/en/divine-adorable-spiritual-geishas-and-victims-dress down.
https://zuluvent.com.
howtoplay.splashit.com/NYUhomecomingqueens.

2:01 a.m.

https://www.zuluvent.fr/e/disruptionofthieves-series-maria-shriver-lookalike-tickets-11143466089243?aff=eand-avoid

https:www.zuluvent.fr/pleasejoinvernissage/
Trippysworks/clickhere

Next up: http://thepaperchasers.ca/tickets/key/lmno^p021918-vip?unii-access-key=pimp021918-VIP

https://www.zuluvent.com/e/gdpr-for-roadshow-new-york-42707988744Vidastoreopener

https://www.zuluvent.com/e/the-memory-of-68-in-czech-43021207590?aff=erelconmlt

https://mailchilla.mp/c22556.3568/tex-out-motion-presents-the-art-of-trippy-5326853?e=0d8f7b4c13 register: https://www.zuluvent.fr/e/wall-street-access-asset-management-client-event-create-timeless-designing-for-your-ass-tickets-42997050335

https://www.zuluvent.fr/e/hottest-ticket-bondage-show-week-titsout-exhibition-vip-party-413163964545588

https://www.zuluvent.fr/e/tres-bitchery-2003-new-york-trade-tastingeachother-414444986118555555

https://www.zuluvent.com/e/hottest-ticket-sluts-show-shrimpsandoysters-vip-party-tickets-41316396454?aff=eaf2

https://www.zuluvent.fr/moneybuilderstrat.com/us/82278/events/the-oscars-pretendviewing-party

https://www.zuluvent.fr/e/living-breathing-in-new-york-after911-tickets-522556542675966966

https://mailchilla.mp/jamessucksitbigtime/top-100-italianchicksand nails-9657705?e=7392309976

3:01 a.m.

[Message clipped] View entire message

There it was, the famous list.

Upcoming events.

The original email was much longer, but Zulu clipped it, sending Dave just enough links to digest. Dave assumed that Zulu's parties were weekly one-offs, but little did he know there was a well-defined schedule of events every night of the week, every month.

Dave read the email carefully. He noticed that each event had its own theme. Success relied on who would show up, that was the catch. Was it a charitable event and for what cause? Or was it just a promotional party? Who might be there? Affluent art collectors? The theatre crowd? Fashionistas? Rock stars? Movie stars?

Dave's first thought? Free food and free gear.

How to get in? His mind ran amok. This strange world of freeloading wasn't so easy to navigate. It was a puzzle, a maze, an endless well of good times and free stuff. All Dave had to do was click on a link, enter his email address and confirm it. It would get his name on any guest list.

Access.

Zulu's email offered no instructions on how to actually RSVP to events, but all the links he forwarded went directly to invitation portals. There was only one thing Zulu asked Dave for in return:

"Hungry hippo, if I am hosting an event on the schedule, you have to be there. Attendance mandatory. That's the cost of friendship," he wrote, "I don't care if you have any conflicts or other plans on the evening of *my* events. My parties are *must-attend*. You know how much I love my events. If you miss one, if you can't attend for any other reason than you're dead or dying, then you are off the list and permanently excommunicated. No more invitations, no more friendship."

Friendship? That could use some elaboration. Mandatory? That was a big word.

Dave over-analyzed everything, tapping on his own nerves with a zealous imagination. He was pretty paranoid. Was Zulu the head of a cult? Was Trish his High Priestess? Mandatory attendance seemed out of sorts. Why the pressure? Zulu was an odd egomaniac. Still, there had to be a damn good reason why he'd insist on Dave attending his personal events. Why would Zulu feel the need to keep track of him? The whole thing felt like it had a serious, underlying caveat: if you didn't read the fine print, you'd miss something important. Cinderella and midnight.

Dave replied to Zulu, confirming he'd received the list. He told Zulu he'd "look into which events to attend, if any, in the near future," and thanked him for their new friendship. Dave closed out his reply by reminding Zulu how much he appreciated the consideration. Simple. A little too simple. Zulu replied instantly.

"What do you mean, *if any, in the near future*? Pick your events. Attend this week. No hesitation, Dave Stevens. Don't waste my time. I'm watching you. To help you get off to a good start, I'm having an investors' gathering in the Brooklyn Navy Yard tomorrow night. It's on the list. Click that link, boy! Wear some clean clothes, Hippo. Casual, but don't roll up like a bum. I want you there. I have a lot to teach you about this game that we're about to play together. Mandatory."

Zulu's email to Dave was quite personal, leaving Dave unsure whether Zulu's definition of friendship was what he had in mind. Dave found himself on a parallel trajectory with Zulu. Whatever implications lay ahead could not be stopped; Dave was on a runaway train. How did this massive man build such an intricate cobweb? It was bizarre, intriguing, and as Dave's curiosity grew, so did his desire to dig deeper into Zulu's world. He found the link Zulu was referring to:

https://www.zuluvent.fr/e/Mumbai-Beijing-Evening-of-delights00043000000120 crash:https://www.zuluvent.fr/-leap-wine-down-mandatory-brooklynyard-42846778890?aff=eand

Click.

"Enter my email…"

Send.

"Zulu, thank you, I'm grateful for the invitation and I look forward to seeing you there."

Click.

Send.

Dave scoured the internet, Google, but he couldn't find anything about Zulu, his events, or Trish for that matter. He called Billy back to share his findings about Lorena's weird gal pal, but as usual, Billy's line went directly to his voicemail. Zulu's email went in so many directions it was scary and stimulating all at once.

"What makes more sense?" Dave wondered, "Should I click on every link that Zulu just sent me, or should I just pick up another knife, stick it my chest again, and finish the job?"

Chapter Ten

"Oh, let the sun beat down upon my face, and stars fill my dream, I'm a traveler of both time and space, to be where I have been, to sit with elders of the gentle race, this world has seldom seen, they talk of days for which they sit and wait, all will be revealed." -Jimmy Page/John Bonham/Robert Plant

Blown away. Without the sirens this time.

It was the only way to describe Dave's confusion.

He never received an email like Zulu's before. It burned lasers into his retinas. He clicked on a random link which led him to a webpage and an invitation to a Wine and Cheese gathering at a quaint spot on 36th and Lexington. Its purpose? Human rights discussions and professorships. Dave scrolled down further and clicked on another link. This particular event was for a book signing down in SoHo. Some obscure musician had written a vanity biography. By invitation only. Private. Click here. He did. It prompted him for his email address.

"It's all I have to do! Then what? Just go, I guess. Wow! I'm on the guest list!"

Dave's mood quickly shifted from doldrums to delight. Like a puppy with a bag of bones, he clicked link after link after link, having no idea what he'd find next. He digested the information, studying it like a Wharton grad.

"Why the hell am I doing this in the first place?" Dave thought, in a rare moment of clarity, "I should be job hunting."

Zulu's list was abundant with cool things to do every night. On one evening alone, there was a magazine launch with free coffee and cake to go to, a software company gathering, an interior decorators' conference, a Wall Street asset managers' *whiskey and lecture*... Asset managers? As appealing as that event sounded to him, Dave knew that if he went, he'd inevitably run into someone he knew there, someone who would bring up 9/11. It taught him to be discerning; there were plenty of other places to go.

The choice of events to attend was actually brilliant. The gamut was unlimited. There were links to exclusive fashion designer line launches, endless art gallery listings, artist after artist exhibiting sculptures, paintings...*vernissages*. Where free wine flowed, free food was served, free samples were given, where free everything reigned, free, free, free ...

All Dave had to do was *click*.

"Ahh, an evening with a private speaker, some Kennedy. By invitation only. Huh."

Zulu's links put Dave at the epicenter of an underground, unchecked, limitless circuit of fun. Choosing where to go, when and why, was no easy task.

"Immediate access, click here, to what I'm not so sure, but I do have access, that's a big deal. I'm as golden as Trish," Dave surmised. He read on.

"Treasure maps available upon request."

Treasure maps.

He'd indulge himself further, but that indulgence would have to be left for another day. There was Zulu's upcoming event to focus on, to prepare for; *"Zulu: An Evening of Delights,"* hosted by foreign investor friends from Mumbai and Beijing.

Held in a warehouse a stone's throw away from Flushing Avenue in the Brooklyn Navy Yard, it was Zulu's personal event, so it was bound to be a big deal.

"It's tomorrow tonight."

He called, then texted Trish several times, but to no avail. Dave sought some intel on Zulu that he believed she could provide and he also wanted to know whether she'd be there since Zulu's affair was *mandatory*. No reply. Dave was on his own for this one. He could have asked Billy to come along for the ride but he didn't want to bring Billy into the discussion. Dave was certain Billy didn't know about the list or the party circuit and even if he did, Dave didn't want to run with Billy as a wingman for the rest of his life; he didn't find Billy to be all that worthy of *access* anyhow.

Dave lost his way. He wandered around like Chuckles, looking for food and safe harbor. His heart was filled with desperation and lust. His sudden change of perspective was extreme. A decent kid from a good family contemplating a life of freeloading? Fulfilling wanton pursuits? Filling his pockets with hors d'oeuvres every other night of the week?

He was a stray cat for sure. Still, in his fragile state, Dave was able to weigh the pros and cons of his situation.

"At least I'll never have to worry about a meal again for the rest of my life, but it won't help much with the rent. I'll use this to network. Certainly not the career choice I planned. Wasn't a career choice at all a few days ago. This is crazy," he thought.

Somewhere in his lost soul he had deep reservations; a voice called out to him. It tried to tell him that all this wasn't a means to an end, just a momentary lapse of reason, a way for him to numb his pain. The nightmarish cold sweats, loss of friends, loss of love, loss of income, loss of a great future? Nobody could relate to Dave unless they'd died on 9/11 like he did; he felt isolated.

By no fault of his own, Dave became a self-deprecating, depraved, mentally unstable, dangerous person. He wasn't an alcoholic or a drug addict, he was just a bad, bad vibe. He couldn't be blamed for his negative mojo. He didn't ask for sympathy, a fucking pat on the back, or a thank you for being a World Trade Center survivor. He was tired of struggling and just wanted some semblance of his old life back.

Dave went all *Johnny Cash* that night, dressing in black from head to toe. Slim black dungarees, a black button-down shirt, his shrimp-smelling tuxedo jacket and his reliable, black cowboy boots brought out the Pennsylvanian boy in him. His dad loved music and used to fiddle with a guitar back in Vietnam. Dave fondly remembered his father playing guitar for him as a child; Cash's *Folsom Prison Blues*, Elvis Presley's *That's All Right (Mama),* Marty Robbins' *El Paso* and countless Beatles songs were among his favorites. Daddy was a *guitar man.*

Dave felt like a country music legend, and it gave him a boost of confidence. He felt cool, gunslinger cool. He shrugged at the mirror, tousled his hair a bit, and then he left for the *Evening of delights.*

"Thank you. Thank you very much!"

Lock.

Key.

Uh-huh.

"You leave window open? You put away food in refrigerator? You clean up the place a bit?"

"Oh geez! You startled me again! Freaking Gigi!"

"What? What? What I do?"

"I'll tell you what you did," said Dave, as he gave Gigi a gentle hug, "you were nice to me. Stop being so nice to me, Gigi. I don't deserve it. Believe me."

"Oh, you just single, a lonely guy. Need somebody to take care of you. You know I watch after you."

"I know you don't mind your own business."

"You, Dave Stevens, you my business. Believe me," she insisted.

"Thanks Gigi, but maybe you should be somebody else's angel instead," he said, blowing her a kiss as he glided down the stairs.

"You look cool. *Too cool*," she said, sensing something was different. "You in love? You find a girl?"

"You're my one and only. You and Chuckles, I mean."

Gigi's compliment warmed Dave's heart. He felt good. He hit the pavement and went about his next great adventure, a *Zulu-mandatory-attendance* adventure at that.

It was a pretty muggy evening. They forecasted rain. A major downpour was coming sooner than later. Dave thought little of it. Instead, he hurried his trek through Midtown, walking along FDR Drive until he arrived at the Brooklyn Bridge. He spared little time. A man with no money or prospects had justifiable reasons to rush.

Walk. Run. Think. Don't breakdown. His journey was long and introspective. Every step was a step closer to full recovery. Fresh as a daisy, sharp and well-dressed, Dave walked proudly. He felt strong.

Halfway across the bridge, he got caught in a downpour; a *hard, thick* rain. With no umbrella and no idea where he was going, Dave ran blindly, like a bat out of hell, but somehow, he managed to find the Brooklyn Navy Yard in no time. When he arrived, he was soaked, like hands in Palmolive.

The Navy yard was massive. Dave had no idea where to go or who he was supposed to meet there, all he knew was that he was there at Zulu's request. He wandered aimlessly until he was flagged down by a uniformed security guard on a golf cart.

"What you looking for, bro'?" asked the guard.

Dave, lost and confused, remembered the name of the event from the list.

"I'm looking for the *Mumbai-Beijing Evening of delights* meeting, please."

"A mumbo-jumbo what-cha-ma-call-it?" replied the guard, with a hearty laugh.

"Yes. I was invited by *Zulu*? There's a guest list," said Dave.

"Ah hell, you mean the bank gig? Marty's thing!" replied the security guard.

"Yeah, that's it, exactly," said Dave, "*Marty's thing*. My Beemer broke down about a mile and a half from here, I had to walk in the rain, can you imagine? I'm drenched, man. Can you please get me there as soon as possible?"

It was a lame, bullshit story. Dave didn't know any *Marty,* nor did he own a fancy sports car. The guard knew Dave was lying as well, but he knew Dave was, at least, an invitee, so he played along.

"I'm the gatekeeper, man. You on that *guest list*? Oh, that's special. You must be really important. What's your name, man?"

"Dave. Dave Stevens."

The security guard called his partner and asked if there was a *Dave Stevens dude* on the guest list. Confirmed. The guard then waved his arm and shouted anxiously.

"Come on man, I have to get you there right away. You're some sort of a *VIP*, Mr. Stevens."

Dave went from being a wet dish towel to a wet dish towel with VIP status in a matter of seconds. He could not believe his good fortune.

"Come on now, get in this golf cart. Lickety-split, no delay man, otherwise it'll take you about 20 minutes to walk there."

The guard drove to an old warehouse far away from the entrance. He parked the golf cart, got out and opened a padlock, peeling away a large set of rusted gates. Behind them, there was a corridor with a freight elevator at the end of it.

"Y'all gonna go from here yourself. I ain't *invited*, ha! Walk on down there, mister. Hit the number 5 button. It'll take you up to where you need to go," said the guard.

"Hey, thanks very much," replied Dave, gratefully.

"You have fun, man," said the security guard as he slammed the gates shut. "I don't make waves with you rich people like Marty does, but I've had my share of wild times. I'm just too old for that shit. I love a good party, though. Uh huh. Oh yes, indeed! *I love a good party!*"

The sound of the rickety ride up the elevator soothed Dave's soul. He peered through its grilled roof and saw a heavenly light shining from the fifth floor above. The wood and steel hulk slowly landed. Dave lifted its cumbersome doors and exited, finding another endless, nondescript corridor to walk down. A to Z, then AA to YY, he passed door after door until he arrived at his destination, the last door, ZZ.

He knocked.

The door opened.

"Invitation only."

"I'm on the list," said Dave confidently. "Dave. Stevens. Dave Stevens."

"Why, yes, Mr. Stevens, we have been waiting for you. Follow me."

Open sesame.

The maître d', a tall, half-naked man wearing a gold sequined turban and gauzy harem pants, greeted Dave warmly.

"Welcome, Mr. Stevens. Welcome. You are an esteemed guest of Zulu. Allow me to take you to him," he said, smiling wildly.

He opened two thick, burgundy-colored, velvet curtains and revealed an exquisitely decorated room draped in brightly colored metallic taffetas and pearl crystal organza. It was meant to resemble an elaborate Middle Eastern palace. Persian rugs had been laid down from wall to wall, pillows and tables were thoughtfully spread about allowing for maximum comfort, and adding further to the ambience, the sweet smell of shisha and hashish filled the air. There were dozens of guests in attendance. They ate and drank, smoked, and were having nothing short of a wonderful time by the look in their eyes.

"Mr. Zulu is right over there, Mr. Stevens," said the maître d'. He pointed toward a small tent. "Have a wonderful evening. If there's absolutely anything I can do for you, *absolutely anything*, seek me out. Even if I'm busy, I'll accommodate you. Zulu's orders."

And so, there he was: the unavoidable Zulu. He sat on his pillow throne, surrounded by his court, three beautiful Indian women to his right and three handsome, young Asian men on his left. There was one empty seat around the low-rise table: the one next to the giant man himself. Zulu had been waiting impatiently for his special new friend to show up.

Dave was unaccustomed to opulence. Throughout the evening, waiter after waiter, all in tux and tails, delivered platters of every Moroccan delicacy one could imagine: couscous, tagine, harira, many types of seafood, large teapots of mint tea; the supply was endless. And of course, there was champagne. Zulu's guests drank Dom Perignon, older bottles only.

"My hungry, hungry hippo has arrived! Dave Stevens! Look everyone, Dave has arrived!" exclaimed Zulu, as he rose to greet Dave with open arms. "Where is my little friend, Teepee?"

"Thank you for having me, Zulu. I haven't spoken to her. I wasn't sure if she was invited. Was she?"

"Dave, here, such a humble boy." said Zulu to his flock. "Come. Sit. Get comfortable. Yes. I've not been in touch with her myself. She might drop by. Not mandatory for her. What matters is I wanted *you* to be my guest tonight. You, specifically."

"What does he want?" Dave wondered.

As the evening wore on, discussions around the table centered on Dave. He retold his story over and again, sharing all the now-meaningless reasons why he came to New York City and all the good intentions he had before 9/11. It was fascinating for everyone, except Dave, of course, who was made to feel like a caged animal on display. He hated revisiting 9/11 every time he met someone new.

Zulu knew Dave was weak and easy to manipulate, that Dave's mind was still stuck on free food and free stuff.

"Let me say this, Dave Stevens; I'm no different than you, my friend. You see, darling, I was born in Alabama. Man, life there was really black and white. What kind of life do you think a 6-foot, 8-inch, bisexual black boy could have down there, y'all? I mean, shit! If it wasn't those low-intelligence, Nazi, white-boy, cracker motherfuckers trying to lynch me, it was my own kind coming at me because I was different. The day I turned 15, I found me a sugar daddy and he gave me a ride up to New York City. I spent a couple years being that freak's receptacle before I got lucky and someone invited me to a party one night when I was down and out. I was down, bro', like a dog, but just like that, I met a cool dude who put me on a list, and I never had to worry about my next meal for the rest of my life. But it has nothing to do with that. It has everything to do with the people that you meet, and how *you* can help *them*. Let me tell you, when you give, it makes all the difference. If you help somebody, sooner than later, they'll reciprocate. I make a living from some of those old connections because I was helpful, giving. Just look around. This is what you get for hard work, believing in yourself, and giving, my man."

"You're paying for all this?" asked Dave, still skeptical.

"Something like that," said Zulu, "something like that."

"Ah. Hmm."

Zulu's colossal frame rose from the table. His three young Asian friends joined him, following him like ducklings, Huey, Dewey and Louie, the lot of them. One of them was quite different in nature from the other two. He had a dour expression on his face for most of the evening and he didn't seem to have enjoyed himself at all. As he left with Zulu, the man stared at Dave. It was an odd thing to do, and it left Dave feeling a little uneasy.

"It's late, Dave Stevens. It's been a hell of a night. I know your soul now. Why don't you take a look at that email I sent you, make some super fresh decisions about what you're going to do with the rest of your life, my man. Nothing is what you think it is. Nothing. The sooner you know what you want to do and, most importantly, why you want to do it, the sooner you'll be your old self again. Trust me, everybody's got a story, you ain't a thang. Story doesn't move forward until you start being honest with yourself. I hate liars. Everybody hates liars. I'm just giving you a roadmap, fork in the road is your decision."

With those brief words of caution and wisdom, Zulu left Dave in the *Bedouin-to-Brooklyn* pillow tent with three beautiful, female leftovers by his side. Alone and shy, Dave didn't feel very sexy.

"Zulu said you're a very lonely boy."

"I'm not lonely," said Dave coolly, "I just keep to myself. Lone wolf, I guess."

"Cool! The truth is, we're not really into men much. Zulu wanted us to do you, but we don't owe him any *tribute* right now, to be honest. Mind if we leave? We've got better things to do."

"Yeah, cool, I don't care…"

Dave was exhausted, he was happy the women left. *'Wham, bam thank you ma'am'* was never really his style anyhow.

Once Zulu left, the air left the balloon so to speak; the party was over. Dave beheld an abundance of food and alcohol sitting on the table in front him, wasting away. He found no justifiable reason whatsoever for leaving it there when he knew his refrigerator at home pretty empty, save for some rotting shrimp. Dave decided he'd take home as much of the food as he could carry, so he asked the maître d' if it was possible to get it wrapped up. The maître d' smiled, surprised by Dave's humble request.

"Mr. Zulu made preparations for you in advance, Mr. Stevens," he said sweetly, "all you have to do is to go to the gate in the yard. When you leave, there will be a car waiting for you, like all the other guests. You didn't know?"

"Well. Isn't that something? I must have forgotten, dear me," said Dave, surprised by the consideration and detail shown. "That's wonderful. Can you direct me to the men's room? I think I'll wash up then, before I go."

"Down to the left, everything you need is there," said the maître d', anticipating a tip, one that never came.

Dave walked into the men's room and was greeted by an attendant who wore a white tuxedo jacket with black lapels, a bow tie and gloves. The attendant had an assortment of wonderful smelling colognes, soaps, shaving products, towels, and condoms.

"How can I help you, sir?" he asked.

"Just here to relieve myself and wash up before I leave," replied Dave.

Their brief encounter was interrupted by loud groaning and an interesting conversation emanating from one of the bathroom stalls. The voices sounded familiar; one of them was definitely Zulu's.

"...*that's how it's done, baby!!*" preceded the sound of two men having a simultaneous orgasm.

Dave felt a little uncomfortable but he kept his silence. The attendant, on the other hand, went about his usual business, folding his towels and rearranging his soaps and bottles. He was very professional, having experienced similar situations in the past.

Dave washed his face, using one of the many bars of soap made available next to the sink. He took a towel from the attendant to dry up and then used it to dry up the bar of soap. While the attendant wasn't looking, Dave slipped the soap into his jacket pocket. The attendant knew it had gone and that Dave had taken it. He'd been working there for years and had every single bar of soap and razor blade accounted for, but he didn't say anything.

Dave stared into the mirror and doubled down, this time taking not only another bar of dry soap but a bottle of cologne as well. He slipped them into his jacket slowly, but his attempt to be inconspicuous drew the attendant's attention. The man had seen enough. As Dave made his way toward the exit, the attendant stopped him from leaving.

"*What the fuck you doin'? Taking my shit?*" hollered the attendant. He shoved Dave into the wall.

Zulu and his young lover came out of the bathroom stall, buttoned their trousers, and witnessed the melee.

"You *pathetic*, cracker motherfucker!! Get the fuck out of here. Go take that soap and *shove it up your ass*!! That ass gonna smell fresh every time you decide to fuckin' steal something, fucking cracker!" the attendant screamed.

He pushed Dave once again and was about to punch him when Zulu intervened.

"Yo, yo. Calm down," said Zulu, intervening. "Don't be so hard on my boy, here. That's *my* boy."

"Mr. Zulu! I'm sorry, sir. I didn't know. I never seen him before, he's not one of your *usual* guests. He was stealin' my shit, man." replied the attendant as he backed down.

Dave, flustered, emboldened yet belittled, apologized. He'd been caught red-handed.

"I'm sorry, sir. I'm so, so sorry. What was I thinking? What is wrong with me?" Dave hit a new low.

"If you ever see Mr. Stevens again, you make sure he gets anything he wants and needs," said Zulu, "*anything.*"

"No hard feelings, Mr. Stevens," said the attendant, "I mean, you *new*, man. Never seen you. You don't have to do that. It's free."

"Sir, I am so embarrassed," replied Dave.

"You get along now, hippo," said Zulu with a smile. "I'm going to have a little chat with our attendant here before me and my boy here split."

"I don't know what to say," replied Dave.

"It's not what you say," said Zulu, "it's what you do. Do good things, Dave. Get your head out of the gutter, for fuck's sake."

Out the door and down and out, Dave took the freight elevator to the exit where a familiar-looking golf cart was waiting for him. The man charged with driving him back to the front yard was none other than his old acquaintance, the gatekeeper.

"Oh boy, you must have had a real good time by the looks a you, sir," said the gatekeeper jocularly.

"That was one of the strangest times I've ever had in my life," said Dave.

"Oh yeah, Marty, I mean, *Zulu*, you know. Can't be callin' him *Marty*. He throws shindigs for just about anything and everything, in some of the strangest ways you can imagine, too! This ain't the first time he's had some crazy party out here," replied the gatekeeper, as he pulled the cart up to the entrance. "So here we are, man. That limo over there is waiting for you. Take it to your broken Beemer, right? *Broken Beemer! Ha! You funny, mister!*"

Dave got into the back seat of a long, black Lincoln Town Car. A bounty of leftovers, all neatly packed in Styrofoam boxes and plastic bags, were prepared and waiting for him on arrival.

God bless Zulu, or *Marty*, or whoever he really was, at least he kept his promise.

"Hello sir," said the driver. "Mr. Zulu instructed me to take you anywhere you need to go. Destination, please?"

"Destination?"

Chapter Eleven

"Jenny said, when she was just five years old, there was nothin' happenin' at all, every time she puts on a radio, there was a nothin' goin' down at all, not at all, then one fine mornin' she puts on a New York station, you know, she don't believe what she heard at all, she started shakin' to that fine, fine music, you know her life was saved by rock 'n' roll."

—Lou Reed

The opening salvo of Gulf War II was described as *Shock and Awe*.

Dave's world was not too dissimilar: Shock and awe.

The US military purportedly provoked shock and awe in Iraq. Dave's sanity barely survived Bin Laden's shock and awe. Dave went from starving and destitute to having a refrigerator filled with enough food to feed a Moroccan family of six for a week, simply by meeting the *right people*.

Access.

Shocking. Awesome.

The world of stocks and market manipulation, along with the miscreants that came with it, were in Dave's rearview mirror now. He willingly embraced the new villain he'd become. This was it, his new career: Party crasher. He had no idea how to master the craft. He'd only been out a few nights, but his sorties were significant. Zulu gave him the keys to the circuit, and now, he'd learned, at the very least, enough to know better.

Dave slept well. He woke up the following morning feeling refreshed but anxious. He covered himself in his plush bathrobe, made himself a cup of coffee, and gave Chuckles some couscous. He then sat down at his computer to study Zulu's email intently. Now equipped with more caution and a clearer perspective, Dave learned quickly. He was able to break down the list of events into different categories and subcategories in short time. It was all foreign to him initially, like cracking a new client, but he got into a groove.

He found a bevy or free parties and promotional events on the list; free alcohol, endless free food, free stuff. No catch. They were giving away brand-new iPods at one party; you couldn't find an iPod within 100 square miles of Manhattan at the time. The event's description insisted guests could have as many of them as they wanted! Insane indeed, but that suggested to Dave that the guest list was very limited, the event small. Still, he had a golden ticket, he could go if he pleased. Every event promoted something different, a lecture, a product, a painting. The event promoters were eager to give things away.

Always *food*.

Free food events had instant appeal to Dave, but they didn't seem like *the* priority anymore. Getting free stuff could go a long way. Who knows? He could start a little side hustle, sell stuff he got for nothing on Craigslist, make a little bank, cold, hard cash. It was something Dave was sorely lacking. Suddenly, he wasn't as hungry as he used to be.

"Okay," Dave thought aloud, stretching out his arms and folding his hands together, "let's get to work. Soho. Loft. Wine and cheese. New magazine launch. Boring. Lots of goofy looking people, sitting around, odd discussions. No thanks. Oh. Hey, now! Italian leather goods and fashion brand launch. Vida. That seems very interesting, but that's on Friday, today is only Tuesday. What's going on tonight? What's going on? What's going on? Japanese sashimi and Kabuki-style theater event to support the victims of the Algerian earthquake. Yep! Sounds delicious! That will be my Tuesday night."

He chose well. It was quaint, a softball affair. A Kabuki theater *thing*. It was all new to Dave, so it served as the perfect backdrop for him to wade into shallow waters.

"Vernissage, vernissage," Dave rambled, as he scrolled down the email, "ahhh…Wednesday. NYU faculty new semester launch party. Faculty. Home-baked cookies. I'll go there early and have dinner. If it doesn't work out, I'll just go to one of the gallery events and have a bite there. Thursday. Record launch, new store opening, another benefit for refugees, and oh, launch of Freedom Fries. Going to be a lot of good food at that one. Thursday will be a lot of fun. Friday is that Italian leather goods thing. Yeah, Fashion Week. There's going to be a lot of beautiful people, hot chicks, good food, expensive giveaways at the Vida thing. You are set, Dave Stevens. Things to do, places to go, people to see, food to eat..."

With the ability to process things quickly and the luck of a man who fell from the top of a tower, landed on the pavement and survived, Dave now had complete access and it meant he was getting in wherever he wanted to go, and whatever *in* offered, he wanted it. He tailored his plan. An excellent pupil, by the end of his first week on Zulu's field of dreams, Dave was set on becoming a pro at the game. The star student from Wharton wanted a Master's degree in Party Crashing. Class was officially in session.

As far as staying under the radar as Trish insisted, Dave shrugged it off, he couldn't care less about any radar. If he was going to go down in a ball of fire, it was going to be of his own volition, not Osama bin Laden's.

He clicked on several links, making reservations for the events he selected to attend and once they all confirmed, he clicked on a dozen more links and repeated the process. Those events would serve as his back-ups just in case the events he chose weren't any fun or profitable.

Ding! Ding! Replies. Confirmations. He was in.

As he prepared for the night out, Dave had a dilemma. He wasn't entirely sure what to wear. His wardrobe was quite limited. It consisted of Brooks Brothers suits, basketball shorts and tank tops, a few dirty, pleated trousers, button-down shirts, and his now infamous, smelly tuxedo jacket. Dave's initial plan was to grind and grind away for five years, get a partnership, and then start a family. There was never going to be any fun, just calm and kids. Bland. That's what Dave Stevens wanted, a stability he never had in West Mifflin. Suddenly, he was a hedonist, navigating a world where having fun was the primary mission. He had a reason to *get dressed up and lipsticked* as Shawna used to say.
  "Japanese Kabuki people supporting Algerian earthquake victims. What to wear?"

He chose a pair of khaki pants because they had large pockets. Their classic fan-pleats had enough room in them to fit two soft balls. Plenty of room for sushi. All you can eat. All you can carry.

He wore an Oxford-blue button-down shirt to match his pants. From Dave's perspective, he had to have the look of an *intellectual*; blue Oxfords always met that criterion.

Topping off the outfit, Dave chose a white V-neck, Slazenger tennis sweater. He and Ellery had planned to play tennis one morning later *that* week, so Dave bought it, just in case it would be cold because it was September after all, the weather tended to be unpredictable. They never got the chance to play Dave recalled, as he threw the sweater over his shoulders.

He then slipped into a pair of hard, uncomfortable penny loafers. His look was stylistically 1990s preppy, but he was a fashion failure at best in 2003.

Dave glanced at his mirror and acted like Robert De Niro, building up his self-confidence. Yes, he was talking to himself. He was talking to himself.

Gigi peered through her door as Dave was leaving. She wanted to know where he was going because she had not seen him dressed up like a normal person would in some time. Something was out of sorts.
"Woo-hoo Dave! Look at you. Wow! Wow! Very nice. Handsome, so handsome," said Gigi, as she bolted out of her apartment. "Must have a lady friend. You are going somewhere fancy, huh?"

"Something like that," replied Dave, startled as always, echoing Zulu's words.

"Oh, so you can't tell me what's going on, huh?" said Gigi, laughing.

"Well, if I get lucky, you'll certainly hear something, huh?" Dave replied, "My business, not yours."

"Dave, I am always minding my own business. You are so lucky to have good neighbor like me."

"Thank God you're here Gigi, thank God you're here. Hey, I'll let you know how it goes," he said, cutting short what could have become a long conversation. Gigi was always inquisitive.

His heart pumping, his blood rushing, his eyes bright as two moons, Dave raced carelessly towards the stairs, tripped as he'd done so many times before, and tumbled down the staircase. He hit the banister when he reached the bottom and barreled into the vestibule.

"Dave???" Gigi hollered, "*Again?*"

"I'm okay! I'm okay!" he replied.

Dave wanted to take a cab, but it wasn't like the good old days when he could afford it. He walked a few blocks but his loafers began to irritate his heels. By the time he arrived in West Harlem, Dave was unable to walk any further, so he hitchhiked.

As he waited, hoping for some good fortune to come his way, Dave looked very much like a lost time traveler. In no time, a stretch limousine pulled over next to the curb where Dave was pacing.

The rear window rolled down. An eccentric, aristocratic businessman offered him a ride. Dave recognized him immediately.

"Where you going, fella?" the man asked. "You look down on your luck. A loser."

"I just need a ride downtown, sir," Dave replied.

"Anything so important that you actually have to hitchhike, son?" asked the well-to-do man. "Don't you have any money? A job? No?"

"Well, I'm actually on my way to a charitable event, and it seems I forgot my cash and cards at home. The car that was supposed to come pick me up never arrived. I'm very upset," said Dave, rather convincingly.

"Charity? Well, I'm very charitable. The most charitable. *Very, very charitable.* I can help you with that, jump in." He opened the door. Dave got in and sat down.

"Well, thank you, sir," said Dave, relieved walking would no longer be necessary.
The well-known businessman was the purported owner of large swaths of the Manhattan skyline. He'd recently hosted a successful television show, so his face and brand were on practically every billboard in the city.

"Okay, well, where you going, son?" he asked.

"If it's not too much trouble, I'm going down to Battery Park, sir, I mean, if that's convenient for you," Dave replied.

"Seymour, take us down to Battery Park, you can take the west side, it'll be faster."

"Yes, sir, Mr. T. Yes, sir," replied the driver, rather unenthusiastically.

Dave sat face to face with his *savior,* for lack of a better description. Between the two men, the businessman was probably the one who needed saving the most. If anything, the businessman seemed to require some sort of psychiatric evaluation, given the look on his face and his odd behavior.

It was a typical New York late-summer's eve. The weather was hot and humid. The limousine was air-conditioned, but it barely helped matters. The backseat of the car was warm, like a foggy sauna and it reeked from the businessman's nauseating cologne. He was dressed in a navy-colored, double-woven wool suit, a crisp white shirt, and a fire-engine-red tie wound tightly around his neck; it was astonishing that he could even breathe. His hair was hectically combed, like a fiery tornado. The guy, however, didn't sweat a drop despite the lack of circulation in the limo and the fact that it was hot enough outside the car to boil an egg on the pavement.
The limousine passed by the remains of the World Trade Center. Reconstruction had begun on the site so it was tricky to drive past the myriad of pylons, police and heavy machinery.

"Did you grow up here in the city, kid?"

"No, sir. I moved here a few weeks before 9/11. I never really got a chance to lay down my roots, but I guess I call it home, at least for now," Dave replied.

"It's a shithole, this city. An absolute shithole. Terrible. Terrible. Just terrible. I can turn it all around. My buddy Rudy turned it around. He's done a great job, great job. Pathetic what's happened to this country. Caught like that. Sleeping. Shame. Just a shame," decried the businessman.

Dave knew when to keep quiet and learn. He let the madman spew his guts out but it was hard for Dave to sit and listen to him.

"I hate losers. Losers. Just hate them. You don't look like a loser," said the businessman. "You look like a winner. I mean, I thought you were a loser. Penny loafers. Sharp. Bush. He's a loser. At least he's taking it to Saddam. I hate those guys. Bad guys, I tell you. Got to keep them out of our country. Bad people. Bad. Bad. Bad."

Dave just couldn't shut up.

"I'm not really political, sir. I was in the second tower when it got hit. I'm a survivor. I have very mixed feelings about the war."

"*You were in the towers? You were in the towers?*" asked the businessman, excitedly. He turned into a rabid dog.

"Why, yes, sir," replied Dave calmly, "but I really don't like to talk about it."

"Talk about it? You don't have to talk about anything! You're a hero, son. An American hero. You deserve a fucking medal. All you people deserve a medal. I'd make a medal for 9/11 people, I swear. Good people. Tough. It's people like you, natural-born Americans, who are going to make America great again one day, you'll see."

"Natural-born, sir?"

Dave sat through the businessman's lengthy diatribe about the Mayflower, and how *they all must have been so brave*. Then, the businessman went on a rampage about immigration policies and how the American political system was failing the American people. He blamed the Clintons, President Bush, the Jews, the Arabs, the Russians, Europeans, Mexicans, African Americans, and especially the Chinese, for all the United States' shortcomings. He raged against the Chinese people more than anyone else for some reason.

"China. *Chiii-na*. We're too good to them. They rip us off. Everybody is ripping us off. Everybody. Where are you from, son?" he asked.

"I'm originally from Pennsylvania, sir." Dave replied.

"Oh, Dutch. Good people. Good people. They fought the Nazis. Oh, they gave up, yeah. I mean, the Nazis, they were good killers, at that and more, but y'know, the Dutch, they kept on fighting until America saved them. It's going to take a lot of good, white, Christian American boys to turn this country around. We'll be chasing those terrorists for years. Years, I say. Maybe decades. Maybe not. Who knows?"

As the limousine pulled into Battery Park, Dave could not get out of the car soon enough. He knew that the huckster-celebrity who had afforded him the ride was a dangerous person.

"I'm not Dutch, sir."

"Well, you seem like a patriot, kid. And you look Dutch! That's why we need you. We need to make America great again…"

"America is already great, sir. Thanks for the ride, it's really appreciated. I learned a lot," said Dave.

"Oh! You learned something?" Impressed, the man reached into his billfold and handed Dave his personal business card. "You know who I am. You're a nice kid. Why don't you drop by the tower someday? I'll call up for some sandwiches, maybe some burgers? You seem useful, very useful. I can use you somehow…"

"Thank you, sounds like a great opportunity. I don't know what my future looks like right now." Dave was bluntly honest.
 "The future? It'll be an America for Americans who love their country. Great Americans like me. They should all be like me, really. I love this country, more than anybody in Washington, that's for sure. Are you sure you are okay, son?" said the man. "You still seem nervous. I know it's a big deal meeting me; a really huge deal. *Huuugge*. I get it. I'd be nervous, too." The

businessman then turned to his driver. "Seymour, do I make you nervous? Y'know, they always get nervous when they know I'm going to fire'em! Are you nervous now, Seymour?"

Perplexed, Dave stared blankly at the limousine as it drove away. He stood on the curb outside his destination, stunned as he stared at the businessman's card, certain the offer he had received from the crazy guy was phonier than a three-dollar bill. Dave ripped up the card and threw it down a drain.

Gathering his thoughts, going over the game plan a million times in his head, Dave readied himself for the unpredictable.

"Okay. Okay. Okay. The National Japanese American Foundation. Raising funds for Iraqi refugees. I got this. I got this."

Dave took a deep breath, exhaled, and walked across the street. His feet were heavy, *cement-boot* heavy. He had the right address. The location was supposed to have Toro lamps hanging outside the entrance. There they were: Red and white Toro lamps.

He walked up the stairs, opened a large oak door, and entered.

"Welcome!"

Greeted by two comely women dressed in authentic geisha wear, Dave quickly noticed the women were charged with gatekeeping and guarding the donation and tip jars.

"Good evening. Name please?" The geishas had thick, whimsical accents.

This game was all going to work out for Dave or it wasn't, plain and simple. He stepped in and took a swing at bat.

"Stevens. Dave Stevens…"

"Steven. Stevens. Yes. Oh, yes, Dave Stevens. You confirmed via email, correct?" asked the alluring geisha.

"Yes, I did, of course," replied Dave.

The skies opened up. The seas parted.

"It is so nice to have you here this evening for such an important cause, Mr. Stevens. Are you related to any Japanese?"

"Not directly, no, but my grandfather was stationed in post-war Tokyo. He helped rebuild Japan after we destroyed it with the H-bombs."

Smooth. Not. It was the best answer he could come up with, better than no answer at all.

The geisha grew flirtatious and giggled.

"Well, Mr. Stevens, come in and have a very nice evening! Brush up on some Japanese culture while you're here," she said. The geishas then bowed and smiled through their lovely painted lips and powdered faces.

Dave saw the donation and tip jars and licked his chops like a wolf. He had nothing to give so he proceeded into the gathering unashamedly, leaving the geishas rather miffed.

The dimly-lit room where the event was held had once served as a cigar lounge. It was complete with walls of antiquarian books, chaise lounges, couches and coffee tables. There were a hundred or so people in attendance at the gathering. The crowd consisted of mostly, but not exclusively, Japanese and Middle Eastern people.

Dave recognized a few of the folks from the other events he'd been to before. One of the people, ironically, was Zulu's young Asian lover from the Mumbai-Beijing party. Dave never got the man's name.

The man stared at Dave with the same contemptuous look he'd given him the night before at the warehouse. The man glared at Dave wildly and ran away as quickly as he could. Dave felt a misguided kinship with the man and hoped to strike up a friendly conversation with him, but he shrugged Dave off, and rather unpleasantly. It was an extremely awkward moment. Dave doubted himself and thought that perhaps he had the wrong guy, but it had to be Zulu's lover. It *was* him, 100 percent.

Dave had to stay focused and on point, so he walked around and engaged in small talk and meaningless conversations. He didn't belong there and he knew it. Of course, the other party guests, the ones he'd recognized, didn't belong there either. They had no idea who he was, what he was doing there, and no really one cared, except for Zulu's friend. Why he seemed uncomfortable around Dave was anybody's guess.

For the moment though, Dave was just another face in the crowd and he felt empowered by that anonymity.

Not surprisingly, Trish was also at the party. Dave was excited to see her so he made a beeline through the crowd, only to be brushed aside once again. As he walked towards her, Trish gently waved to Dave and nodded her head; she wanted to be left alone. Her body language implied she was busy. Deeply engaged in conversation with two Middle Eastern men, Trish ignored Dave's advances, treating him as if he was a stranger.

"It must be an access thing," Dave thought.

By the look on her face though, Trish didn't seem at all surprised Dave was there either. Dave picked up on her wishes, stayed in his lane, and continued his journey of nods, hellos, and plastic smiles.

Then, Dave saw something rather alarming.

His fellow party guest, Zulu's lover, pickpocketed another man right in front him, in broad daylight. The victim was in deep conversation with a waiter regarding a plate of escargot in brioche, unaware that Zulu's pal had just made quick work of him. The victim's attention was focused entirely on the snails; the second he turned his back, in came the predator and voila! Snatching his wallet was a cinch. Dave was aghast but somewhat impressed. Zulu's lover then turned around and noticed that Dave had seen him do it. He gave Dave his now-familiar nasty gaze and left the room stealthily.

He had a message for Dave: *mind your own business.*

Having witnessed the petty crime, Dave stood in suspended disbelief, it was really quite shocking to see it go down just like that. His utopian party world took a dark turn. Dave was there for all the wrong reasons, surely, he wasn't the only one, that was now clearly confirmed, but he wasn't there to rob anybody.

Dave had to tell someone what had happened, but what was he going to say? "Hey, I'm Dave, I'm here to steal food, but I just saw somebody have their wallet lifted?" He had a moral dilemma on his hands and twitched nervously, uncertain what to do.

Thankfully, Trish came around to talk with him.

"Hey, handsome, what are you doing here? she asked. "Oh! Shaky? What's up??"

"Well, what a surprise. Thought you didn't know me. I am into charitable things, this seemed like the right thing to do," said Dave, matter-of-factly, "I guess I'll make a big donation to the National Japanese American Foundation before I leave. I've been supporting them for years."

She laughed.

"You're so full of it," said Trish. "I'm guessing you were in the mood for some sushi for dinner tonight and that's why you're here."

"Maybe, just maybe," replied Dave.

"Zulu sent you the list, huh? You're going to make good use of it now, right?"

"Well, isn't that what you did?"

"Dave Stevens, just be happy that I introduced you to Zulu. Maybe going out, it'll get you right, sooner than later."

"Yeah. Right. Trish, listen," said Dave with trepidation, "I just saw something *very, very* strange happen."

"I don't think I want to know," she replied.

"Yeah, well, I have to tell someone. I was just standing around the hors d'oeuvres tray like a one-eyed cat in a seafood store and..."

"Oh, that's cute!"

"Oh, no. Not cute at all. I saw a guy have his wallet stolen right out of his back pocket. He was standing right next to me, picking away at some escargot..."

"Did you say anything to him?"

"No, I froze, and then he took off with his snails."

"Did you get a good look at the thief?" asked Trish, unfazed by Dave's declaration.

"Well, yeah, and I've met him before, at Zulu's party last night in the Navy yard. You weren't there. He's one of Zulu's lovers."

"Dave, Zulu has a lot of boyfriends and girlfriends. You can't assume Zulu is involved here. Do we really know who he sends the list to?"

"No, but I'm pretty sure Zulu would not approve of list recipients using it to come to these parties and rip people off," said Dave, "I mean, what the hell just happened here?"

"Zulu doesn't care what people do with their invitations. If Zulu gives you the list, he has his reasons." Trish replied.

"Yeah, but this guy was, like, so fuckin' brazen," said Dave.

"Says the man with a half a pound of sushi in his pockets," Trish noted.

"Yeah, but it's not the same," Dave insisted.

"Oh. It's not?" asked Trish, "How is it any different?"

Dave was at a loss for words and didn't reply, he just stared at his penny loafers and felt quite ashamed.

"Listen to me, Dave," Trish continued, "people come to these free things for all kinds of reasons. Some need to socialize, some need to eat. Zulu doesn't ask questions. He told me all about you and the bathroom attendant. Dave Stevens! That was fucking hilarious! You are pathetic!"

Dave never found it amusing to be belittled, but her words rang true. He was no more a fuck-up than he was before, he was just getting better at it.

"I was so embarrassed," said Dave, "Luckily, Zulu bailed me out. He told you?"

"He emailed me almost immediately after you left."

"That soon?"

"Quite a performance, David. He said he'll laugh about it for years to come. Years. Soap?"

"Two bars. And cologne!" said Dave, not so proudly.

A geisha came around and offered them each a glass of champagne. They heartily accepted and toasted to their new friendship.

"*And cologne*? Impressive. Here's to you, Two-bars-and-a-bottle-of-sweet-water Stevens! Born again! An unwelcomed guest! Enjoy!" said Trish blissfully.

"And to you, Teepee! My wild, schizophrenic Pied Piper! How many other events will you be attending this week? All of them?" he replied.

"Maybe one. Friday night."

"Only one? The Vida thing in Little Italy?" asked Dave, hoping to impress her.

"How did you guess?" Trish coyly replied.

"I was looking at the list and..."

Trish cut the conversation short as something began to smell fishy.

"You, sir, are brighter than I thought, Dave Stevens. There might be some hope for you after all. I've got to get back to some people I was talking to, and you better run before your sushi goes bad. It's been sitting in those pockets for a while now, I'm guessing?"

"Hey, I completely forgot," replied Dave, also noticing the aroma. "Yeah, I suppose I should go now, before I smell like the sea. So, I'll see you Friday then?"

"Fridays are usually really busy for me. I'm not 100 percent certain. I'll keep an eye on it. If nothing else comes up, then, yeah, of course. I'm sure a few people I know will be there. No promises, though."

"Doesn't sound like a plan."

"You are doing just fine without me," said Trish, reassuring him.

Dave smiled as he watched Trish wander back into the crowd.

"Man, I'm glad I met that girl," he thought.
Dave passed through the vestibule on his way out. The two geishas he met at the door when he arrived were now tucked away in back behind the coatracks, smoking cigarettes. He smiled and waved goodbye to them but they ignored him. He walked out the door with his pockets full of sushi, but remembered his ride downtown, and how his small issue of

having no money for a ride home had not been resolved. Small issue.

He paused to consider his options.

"What to do? What to do?"

The solution to his problem was simple. He was desperate and knew what he had to do, it was clear, as clear as a morning lake.

Dave returned to the party. He walked into the vestibule and looked around. There were no geishas in sight. They had left their honey pots, the donation and tip jars, unattended. Dave reached into the tip jar and quickly grabbed a handful of cash and change, as much as he could gather with one great claw, and then ran out the front door.

And ran, consumed by guilt.

And ran, consumed by failure.

His tennis sweater slipped off his shoulders and fell to the ground. Dave's feet got caught up in it and he wiped out. As he was rolling on the ground, he ripped flesh off his knuckles, but he was so overcome with fear, he didn't feel a thing. He got up, collected the sushi that fell out his pockets, and he kept on running, maniacally, through the streets of Manhattan, bumping into people and stopping traffic.

By the time he stopped to catch his breath, he'd arrived in Columbus Circle. Dave was almost halfway home.

He fell to his knees, wiped his cheeks and forehead, and looked at his bloody hands.

"Yeah...fuck, yeah…"

Unhinged, thoughtless, fearless, Dave had never been the *guns-a-blazin'* type before, his world had processes and order, calculations and expected outcomes. Nothing was ever *snatched*, it was earned. Recklessness was a recipe for disaster in the world of finance.

Old habits. Bad habits.

Dave took what he wanted when he needed it, and he got away. He stole something. Robbery is a crime, and Dave crossed a line.

He was a *top-fiver,* after all.

Chapter Twelve

"I'll light the fire, you place the flowers in the vase that you bought today, staring at the fire, for hours and hours while I listen to you play your love songs all night long, for me, only for me"

—*Graham Nash*

That's not what they taught him at Wharton.

Overcoming desperation and karma-caused insolvency was not part of their curriculum.

Dave's journey home was filled with thoughts of the petty crime he had just committed and little else. He felt very guilty, but it didn't change the facts. He took his first baby steps.

"I'm a petty thief," Dave conceded, *"Dad would be so proud."*

It was a bit nippy that evening. Dave shivered in silence, listening only to the click-clack of his feet on the pavement and his conscience telling him he'd crossed over to the dark side. When he arrived home, he kept his head down low and scooted up the stairs to avoid Gigi, but as always, she caught him at the lock and key. Dave looked like a dead rose, far from the fresh, vivid knockout he was when he'd left earlier.

Gigi stuck her head out the door. Always intuitive, she rarely missed an opportunity to say something to Dave, sarcastic or comforting, depending on how he was feeling that day.

"Wow, movie star, you must have struck out, am I right?" she observed. "What happened to your hand?"

In no time, Chuckles darted out of her apartment. She purred and clawed at Dave's pockets, picking up the fishy scent that came from the sushi he brought home for them to eat.

"It wasn't anything fancy, just a meet-up with a few friends," Dave replied. "I fell. Clumsy me, right?"

"So why you dressed up so fancy? You don't have any friends, except me and Checkers," Gigi declared.

"Had to get out of my basketball shorts sooner than later," said Dave.

"Yeah, sure." Gigi didn't believe a single word. "Don't forget to take the sushi out of your pockets," she said as she walked briskly back into her apartment. "You really are *fucked up*, Dave Stevens."

Chuckles took a couple of pieces of sushi for herself. She was quite content. It was salmon. She loved salmon. So much for being cool. Dave was exposed. Chuckles blew his cover.

Gigi stood steadfast in her doorway and looked at Dave with utter disdain.

"Dave Stevens, I tell you to always leave your window open in your kitchen. Checkers can't get back into your apartment. Now I have to feed her? It costs a lot of money to feed animals," she said. "Your apartment smells like a fish market. Gross. Clean up, Dave Stevens. Clean up. Don't forget the window. You forget the window one more time, I'm keeping your Checkers."

"The hell you will," replied Dave with a laugh, "Chuckles knows why my apartment smells fishy. It has something to do with your damn cooking, I think."

"Your apartment is just a disaster waiting to happen, Dave Stevens!" said Gigi angrily. She slammed her door shut but continued to lecture him.

Boom!

"The window! The window! Don't forget! Don't forget!"

"The window! In the kitchen!" Dave hollered back; certain she heard him.

One of Gigi's unique abilities was being able to bring Dave back down to earth.

Dave quietly settled in and slowly removed his shoes. His heels hurt from all the running he'd done. Dave still had sushi in his pockets, but by now it had melted into a puree of sorts. He reached into his pocket and shoveled a handful into his mouth, slobbering the rice and fish all over his lips. It was still early enough to venture out into the city again, the list had dozens of other parties on tap that evening, but Dave had failed so miserably, he wasn't going anywhere, he had to reset. His mind raced.

"There's got to be more to this," he thought, "there's got to be more. What am I doing wrong? Why did I lose my cool? I can do anything. I can survive anything. I'm invincible."

Invincibility. His therapist said that might be a problem.

With heightened resolve, and a fresh slice of courage courtesy of his geisha adventure, Dave forced his dead weight off his couch and took a long shower. He needed a thorough cleansing.

Showering was the one activity that gave Dave true solace. Standing there, naked, listening to the pitter-patter of the droplets on his forehead, Dave's shower stall was the only place on earth where he could think calmly and clearly. It was where he reconnected with Shawna, where he reached out to her soul, heard her whispers, remembered her touch. It was mostly a dream, their life together, a vivid memory Dave manufactured while in a coma, but Shawna's voice, her words, kept him alive. He could have returned to the light, but Shawna's voice told him he had a purpose. She sent him back to the world of the living.

"*I love you, Steel-town.*"

"I wonder if she'd still love me now," he thought.

Dave toweled off and walked into his living room. He'd forgotten his khakis on the couch. Chuckles cleaned out the pockets of every grain of rice and fish. She also managed to empty the other pocket, the one filled with the geishas' money. Dave got down on his hands and knees and struggled to pick up the change as most of it had rolled under the couch, courtesy of his anarchistic feline roommate. Dave retrieved every last penny. Once counted, his new fortune amounted $14.12.

"I'm a baaaaddd man, Chuckles! A regular Billy the Kid," he thought shamelessly.

Dave could self-deprecate all he wanted to, but he knew, in earnest, that $14.12 just wasn't going to cut it. He justified his behavior by convincing himself that this *quick borrow* from the geishas was a one-off. In reflection, Dave knew that Zulu's lover boy-cum-pickpocket was bad news, but that his activities were probably not unique. It didn't make Dave feel much better about himself. It was obvious that Zulu's list could get into the hands of anybody, for better or worse, even tip-jar thieves.

Dave knew he got away with one. He wasn't going to press his luck and hit the circuit for the purpose of stealing. His initial motivation was to network and find the *right people*, place and time to resuscitate his career. Incremental growth. Patience. That's what they taught him at Wharton. It was preached to him by Ellery McTier as well, but Dave learned how to say *fuck it* from bin-Laden, and that changed everything.

Landing a new job with an investment firm that would allow him to hang his hat and fill up a cubicle now seemed counterintuitive. Embracing this strange and tantalizing Zulu-given opportunity was too sexy to pass up. *Wall Street* or *Open-Sesame Street* were Dave's choices.

"People do this," he reassured himself. "I'm not the only one."
Clearly, Dave's rehabilitation had failed him.

He flipped.

Dave went online to check up on the financial markets and read the daily news. It was unhelpful. The headlines were bad and things were getting worse by the day. The occupation of Iraq, suicide bombings galore and the war on terror; it was all senseless violence. The President assured the nation the war was over. Dave's war would never end. His therapist told him to stay offline if he could. The therapist said going online could accelerate depression and suicidal tendencies. She recommended that Dave keep it light, to not underestimate his own fragility. It was exactly why she gave him the meds and exactly why he never took them. Dave needed to stay anchored in reality. War, death and destruction were just redundant, shitty news to him. There was no escaping it. Bad news just annoyed Dave, like a relentless wasp, masking it with meds would be no different than going back into a coma.

He may have been victim, but Dave Stevens was all about winning or learning. He expected to suffer from time to time. *"A few strokes of the lash on your back will only do you some good, son."* That was his late father's philosophy, the kind words he shared when Dave's team lost a high school basketball game or when he came home with a poor grade on an exam. Those fatherly digs were extensions of his dad's memories of his own capture in the Mekong Delta. The lash.

The Vietcong lashed his father thousands of times until he managed to kill them and escape. The voice of the man who won a Purple Heart, the man Dave could never live up to, spoke to his soul and fueled him to re-open Zulu's email and get his world in order.

"Go-time, son."

Dissecting every single link Zulu sent him, Dave tried his hand at *party-crashing 101* but it wasn't as simple a game as it appeared to be, it required research. Where to go and why? Who would be there? What could be gained? Dave set up a calendar and kept notes. People were going to ask him questions. He needed credible answers. He also needed proper attire and accessories to blend in and look believable. Even though Zulu was 6-foot 8 and possibly the most flamboyant transvestite in New York, Zulu found a way to blend in naturally, like a crystal chandelier. He was beautiful, if you gazed up, that is. Dave could blend.

"I have to master this shit, man," he reasoned. "I need money. I need food. I need a way out of my head."

Dave re-read the NYU link. He chose to attend that event because he knew that if the link came from Zulu, and it was academics-related, it was bulletproof. Doubling down, Dave then reconfirmed himself for the three other parties for which he had already registered. The other parties were being held at art galleries in the vicinity, so Dave had options, a multi-faceted plan, at his disposal.

The NYU event was held for faculty and alumni. It was the university's staff Rush Week, if you will. The party kicked off the new school session with a bang! Academic types were Dave's wheelhouse. He could talk shit to the best of them and play them like fiddles. Faculty. Grants. Submissions. Papers. All leading to more grants. Money. Schools used to hound Ellery McTier for huge amounts of grant money. It was a business all to its own. The game? How to live off wealthy people's gratuity in the name of academia. Dave viewed academics as egotistical people who deserved a shakedown so they could learn a thing or two. Dave was a Wharton grad, NYU people were easy prey for him.

"I'll have a field day," he thought.

Comfortable with his game plan, Dave closed his eyes to take a quick catnap. He was exhausted from all the excitement. He smiled contently and woke up the following afternoon. It was actually time to get ready to go out; he'd slept away the entire day.

To immerse himself in character that evening, Dave wore his usual fare, but he added a piece of ammunition to his outfit: a bow tie. Colorful. Paisley. It was the cherry on top of a suitable guise, worn to impress his soon-to-be *audience*. Dave looked smart.

With plans set for later if the faculty affair didn't produce enough bounty, Dave's bow tie gave him the flexibility to play different roles, professor or perhaps, art critic. Dave planned abstractly.

Intent.

Dave learned the hard way that preparation was indeed a fool's game. No one knows what happens next when you walk out your door, get in a taxi, take a train, board a plane, or walk into a boardroom for a meeting, but at least Dave now knew what he was doing and how his endgame was supposed to play out.

With one final, confident, De Niro-inspired wink in the mirror, and a slight adjustment of his bow tie, Dave was raring to go, but he couldn't ignore the stench of Thai food and the previous evening's sushi in the air. Chuckles purred gleefully, pleased that Dave had left such a mess for her to enjoy.

"You know I love you, Chuckles. I'll do my best to bring something good home for you to eat. You must be tired of shrimp."

Chuckles meowed. She could never tire of shrimp.

As he left, Dave doubled back to the kitchen and opened the window that led to the fire escape. Chuckles darted out quickly, making her way up to the roof where Gigi's chickens, roosters, birds, and probably Noah's Ark, resided.

"Dave Stevens!!!"

"Damn," said Dave, startled once again. Gigi stood in his doorway.

"What kind of crazy idea you have today, Dave? You go from staying in your apartment for six months to going out every night like New York big shot celebrity all of a sudden??" Gigi was keenly aware he was unhinged. "Vampire, huh?"

"Hey, I told you! I know people. I've got friends. People you don't know, people you've never met. Friends. Real friends. I'm feeling better. They want me to go out with them," Dave replied.

"I don't want to put salt on old wounds but didn't you tell me you don't want friends anymore because all your friends are dead?"

"Well, *you* are my friend, Gigi."

"Yeah?"

"Well, yeah. Kind of," replied Dave.

She blushed. Those were sweet words.

"Well, okay, *friend,* you just go have your good times, but be careful. I don't know these *friends* you know that I don't know, that I've never met." she forewarned.

"Gosh, you're so kind. If you're too careful Gigi, you'll miss everything and never have a good time. No sense waiting anymore for the good times to roll. I just needed a push down the road, that's all. Maybe you need a push, too."

Rolling like a boss with the hefty $14.12 in his pocket, walking 80 blocks was no longer necessary. Dave took a cab down to Washington Square. His newly-acquired wealth proved taking a cab was no longer a luxury. In fact, the

$14.12 took him as far as he needed to go. The event was just around the corner from his drop-off point, making it a short, easy walk for Dave the rest of the way.

With a tug on the lapels of his blazer, he fell into character as Dr. David Stevens, professor of Business Administration and Finance, University of Tacoma. His reason for being in New York City? A conference with Dr. Paul Rodríguez. Yes, Dr. Paul Rodríguez. It was a generic name, like his own. If that didn't sell it, nothing would.

As he arrived at the NYU entrance, Dave was greeted by a young, whimsical, bespectacled freshman. She wore a short, pleated kilt, and a warm, inviting smile. She was a knockout, a sexy little kitten.

"NYU! Here for you!" she cheered.

"Is that some sort of secret password? Well, I'm NYU! Always here for you!" Dave replied, with a wanton look in his eyes.

"Oh, I love all you alumni," said the freshman. "Are you on staff or just here meeting colleagues and former classmates?"

Dave grew impatient, annoyed by her prying. "Which room is the event being held in? Faculty Rush?"

The freshman picked up her clipboard and pressed it tightly against her chest.

"Fourth floor, room 418...And, oh yes! Name please, cutie pie?"

"Stevens. Dave Stevens."

"Yes. Here you go. Hold on a moment." She handed Dave a bracelet.

"What's this for?" he asked.

"Just wear it when you're inside. All food and beverages are complimentary. On your way out, you hand in this bracelet for recycling and then they'll give you your homecoming gear. Don't forget to recycle, Dr. Stevens! No recycling? *No gear*!"

"How do you know I'm a doctor?" asked Dave. "Is it written on your list?"

"Well, mostly everyone who's attending the event this evening has a PhD, right? It's true, though. You are kind of young to be a doctor, hmmm?" replied the freshman, precociously.

"Oh, yes, of course, of course. I get that from time to time. What kind of homecoming gear are the alumni receiving this year?" asked Dave, salivating with curiosity.

"Cozy sweatshirts, hats, books, all in a huge duffle bag. A really nice bag, too! You get them every year you attend, don't you, Dr. Stevens?"

"Yes, yes," Dave chuckled, "I totally forgot. The years just fly by."

"Well, have a nice evening, handsome Dr. Stevens," said the freshman as she blew Dave a kiss.

Dave read her name tag. "Thanks, I will. You too, *Maybelline*? Maybe we could have a cocktail later?"

"Oh! You read my name. Yes. My friends call me *May-Day*. Dr. Stevens! My goodness!" she said with a giggle. She pointed over her shoulder to a staircase. "It's just up there, to your right. It'll get you up to the 4th floor."
Dave seemed legit. Victory.

Garbed in a filthy tuxedo jacket, pleated pants and a bow tie, Dave looked rather Chaplin-esque. He gazed at the bracelet of manna on his wrist; it came with a *pay-out*. He looked around the room and formulated his *half-an-hour-in-and-out* plan: "Settle in, get a drink or two, make small talk, check out what food is available. Fill up if it's good, fuck off if it's not."

The party was bland. Desperate for a meal, Dave looked to nibble on something, but his mind was fixed on the parting alumni gifts and the freshman's kilt. "It's not just a fridge-filler. There's free stuff. It won't be a total bust."

Dave needed a reason for attending, so he walked around, contemplated, schemed, and honed his acting skills. His bullshit skills needed sharpening. Dave wanted to play the game like a professional, but was he like Icarus getting a little bit too close to the sun? That could spell disaster.

The gathering was quaint, but Dave managed to recognize a couple of obvious list recipients in attendance, a woman he'd seen at Fight Club, and Zulu's lover, the thief, who was on the trail once again. His presence made Dave feel uncomfortable.

Snaking his way through the throng, Dave stalked a server who had a tray full of spring rolls. He swooped in and grabbed them all, taking a stack of napkins as well to wrap them up. The spring rolls fit snugly into his left pocket. Dave then sauntered about clumsily, taking stock of what other food was available for *take-out*. Dinner would not be complete without dessert, and Dave had a sweet tooth. Just as he anticipated, there it was, in plain view: a table overflowing with home-baked cookies and muffins. Dave knew his shit! It confirmed his research. Zulu put the NYU gig on the list because it was a *grocery* stop, for people who were hungry. The problem was that the party itself just wasn't much fun.

"Two of *Kathy's double-chocolate muffins* and I'm leaving." As he reached for the rich treats, Dave was interrupted by an odd fellow.

"Ahem, excuse me sir, is it you, *MacTavish*?"

A gentleman with an imposing, well-coiffed moustache tapped Dave on his shoulder and startled him. Dave nervously laughed at the man but quickly reminded himself that he had to remain in character.

"Dear sir, no, you must have me mistaken with someone else," Dave replied, enunciating every letter. "I'm Stevens. Doctor. David Stevens. Tacoma University."

"Pardon me, Dr. Stevens. Tacoma. Tacoma? What brings you all the way here to New York City this evening, Dr. Stevens? Are you an alum?" asked the gentleman.

"No, no. Following up on some research by my colleague Dr. Rodríguez here at NYU. Yourself?" Dave replied.

"Oh me? I'm Dr. Mahone. P.G. Mahone. I'm trying to drum up some grants, you know, for ancestral Irish lineage research connected to New York. Is Dr. Rodríguez in any way responsible for grant disbursements this coming session? Do you have an in, I mean, *for the money*?" the gentleman asked, unsubtly.

Dave knew Mahone was playing some sort of game. Everyone, it seemed, was a scam artist, everything had a hitch, so Dave took his own game up a notch.

"Why, yes, Doctor, I do. Could you repeat your name again?"

"Mahone. P.G. Mahone."

"Well, I suppose I could speak to Dr. Rodríguez. Do you have a contact where I can reach you? An email? Perhaps a cell number?"

Mahone reached for a muffin, looked at Dave, and took a large, unseemly bite out of both of them, knowing full well he'd been handily dismissed. Dave was not as naïve as he looked. His mouth half-full, Mahone bowed out with pleasantries.

"Good luck to you there, Dr. David, with whatever you're doing. We'll exchange that contact information later, if you're still around, I mean."

Mahone knew he'd delayed Dave's departure, so he backpedaled his way into an adjoining conversation and flashed a mischievous smile. Dave admired the moment and wondered if he himself was now a bonified player or if he'd just been played.

The NYU party was a fiasco. Dave had run out of patience. He took a few chocolate muffins, wrapped them up, and stuffed them clumsily into his right pocket, causing his pants to bulge. His grocery shopping complete, it was time for Dave to check-out. "This shit is lame. I knew this would be a dump. Stale muffins, crappy wine, *and freaks*."

As he left, Dave bumped into a man making his way into the NYU affair. The collision caused the muffins in Dave's pocket to fall to the floor. The man gave Dave a stern look.

"Hey! Watch where you're going, man. Those are my muffins...!" Dave shouted.

The man clearly didn't care; he growled, shrugged and kept walking without apologizing. Dave picked up his muffins, certain he'd seen the man somewhere before, but he couldn't remember where. It was an eerie feeling, once-faceless people all began to look familiar.

Actually, a lot of things came into focus for Dave. For one, Zulu's email list wasn't all that exclusive. Tons of people got it, and tons of people used it. Zulu controlled it, but the list had been circulating for a while, a long while. Also, it seemed as if everyone attached to Zulu was under some sort of spell, a crazy *chocolate muffins and spring rolls in your pockets* spell.

To make matters worse, Dave forgot about the bevy of gifts his piping-hot young friend at NYU had waiting for him, the *really huge, nice bag*. He could have used it, but it wasn't worth enough to him to run back to the lifeless gathering. Dave was already flustered by Mahone's suspicions. The fact that Zulu's boy, the pickpocket, was at NYU made Dave's decision to leave the place an easy one. He'd already put his name down all over town, there were other spots to check out, so Dave ripped off the manna bracelet the freshman had given him, and he threw it to the ground, essentially littering. He didn't recycle it, that's for sure.

Dave's chosen backup gig was at an art gallery close to the NYU party. He took a shortcut through Washington Square to get there. As he strutted on, oil from the spring rolls in his pocket began to seep through his pants. It dripped down his leg. Something had to be done.

Dave passed through the Washington Square arch and onto Fifth Avenue. He was looking for a garbage can to throw out the gnarly food when he crossed paths with a dog walker. She had a dozen or so dogs of all shapes and sizes under her strict command, strict that was, until Dave showed up.

The pups smelled Dave's food instantly as he passed them by. They barked loudly and pulled on their leashes, so much so, the dogwalker begged Dave to leave.

"Hey, they don't usually act up like this. Could you please, um, move on, sir?"

Dave had left the NYU party because he was bored, dissatisfied, and bent on destruction. He reached into his pockets, pulled out the spring rolls and muffins, and he threw them to the dogs. The poor animals went nuts and snapped viciously at the food. They slammed their walker to the ground.

"*Jesus! What the fuck is wrong with you, man??*" hollered the dogwalker. "*You fuckin' asshole!!!!*"

Dave gingerly walked away, nefariously pleased with the chaos he had caused. His behavior was malicious and completely out of character, as if he had suddenly turned to darkness for comfort.

"Sometimes you win and sometimes you lose. Dog eat dog world." he thought. "*Let's become the Alpha. Let's go get a win now.*"

Chapter Thirteen

"Well, you gave me all your loving, and your turtle doving, all your hugs and kisses, and your money too, you know you love me, baby, still you tell me maybe, that someday well, I'll be through."
　　　　　　　　　　—Norman Petty/Buddy Holly/Jerry Allison

It was dusk in Soho. The gallery's exterior was decrepit. The windows were filthy, no hose or squeegee had been applied to them in decades. The wood framing of the windowsill had chipped away from years of neglect and carpenter ants that fed upon it. The building's exterior paint was layers thick; the culmination of shabby jobs done on top of shabbier ones. The building itself was art, not simply the contents of its gallery.

"*Trippy's Masterpieces.*"

Dave peered through the window with the fascination of a child. The interior lighting was as lucent as the North Pole. Trippy's masterpieces were uniquely displayed, the lights so blinding no one could miss the very tiniest detail of Trippy's talent. It was the *pick of the list* spot that evening. Dave was sure he had a lucky number. His pulse raced. This was the type of party he absolutely wanted to crash, the one he dreamt of attending when he first received Zulu's email.

"Cool people. Finally. Looks like great food and free booze. Nothing to do but stand around, act cool, and make conversation. Chill, Dave, chill."
Dave found himself that mythical *good time*.

No pressure.

He took his party crasher initiative down a notch and casually walked up to the entrance where he was greeted by
two thin men with pencil moustaches. They wore zoot suits. One man's suit was red, the other man's was emerald. Both men had matching buckskin shoes. They weren't the least bit intimidating. Still, Dave thought to approach them with caution. Getting in had been easy up to this point. Registering in advance was working like a charm. Dave saw no reason to do anything different.

"Good evening, gentlemen."

"Yeah, good evening. Who are you?" asked the red zoot suit, rather rudely.

Uh oh. Game on again. Dave had to fall into character, and with a bow tie on, the transition was easy.

"Dave Stevens, San Francisco *Chronicle*. Art critic. I'm here to see Trippy's latest masterpieces."

"Are you a friend or colleague of Trippy's? We weren't expecting any press tonight," said the emerald zoot suit as he lit a long, thin cigarette.

"Neither. I'm an art critic. What don't you understand? I was referred to this exhibit by a dear friend of mine at the *Village Voice*. You are familiar with the *Voice*, I presume? I'm supposed to be on a guest list." said Dave.

Village Voice. It was sufficient. The men straightened up and became much more accommodating.

"You're on the list?" asked the red suit.

"Yes, most certainly!" replied Dave, angrily. "Do you think I would fly all the way out here from San Francisco if I wasn't on that nasty little list of yours?"

Dave moved them along; giving the men a little attitude made all the difference. The evening was another hurdle to build his confidence. He'd never been the pushy type before, he'd always been easy going, but overnight, Dave grew into a bulldog. "Are you going to make me wait all evening, boys?" he asked vehemently.

"What's your name again?" asked the red Zoot suit.

"Dave Stevens! Stevens! Dave! Dave Stevens!"

Panicking, the emerald Zoot suit pushed his red-suited confrere aside, ruffled his papers, and let Dave pass.

"Yes, yes. *Dave Stevens.* Right this way. Thank you, thank you very much. Have a good evening, Mr. Stevens, thank you."

Dave plowed through the foolish-looking, inept gatekeepers. He pushed them aside, ripped the gallery's door open, and walked into an obtuse wonderland. His eyes were instantly blinded by bright lights.

As advertised, fourteen *masterpieces* hung on the gallery walls; seven on the left and seven on the right. Bar stations were set up in the middle of the space for the guests to gather, drink and get panoramic views of the exhibit. The paintings had large speakers wired in front of them. Loud house music pounded out of them like a barrage of artillery. The heavy sounds were meant to enhance the overall experience of Trippy's purported genius.

Dave felt his feet tremble. The music's bass was so intense it shook the room like an earthquake, so very deafening no one could hear a thing, let alone one another. He walked up to the bar to get himself a glass of champagne and saw the same attractive woman he saw at the Fight Club, and most recently, at the NYU affair. He was sure she was a list-recipient. Same places? Same night? It was no coincidence. Dave raised his glass to get her attention. She nodded her head and smiled at him.

"Alright, alright Dave, you've arrived!" he thought

He left the bar to wade into the crowd and admire the works of art on display. Pausing to enjoy their uniqueness, Dave made small talk with the other guests and fabricated opinions about Trippy's creations as only a purported art critic could.

Trippy's works were based on Giacomo Balla's abstract *Speed and Sound*. They were essentially forgeries of the original work, but Trippy modified the original scheme by using neon colors and gluing bubble gum wrappers on the canvases. The idea was pretty avant-garde but the pieces were, at best, kindergarten projects, thoughtless and extreme in nature. Nonetheless, Trippy was a big enough deal for someone to back him and pay thousands of dollars to hang his shit on their walls.

It was lively affair, a definite upgrade from the other parties Dave had gone to so far. He was just getting his feet wet, so an evening of chatter, fun, of simply being a party *guest* as opposed to a party *crasher*, seemed like the best strategy.

"Pretend you belong." For the moment, he was calm and content.

"Dave!"

Trish snapped him out it.

Dave wasn't surprised to see Trish there. He called her a couple of times, she didn't pick up, but the list being what it was, there was a pretty good chance they'd to cross paths.

"Hey! Nice to see you here!" Dave hollered over the beats.

"Hey back at ya'! I know Jimmy Shabazz since he was a snot-nosed, little brat in grade school," she replied.

"Who is Jimmy Shabazz?"

"Trippy. At least he thinks he is!"

"Oh, okay. His stuff has a pretty cool vibe." Dave shouted.

"Oh! You're an art critic?" joked Trish. "Yeah. I'm only here because I'm his friend."

"Great place. It's a pretty high-end, classy affair." Dave was impressed.

"Ha! Looks can be deceiving," replied Trish. "Did you know that all the champagne being served is really swill that you can get down at a corner store? It's all been put into fancy bottles. If you think you're drinking the good stuff, you are truly mistaken, my friend."

"How do you know?" asked Dave.

"You go to enough of these gigs, you learn a thing or two, like the difference between good champagne and piss water! Anyhow, I'm going to go speak to Jimmy now. He's having a hissy fit over something. I don't know what. It's nice to see you out here, Dave," said Trish, with a coy smile. "I'm glad that you're making the rounds. Zulu sent you the email because he thought it would be helpful."

"Hey, Trish, thanks for being a friend. If you don't mind, though, when I call you, can you pick up next time? Sometimes, I just need to speak to someone. My nerves, they're a little…" Dave tried to elaborate, but it wasn't necessary.

"Sure, Dave. I understand. Don't feel like you can't reach out to me. I'm here for you, more than you know." Trish replied.

"You really mean that?"

"I do. I know you're going to do something special with your life one day, Dave, something *really special*. Trust me. I just have that feeling."

Trish gave him a hug and made her way over to the bar to spend time with her friend Trippy, the man of the moment.

Soon after, Dave ran into Zulu's boy, the pickpocket. Everyone who had received the list from Zulu was on the same track that evening; the NYU event, the gallery... Dave wasn't crazy about Zulu's young friend or his attitude so he confronted him.

"Hi, how you doing? It was great seeing you the other night. I also saw you at NYU tonight. You were pretty rude. Do we have a problem?"

The man didn't bat an eyelash. Dave wouldn't let him go.

"Don't you remember me? I'm Dave. Dave Stevens. I'm friends with Zulu. We sat at a table for hours the other night, laughing. Together. Remember?" Dave persisted.

"I don't recognize you, ok?" the man replied reluctantly. He stared at Dave with *that look*, that dour, *unforgettable* look.

"The other night, in Brooklyn. In the yard. The warehouse. You and Zulu in the bathroom...Don't you remember? Come on, you're pulling my leg."

"You must be mistaking me for somebody else, sir. Have a good evening."

Zulu's boy stood up from his seat and tried to walk away just as he'd done before. Dave grabbed his arm and wouldn't let him leave.

"I know what you do at these parties."

The man pulled his arm away and pushed Dave.

"Don't touch me! You touch me again, I'll kill you. I don't know what you are talking about." He quickly vanished, leaving Dave somewhat frightened.

"I have to tell Zulu what this guy is doing at his parties. What the hell just happened? I sat there for hours, shoulder to shoulder, between him and Zulu. This guy is a fucking problem." Dave was no longer in a partying mood.

Bad vibes crept up on Dave from time to time. His senses had been heightened as a result of his traumatic head injury and death experience. Rehab taught him how to think and feel once again, but it also rewired his brain. Call it what you will, but Dave had developed antennae and a nose for impending trouble, but his power was very unreliable. He knew that most of the people at the gallery that night were on Zulu's list, but Dave needed to know more. Who were shmucks like him, the *party-crashers*, and who were the *pickpockets*?

Dave approached the woman he'd seen at Fight Club. They never spoke that night because Dave was with Trish, but their eyes locked on one another on a number of occasions, mostly out of curiosity, a *faces-in-the-crowd* sort of thing. They shared a moment, that much Dave remembered, so he felt comfortable enough to talk to her.

A buxom redhead, she sat on a bar stool alone, stirring a raspberry in a champagne glass. Dave waited a while before making his move. She glanced nervously over her shoulder and then settled her gaze back down into the depths of her glass. Dave surprised her.

"Hi, can I buy you a drink?" he asked foolishly. The drinks, of course, were free. Dave thought to open their conversation with some light humor, but his joke wasn't particularly amusing.

"I have one, thanks. Maybe when I'm done," the woman replied, coldly.

"Are you a fan of Trippy's work?" asked Dave, attempting to pry some nugget of information from his Fight Club acquaintance.

She cut him off immediately. "I am actually here with someone."

"Oh, I'm sorry, it looked like you were alone. Maybe some other time?"

She stood up and pulled her handbag away.

"Nice move. Almost got me," she whispered. "Mind your own business, man. You seem like a nice guy. Don't ever talk to me again. Happy hunting." Like mist from the East River on a stormy day, the woman faded away into the night, leaving Dave with more questions than answers.

He needed to share his weird experiences with Trish, but she was nowhere to be found. His new support system had failed him. Dave dealt with his erratic hills and valleys, sans medication, and it was particularly painful for him early on in his recovery, but he made it through. The only time he had minor setbacks was when he felt overwhelmed and overstimulated. Too much shock taxed his system. That night, Dave's intentions were to have good time and relax but suddenly, he felt alone, adverse, shaky, and he needed to get out of there.

The house music pounded into his skull. Its repetitive thumping gave him a terrible migraine. The neon paintings, combined with his sensitivity to light caught up to Dave and hit him like a ton of bricks. Dave was crashing.

His instincts told him to grab some food, put it in his pockets, and get home as soon as possible, but as Dave was trying to leave the gallery, Zulu's boy, the man who'd repeatedly insulted and ignored him earlier, came up to him and grabbed Dave's arm firmly. "Come with me, we'll leave together." He abducted Dave, quite literally, and pushed him out the front door where another man was waiting for them. He, too, grabbed Dave, and the men hustled him down an alleyway. When they were far enough from view, they let Dave go.

"Fuck! I know you! You made me drop my muffins. You two know each other??" Dave shouted.

"Yeah, we do. I'm Remy. Your friend from the Navy yard here? He's Eren. What the fuck are you doing here?" He slammed Dave, rather violently, into a wet brick wall.

"Hey! I was meeting my girlfriend. We came to see Trippy's works of fine art. I'm a big fan. He's a genius!" Dave attempted, in vain, to play his way out of the situation, but he was, unfortunately, out of moves.

"Dude. Don't bullshit me," said Remy. He grabbed Dave by the lapels of his jacket lapels and shook him. "We've seen you everywhere this week. Here. There. Everywhere. What the fuck are you up to, man?"

Dave pushed back. He was the son of a war veteran and on his second life, nobody was going to derail him from doing whatever the hell he wanted to do with it.

Then, Zulu's boy Eren chimed in.

"Don't be so rough on him. He's a friend of Zulu's. It was Zulu that wanted him here. We should respect that."

The beating stopped momentarily. The men took their hands off Dave and backed away. Remy shook his head and tried to process the whole situation.

"So, you've seen me before?"

"Yeah. You bumped into me at NYU. Knocked my muffins out of my pocket. I was sure I'd seen you before that, too. I don't remember where, though. But I've seen you. Both of you. I know what you do," Dave replied.

"Oh. You know what we do?"

"Yes. I saw Eren at work!"

"And you're a friend of Zulu's?" asked Remy.

"Yes. He invited me here tonight." Dave replied.

"Oh, he invited you, did he?"

"Yes. Personally."

"Personally. Don't make me laugh, fuck. Something tells me you're not coming clean," said Remy, "something tells me that you're just one of those people who shouldn't be here."

"No. It's true. Zulu and I go way back, I mean it's been a long time since we've been, I'd say, close but..."

"List," said Eren, bluntly.

"Oh. You're a newbie on Zulu's list, are you?" asked Remy.

"List? Zulu's list? I don't know what you're talking about, man," replied Dave, calmly. The lies weren't working.

"You better come clean, fucker. You know what kind of people Zulu emails his list to, right?" said Remy. He expected some truth to start flowing out of Dave's mouth.

"Sure. People like me. Art lovers."

Dave doubled down and replied sarcastically. It was the wrong answer, delivered smugly and with a giggle. His response wasn't even worthy of being called a *lie*. Remy paused for a moment, lowered his eyes to the ground and tapped his chin with his index finger. He lifted his head back up inchmeal, and he took a good, long look into Dave's lying eyes. Dave's wormy giggle infuriated him, so much so, Remy cocked his fist and hammered Dave swiftly in the sternum, punching him where 9/11 had previously crushed all of his ribs. Dave sunk to the ground like a crumpled piece of origami.

Remy knelt down in front of him.

"I'll be more specific. Do you know why Zulu invites people like us to these events?"

"You're...Art...Lovers...Art lovers," replied Dave, breathless but defiant.

"Art lovers...fuckin' art lovers! This guy just won't stop..."

Eren was incensed. He kicked Dave in the stomach and rolled him over. Remy lifted Dave up and tore his jacket. Once Dave was upright, Remy backed off but he was far from done with Dave. He slammed Dave into the wall once again and barked at him. The stench of Remy's alcohol and tobacco-laden breath was so strong, it practically burned the hair off of Dave's nostrils.

"Three types of people come to these *parties:* people who should be here, people who shouldn't be here, *and people like us*," Remy explained, cold-bloodedly. He slapped Dave repeatedly, causing Dave's magical bow tie to fall to the ground. *"Do you pay tribute to Zulu*? You know what that means? You know what that means?"

Dave was in deep. He had no idea what Remy and Eren were talking about and it didn't bode well for him. He suddenly remembered the women at the Navy yard party mentioning something about *tribute*, but he didn't make anything of it at the time.

Eren jumped in and slapped Dave vigorously.

"Yeah, *tribute,*" asked Eren, "do you pay Zulu tribute??"

"Tribute? Tribute? What the fuck is *tribute*? I don't pay Zulu anything!" Dave insisted. He raised his arms to protect himself from being beaten further.

The ruckus crushed Dave's spirit. He was terrorized, but he didn't regress or lose control of his emotions even though he winced in pain and welled up with tears. You could punch Dave Stevens a thousand times, but the blows would never hurt nearly as much as when he was killed on 9/11. Random hoodlums punching him in the gut? It was a breeze.

The men stopped and looked at one another, realizing they'd made a mistake with Dave Stevens; he was a *nobody*.

"He doesn't know shit. You don't know shit, now, do ya'?" said Remy.

"No, I don't know what you're talking about. Please, man," Dave begged.

"What's your name?" asked Remy

"Dave. Dave Stevens."

Remy slapped him in the mouth.

"Dave? Dave Stevens? What kind of bullshit, made-up name is that?"
"Give me your wallet," Eren demanded.

Dave took out his wallet from his jacket pocket and surrendered it to Eren. He sifted through it and found Dave's driver's license. It had all of Dave's pertinent information. It was all Eren and his associate Remy would need. He handed it to Remy.

"He's not lying. Zulu knows him. Here. Look at this."

"David Stevens. Wouldn't you know it? It's his real fucking name. Wow. West Mifflin, Pennsylvania. I'm going to keep this, David Stevens. I know where your family lives. That's not a good thing for you, I mean, now that you know what I do for a living," said Remy.

"You better leave them alone!"

"I will, or I won't, that depends on you really, and you aren't in any position to negotiate, huh? Listen up. I'm going to expand your horizons, my little friend. It's quite obvious that you're on this list, right? Zulu sends the list out to all kinds of people. Thousands might receive it, or maybe just a handful of us. Who knows? He changes his mind every day. Zulu is in charge, man. He's the kingmaker. He inherited some shitty list a few years ago. The original creator did fuck all with it; he was just some nose-picking geek from Harvard. Zulu has taken it to the moon and now he has the largest information network on the island of Manhattan. He puts together this list, not for the people he sends it to, but rather, for the people who want eyes on their events, understand? The *party-makers*. They are his clients, those attention-seekers. They want the illuminati, the rich and famous, to come out and play at their parties. It's free publicity. It could mean the difference between 10 bucks and 10 million bucks, all from one photograph. Zulu has relationships with all kinds of people. He has his way of showing how he feels about them, different ways of helping them, if you will. As a big fuckin' thank you for his help, we pay Zulu *tribute*."

"You steal and then you pay him?"

"No. No. No. It's not a conventional payment. Zulu has different arrangements with everybody. He benefits? Everyone benefits. Everybody's a winner. It doesn't matter what game you're playing. If you are on Zulu's list, you do your own thing, make your own way, you make your own luck, and then you show Zulu some form of appreciation. That's it. Since you're new and you don't know what the fuck is up, you're in my way David Stevens, and that's disturbing my ecosystem. Like I said, three types of people come to these *parties,* if you will. The ones who should be there? They show up to get their faces in the newspapers and online. The ones who shouldn't be there? Yeah, they do that too, but they're meaningless cake eaters, people like you, who just come for free shit, yeah. Shits and giggles. Zulu probably gave you the list because he thought you were pathetic."

"He's a friend of a friend," Dave confessed.

"Who's your friend? I need to know," Remy demanded, as he picked his teeth with Dave's driver's license. "Zulu's got a million *special* friends."

"I'm not going to tell you," Dave insisted.
Eren threw a punch at Dave's chin but missed. Dave countered, hit Eren in the back of his head, and knocked him to the ground.

"Back the fuck off!" Dave roared.

Remy pulled out a gun, pushed Dave back up against the wall, and pressed the gun's nose firmly into Dave's cheekbone.

"Where do you live?!" Remy howled. "Are you visiting here from West Mifflin, or do you live here?"

"Uptown! UPTOWN!" Dave shrieked; his eyes wide with fear. "Washington Heights. 158th and Riverside. Not too far from the train…"

Remy lowered his gun.

"Perfect, Dave Stevens, you lucky son of a bitch. I won't kill you tonight, you've been enough of a fucking obstacle already, but I might kill your family. Tell you what, tomorrow night? Yeah, you gotta roll with us. We're going to show you the ropes. You see what we do? Thieving? It takes planning. You're going to get your fucking hands dirty and break the law. You're curious? Okay. I'll teach you. I don't need some freeloader getting in the way. I've been doing this a long time. Sooner than later, I'm going to have a list of my own. Then, you'll be paying tribute to me. No newbie is going to fuck that up for me. You see, Dave, we're a crew. Money. Real money. That's what you came for, right? Free shit? Food? Connections? Money, man. You're going to roll with us, Dave. You don't have a choice in the matter. Welcome aboard."

Dave got up and dusted himself off, still convinced he had options.

"What if I just go to the cops? I know who you guys are, what you look like. I could pick you out of a lineup."

"Yeah, that's funny. And what are you going to say? You gonna tell the cops about the list? You think you could just blow that up for everybody? Maybe, just maybe, the cops are in on it. Did you think of that? You don't know. You don't know shit. I'm not going to have you finger me for petty theft and pickpocketing, dude. It's a lot bigger than that. I'm just one of many. There are legions of us. This has been going on for years. You either play along or you get taken out. I'm sorry it had to come to this, but you were just asking for it. You couldn't mind your own business," said Remy.

"Couldn't mind your own business," Eren agreed.

Remy pulled his arm back one final time and let his fist fly. He clocked Dave right across his jaw. Dave fell to the ground, knocked out cold, unable to see more than a reflection of the city lights in a puddle next to him.

"158th and Riverside, buddy. Tomorrow at 6. Wear a pair of jeans, it'll be a fun night." Remy tossed a $20 bill on the ground. "This ought to get you to Harlem. You can walk the rest of the way, you sad fuck. Sorry for ruining your smelly jacket. I'll bring you a new one. Promise. Can't have you walking around looking like that."

Remy and Eren made their way down the alleyway and back onto the street. They left Dave behind, crushed like an aluminum can, gasping for air. He heard Trish as she left the gallery, but he was unable to breathe or get up, let alone holler out to her for help.

"Oh! Hey Remy! How are you doing? Eren! Long time, no see!" said Trish.

"Trish! My girl! I'm doing great," Remy replied.

"I didn't see you in there." Trish noted.

"Oh, yeah, I was there earlier. Great show. Great show," said Remy, comically.

"I didn't know you were an art lover," said Trish.

"Art lover, yeah, that's it. Fine art," Remy replied, "fine art."

Dave overheard their conversation clearly. Trish knew these men? That sobering revelation brought Dave around rather quickly given the bad beating he'd just received. He sat upright against the wall, peered down the alleyway and watched Trish as she, Remy and Eren all left together.

Winded, Dave's ego hurt more than his chest and mouth. He definitely didn't trust Trish anymore nor did he want her *help* any longer, given the mess he had gotten himself into, thanks in part to her and her friend Zulu. Was Remy a friend of hers or did they just know one another from the list? What was her connection to this? Did Trish also pay tribute to Zulu?

"Tribute??"

It took only a few days for Dave to go from a lonely, damaged, friendless man to one whose very life was threatened by the new relationships he'd just fostered.

A stray dog, a Doberman Pinscher, walked up to Dave and sniffed his torn tuxedo jacket. Dave pulled out a piece of a chocolate muffin from his pocket that had somehow survived his journey and subsequent rumble. Dave surrendered it to the pup.

"I know how you feel," he said to the gentle beast, "I know how you feel."

The dog jumped on Dave and barked. It sniffed around and licked him vigorously; it wanted more food.

"Down, boy! Down, boy!" said Dave nervously, "That's all I got, little fellah!"

The pup wasn't friendly by any means. It picked up on the food scent all over the tuxedo jacket, and it sensed Dave's momentary weakness and fear. The dog was relentless. Dave pushed it away, but the dog snapped back and bit his arm.

"Grrrrrr, rrruffff!!!" the dog growled, as it ran down the alleyway.

"*Ouch! Ouch! Ouch! Fuuuuccckkk!*" Dave screamed.

"Oh, there you are, you bad puppy!! You can't run away from mama like that, you sweet boy!" It was the dog walker who Dave had met earlier in the evening; the not-so-sweet hound that bit him had strayed from her pack.

As she knelt down to put a leash on the Doberman, the dogwalker noticed Dave, laid out and bloodied, perched up against the wall at the end of the alleyway. He was a fraction

of the confident and ill-intentioned man who'd caused all the trouble for her in Washington Square.
Dave, beaten and bemused, lazily waved at her.

"Fuck you!" she shouted delightedly, as she left with her furry friend. She raised her middle finger with great enthusiasm, and pointed it at Dave. *"Fuuuuuck yooooouuu!!"*

"Let's get a win tonight, baby, a real big win!" That was the game plan.

Dave spat out some blood and reached over for the $20 bill Remy had left behind for him. He stared at it.

Dave had survived quite an ordeal again. He was getting good at that.

"The night wasn't a total loss now, was it? 20 bucks is 20 bucks, and I have plans for tomorrow, hmmm."

Hmmm.

Chapter Fourteen

"Heaven loves ya', the clouds part for ya', nothing stands in your way, when you're a boy, clothes always fit ya', life is a pop of the cherry, when you're a boy."
—*Brian Eno/David Bowie*

Dave's third night out on the town as a bona fide party-crasher was an absolute disaster. Everything comes at a price. He paid the hard way for his new education. The money he'd spent on Wharton was a bloody waste. Dave would have been better off learning hand-to-hand combat from his dad.

Remy and Eren beat him up, and then they beat him down to his core. Dave had left his apartment that evening with the intention of *tripping the light fantastic* in Soho, but in the end, he wound up in an alley with a bloody mouth, a torn jacket, and a crushed soul.

With $20 in hand, Dave walked into Midtown. He figured that by walking some of the way home, he could save some money and hop on the train instead of taking a cab. The train ticket only cost $5. He'd have some cash left over to buy cat food, at the very least.

Dave caught the train near Lincoln Center. His ride home was torture. More than likely concussed, he felt no worse for wear than he did on doomsday. It had been a sweltering night in the city. Dave's arm had small puncture wounds from the dog's snapping at him, and his hard leather shoes caused his feet to sweat, then swell, from all the trekking. The shoes left him with terribly painful blisters on his heels. The blisters soon ballooned with fluid and popped open. Dave's jaw was sore, his brain foggy, he had the taste of dry blood in his mouth, a ruined jacket, and now, his heels had opened wounds that were *code blue*. He exited the subway station gingerly, almost tip-toeing his way across the street to the bodega.

Dave walked in and nodded to the lifeless shopkeeper. He proceeded to pick up a can of cat food first. When Dave could afford it, Chuckles' food was the always the priority, her needs always came before his own. He then filled up a container with chicken and rice, grabbed a peach Snapple ice tea from the refrigerator, and finally, a box of Band-Aids from the shelf. They slipped from his hands and fell onto the counter.

"$16.25," said the shopkeeper.

"Look, man, I only have $15.00." said Dave, revealing his now empty pockets.

"$16.25."

"Hey, come on. You know me, *and Gigi*. I'm in here every other day. I'll be back tomorrow and I'll bring you the extra buck and a quarter. The subway cost me $5.00; I only had $20.00."

"$16.25."

"Look, man! Are you serious?"

"Serious. $16.25. $16.25."

Dave shrugged, mumbled, and reluctantly placed the Snapple back in the refrigerator.

"$15.05"

"But the Snapple was $2.00!"

"Tax. $15.05."

"You aren't going to cut me a deal today, are you?" asked Dave, angered by the man's rigidity. It was all so unreal.

"No," replied the emotionless shopkeeper, "no deal."

"Not even for a nickel?"

"No."

It came down to the cat food or the chicken-and-rice dish. Barely able to walk across the street with the blisters on his feet now bleeding, the Band-Aids were staying, and so was Chuckles' treat. Dave put the container of chicken and rice aside.

"$13.95. Tax in."

The shopkeeper smiled then reverted back to his usual blank stare. He gave Dave a dollar and a nickel change, slowly turned away, and refocused his attention on his TV and the security cameras behind the counter. The shopkeeper always watched old cowboy movies dubbed in Chinese, flitting off his stool like a grasshopper every time a shotgun went off.

"Thank you," said Dave kindly, but there was never a reply, a *you are welcome* or *have a nice day* from the shopkeeper, he never even blinked.

Dave left the ungracious shopkeeper alone to watch his gunslingers, choosing to sit down on a bus stop bench outside the bodega. He put the can of cat food aside, removed his shoes gently, and winced in agony. He opened the box of Band-Aids. The burning sensation and degree of pain from the blisters was so intense, it reminded him of every other painful injury he ever had: a broken collarbone from football in junior high, a broken leg during prom weekend getaway, 9/11...

Bummer. The bottom. Dave felt as shitty as one could feel, but from where he verily sat, he sensed something was coming to an end, whether it was his luck, or his life, he was unsure. He was numb, deeply alone, applying Band-Aids to dirty, open wounds. Things could not get worse.

"Eeuuuhhh!!"

Grunting in pain, Dave set his feet back into his stiff shoes and walked home, only to realize once he'd crossed the street that he'd forgotten the can of cat food on the bench. He doubled back to get it, but in no time at all, a homeless man had picked the can up and was looking at it with great curiosity.

"Umm, hey, man, I just bought that in the bodega. It's for my cat," said Dave.

"Yeah, well, I got me a cat too, man. Lots of motherfuckin' cats. Ain't got your cat's name on it. Huh! Ain't even got your name on it, unless you Mista Fancy Feast!"

"Look man, don't fuck around, give it back, please." said Dave angrily.

"*Fuck around? Fuck around?* Fuck is a *big* word, homey," replied the crusty, gray-bearded street prowler. He pulled out a shiv. "What's that cat food worth to you, motherfucker, you got to talk to me disrespectfully? What's that cat food worth??!"

"Whoa, whoa! It's just cat food, it's for my cat, Chuckles. Her name is *Chuckles*. Relax, man. *Relax.*" replied Dave, as he backed away. He tried to diffuse what had rapidly become an explosive situation, but it spiraled out of control.

"What else you got, motherfucker?! What else you got??"

Dave had lost all sense of panic and anger at this point in his perilous journey, so he just shrugged his shoulders, put his hand in his pocket, and pulled out the dollar and nickel he had just received from the shopkeeper in change.

"That's it, okay? Look at me. Do I look like I have *anything the fuck else*?"

The delusional man snatched the money from Dave's hand like a pigeon with a bread crumb, but the nickel fell to the ground. Confused and dissatisfied, the madman waved his shiv wildly. His homespun blade passed only a few inches away from Dave's nose, barely missing him.

"Fuckin' dollah-five? That's it??! I seen you walk across the street and then run back. Maybe you live around here. Maybe we go up to your place. You got money there!" suggested the wide-eyed, crack-induced vagabond.

"*Really*? Come on man, give me a *fucking break*," replied Dave. He'd reached his limit with the fellow.

The homeless man muttered, calculated and negotiated with himself until he became judge and jury. He sentenced Dave to a game of chance.

"Pick up the motherfucking nickel!" he shouted.

Dave knelt down slowly and picked up the coin.

"Heads? I just let you walk away. Tails? I'll cut you up into ribbons, motherfucker. Go on. Flip it, man! Flip it!"

Dave's hand was sweaty. He looked at the coin knowing that, barring some miracle, his life wasn't worth a nickel. He flipped it into the air and watched it rotate for what seemed like an eternity until the coin finally hit the ground. It hopped twice before landing on *heads*. The homeless man's eyes, deep, black and soulless, told the story.

"Yo man, Jesus saves! See? You just walk away now, motherfucker, you just walk away." Quite amused, the homeless man tossed the can of cat food over to Dave. "Thanks for the dollah. Going to get me a Snapple."

"Snapples are two bucks with tax, man," replied Dave as he caught the can and gently backed away onto the road, "I don't think you have enough for a Snapple..."

"Oh, that motherfucker going to give me anything I want. I got money. See dis dollah? That motherfucker going to give me anything I want, a'ight?"
Dave looked up at the stars and then watched as the homeless fellow walked into the bodega. Dave crossed the street and soon heard the beginnings of what would become a heated argument between the two men inside the shop.

"I don't give a fuck if it's two dollahs, man! You give it to me for a dollah. You took that dollah from me!! Now give it back or gimme this here Snapple! I'm taking this chicken and rice, too!!"

"Two dollars! $2.32 with tax! $2.32. Tax! Tax! No chicken and rice! No chicken and rice!"

"You give me that back then, motherfucker! You give me that back! You took my dollah! You took my dollah!"

"No dollar! No dollar!"

Dave sat on the stoop of his apartment building and listened to the commotion. He heard cans fall off shelves, fighting, screams, but he wasn't about to intervene. In broken English, the shopkeeper warned the homeless man as best he could, but shots were eventually fired, a sound not too uncommon in the neighborhood. Dave knew the cops would arrive in no time and look for witnesses as they had always done in the past when things went south at the bodega, but he'd seen enough for one night. He turned away from the murder scene and walked into his apartment building, unable to digest much more. The homeless man's corpse laid motionless on the ground, his eyes staring emptily, his blood flowing down the walkway of the bodega, a box of chicken and rice and a peach Snapple still in his hands.

Stomping as he marched up the stairs to his apartment, Dave still managed to evade Gigi's home surveillance. Chuckles was in the hallway, which was rather unusual. Normally, she'd make her way between Dave and Gigi's apartments from the back of the building. Gigi never let her stay in the hallway. Something was amiss; he remembered opening his kitchen window before he left.

Dave opened his door and found the carcass of one Gigi's prize chickens on his living room floor. It had been ripped to shreds. Chuckles ran into the apartment and meowed proudly, displaying the dead bird's head at her feet. She snatched the poor thing from the roof, hustled it down the fire escape and killed it ferociously. If pets could talk…

Chuckles ushered the poor bird in through the kitchen window but not without a fight apparently; there were feathers and bloody chicken bones everywhere. Chuckles was a sly kitty cat, chickens were easy prey, but she had never done that before, killing one of Gigi's chickens, and with such impunity. She was usually quite friendly with all of Gigi's furry and feathered friends. It was a bad omen.

"That's some message from the universe. Gigi's going to lose her shit, Chuckles. I'm glad I'm not the only one in knee-deep shit right now. Gigi is going to skin you alive, and Remy is probably going to put a bullet in my brain. I won't say anything if you don't."

Dave hugged Chuckles lovingly as she licked the chicken meat off her paws. He collected what was left of the mangled fowl and chucked it out the kitchen window. At least Chuckles would have an alibi if Gigi found it.
"There's no escaping harsh reality," he said to his feline companion, "there's trouble on the horizon."

Remy warned Dave about skipping town. Running meant Dave could never return, and Remy still had the ability to harm Dave's family. Running wasn't an option. Ensnared, Dave had no choice but to remain in the city and go along with Remy Hood and his evil sidekick, Eren.

The bathroom mirror never lied. Dave's unkempt hair and slightly bruised chin were a turn-on. His unshaven face, deep-set eyes, wild smile, the dirt; he wasn't shying away from this version of himself. Dave washed his face and brushed his teeth thoroughly, wallowed into bed and stared at the ceiling.

Running on empty with another long night ahead, he couldn't sleep. The ceiling stared back. It was the boy from Wharton with the McTier and Longley acceptance letter in his hand. That young graduate was amped, green, and he had no knowledge of what the future held in store for him. Young Dave Stevens laughed giddily. Dave felt sorry for him. Then, Dave died again, and again, the same way he did every night when he closed his eyes and had his recurring nightmares.

"Meow! Meow!"

Dave woke up the following morning after another night of tossing and turning. They were never just *dreams*. He shook his head and shoulders, rubbed sand from his eyes, and found Chuckles sitting on his chest, pawing his chin on the very spot where Dave had been clocked by Remy the night before. Chuckles knew what had transpired.

"It didn't feel too bad, I can take a punch." Dave had survived the World Trade Center massacre, a punch on the chin seemed palpable.

Chuckles sensed Dave had been manhandled, so she let him be, quietly rolling herself up into a ball and dozing off rather than begging him for a meal.

Having a long day ahead to contemplate what Remy and Eren's next move might be, Dave did recall Remy mentioning something about *casual attire*. That was a clue. The only clean clothes Dave had left were a pair of jeans and a Radiohead T-shirt he bought at a show with Shawna and Lester. He'd wear them, they were casual enough.

Dave sat down at his computer and opened Zulu's email to check Thursday's schedule. Using his newly acquired skills, he deciphered at least part of the scheme.

"Thursday. Record launch, new fire station dedication, another refugee benefit, launch of Freedom Fries. Hmm. Freedom Fries. Celebrities. Corporate sponsor. America. That's going to be a big event, maybe too big, but there will be a lot of good food at that one. At least I'll be able to eat before they kill me."

He may have been saddled with anxiety related to his uncertain fate, but Dave was still determined to stay one step ahead of the game.

"Which one of these events would Remy and Eren target and why? The new fire station dedication near the Trade Center? Lots of political figures, a lot of police. Why would Zulu put that one on the list? That is the last place I'd want to go, period. The refugee benefit? Angry, loud, opinionated people, giving away pamphlets, pushing issues; no money there. Again, why would Zulu put that on the list? Freedom Fries? What the heck are *Freedom Fries*? Lots of food. The problem? A lot of kids, families. Dangerous. Sure, families are easy targets, but if you fuck up a job like that, you're dead. Too many cameras. Too many eyes..."

Dave hashed out the situation, trying to emulate Remy's thought process. Remy had become Dave's new mentor. Dave should have gone to the authorities, Remy snapped a pistol in his face the night before, but Dave knew his family's safety was in jeopardy. He had no choice but to go along for this wild ride. Remy was an extremely dangerous man.

Zulu's Thursday schedule was riddled with smoke screens, diversions, but the record launch? It seemed fun and cool, too cool for school. Remy told Dave to dress casually. It added up; that's where they were going.

Dave painted a picture of the record launch for himself: a small crowd, but sizeable enough, a quaint venue with easily readable people, an inner bubble of untouchables, and an outer bubble of fans and hangers-on.

"Now, those people, they are the right kind of people, but the others? Nah, they shouldn't be there; and then there's us!"

VVVVRRRROOOOMMM!!!
SSSSMMMMMAAASSSSHHH!!!!!!

Us??

Dave had an episode.

"Breathe, Mr. Stevens. Breathe. Mr. Stevens, try and breathe. You are awake, sir. You're alive."

"Reset."

Dave opened his eyes. He needed to relax and catch his breath. Meds would have helped this time, but he was stubborn.

"Reset." It's what the therapist taught him to do.

Dave took a deep breath, widened his eyes, and averted a minor crisis of conscience. He re-read the link to the record launch, but it was too hard to focus, so he closed the email, certain the record launch was their probable destination.

Dave got up and dressed hastily. He reached into a drawer and retrieved an Evel Knievel #1 belt buckle. It matched the jeans and Radiohead T-shirt he was wearing. His outfit was a little loud, but the buckle was a gift from his dad. Dave felt *cool* wearing it even though it was corny and unusual.

With the anniversary of 9/11 just a few weeks away, it was scorching hot in the city during the day, but considerably cooler at night. Dave needed something warm to wear that evening but unfortunately, his smelly, torn tuxedo jacket, his *go-to* wardrobe piece, was done. Remy ruined it when he used Dave as a mop. The only other jackets Dave owned were suit blazers worn strictly for work. "Definitely not going to ruin a *Brooks Brothers* suit jacket," he thought. It seemed the Wharton grad and Wall Street trader in him was not dead entirely. For some strange reason, Dave could not put *fine tailoring* into the crosshairs.

Deprived of food for what seemed like an eternity, Dave opened his refrigerator, but he had little to eat. There was a jar of pickles, some peanut butter, a piece of moldy processed cheese, three pieces of Wonder Bread in a bag, a jar of mayonnaise, and a pan of leftover noodles, a gift from Gigi. The noodles had been on the floor, only a few remained, but he still had plenty of sauce.

"Sandwich?"

Luckily, Dave had two bottles of Rolling Rock to wash it all down.

Breakfast of Champions.

His stomach full and a little nervous with anticipation, Dave had to clear his mind, so he went for a long walk in the city. He prayed for just one peaceful day in his life. The sun was out, the war had been won, the enemy was on the run. Dave was prepared to make the best of the situation. There would be other nights in the future, nights where Remy was but a distant memory, nights where he, Trish, Billy and Lorena could go out and party like royalty for free with no strings attached. *What is now was meant to be* was Dave's mantra.

That peaceful day finally arrived, there was no doubting it, even the air smelled fresh and inviting. Dave felt unshackled, free, light as a feather. He locked his door and then thanked God for his new opportunities. He avoided a nervous breakdown; his episode was only a brief one. Dave was as calm as a gentle stream in a Zen Garden.

"DAVE!!! DAVE!!!"

"Gigi! *What the hell*?!!!"

"DAVE!!! DAVE STEVENS!!"

She spooked him and killed his moment, sinking him like a rapidly-melting Arctic glacier. Her shriek curled up his spine, but she was mad as hell, and for good reason.

"Dave Stevens, do you know what happened to my chicken????" screamed Gigi, crossly.

"You have so many chickens, ducks, pigeons, for Christ-sake, you may even have bunnies! I don't know what chicken you are talking about!" Dave insisted.

"One of my chickens! I found her dead on the fire escape! Your window. Checkers is a good cat? Wouldn't kill any of my chickens? Sure! How you know about the bunnies, by the way?"

"That's Chuckles, Gigi. Chuckles. Like, to laugh, to chuckle. Chuckles."

"Yeah, that's what I said. Checkers. Checkers."

"Chuckles."

"Yeah, Checkers."
"Cha. Kulls. Chuckles."

"Cha. Kills. Cha kills."

"Right! Good job, Gigi! Look, I gotta go. I just gotta go. I'm really sorry to hear about your chicken. Maybe I can buy you a new one, and say, maybe *you* can cook it? Either way, I got to go, really got to go..."

"Yeah, I don't know what you're up to, Dave Stevens. Now you're lying to me. You're weird, man. Just be careful, Dave Stevens. Just you be careful, okay?" she replied perceptively.

Dave darted down the stairs and as usual, he tripped. He rarely, if ever, looked where he was going. He stumbled, fell through the front door, and landed on the pavement outside. He dusted himself off and noticed that the police had cordoned off the bodega.

"Hey, what happened there?" Dave asked a bystander nonchalantly, as if he didn't know the answer already.

"Same shit as ever in this neighborhood! Shopkeeper shot a guy in the back of his head last night over a dollar," the stranger replied.

"Over a dollar?"

"Yeah, dude was walking out with a Snapple or something and the guy said he didn't pay for it in full. They're looking for witnesses."
"Are you serious? Who told you that?" asked Dave, now somewhat nervous, wanting desperately to distance himself from the situation.

"That cop over there," said the bystander, pointing to a squad car parked over his shoulder, "he said the guy came in all crazy high on crack and that he had a knife. Gives the shopkeeper a dollar, they get in a fight, dude walks out with a Snapple and some chicken, then the crazy shopkeeper? He walks out of there with a gun. Caps the guy right in the back of the skull. Executes him. I tell you man, I'm glad I never argued with that guy over a buck. They got it all on camera. He'll claim self-defense and be back at the bodega by the end of the day."

Dave shook his head and kept on walking. He wasn't sticking around, only too able to act as witness to what had happened. Dave didn't do the right thing, he couldn't.

With time to kill and prepared for the unpredictable, Dave made his way down Amsterdam Avenue and sat down on a bench by a playground. Kids giggling on swings, the swish of a metal basketball net drained by a rimless three-pointer, women on their phones speaking in Spanish, honking taxis, moving trucks, sirens in the distance; they all served as orchestral maneuvers, leading to the crescendo of the symphony known as a *typical New York afternoon.* Sounds, things, people, places, everything we take for granted, Dave's soul swallowed them all up in one gulp. He could have just as soon swallowed the sea. Dave never took anything for granted again after 9/11.

He stretched himself out on the bench, taking up space for three. Occasionally, someone would come along and try to sit down next to him, but he wouldn't budge. His odd demeanor made people feel uncomfortable but that suited his purpose. He wanted to be left alone, not an easy thing to accomplish in New York City.

Soon afterwards, Dave walked down to the riverside where Shawna used to live. He gazed out on to the Hudson River to watch the might of its flow, and to think of her. The river's vastness reminded him of how powerful his own energy was when he could harness it, like a dam, like a top-fiver.

He returned to the stoop of his apartment building and waited impatiently, quite on edge, hoping 6 p.m. would come around sooner than later. Dave stopped a man who was happily walking by, listening to music on an old Sony Walkman. Dave tugged on the man's tracksuit jacket to get his attention.

"Hey man, gimme a smoke…" Dave belligerently demanded, catching the man off guard.

"Ok, man. No problem. No problem," replied the fellow, startled and upset, "just ask nicely."

The passerby drew a cigarette from a pack of Marlboro Menthols he had in his shirt pocket and handed it to Dave along with his Zippo lighter.

"Cough!! Hack! Cough! Cough! Cough!"

Dave never smoked. There was the odd cigarette, cigar or joint at a Frat party, but beyond that, Dave found smoking rather disgusting, a despicable habit. His eyes watered up and his complexion turned pale. He hated cigarettes. They, and Agent Orange, killed his dad. Dave hard-gagged, and nearly threw up on the sidewalk.

"Yo, my man. You shouldn't be smoking! You gonna be alright?"

Spit drooled from Dave's mouth as he raised his head and handed the man back his lighter. "Trying to give it up. Nasty stuff. The worst…"

"Today would be a good day, man!" said the passerby as he continued on his journey. "Maybe for me, too, come to think of it!"

Dave kept the lit cigarette in his hand, considered his sudden sense of recklessness, and smiled reservedly. "I'll be okay, this is actually pretty cool."

6 p.m. The car pulled up in front of the cordoned-off bodega on time, as promised. Remy stepped out from the driver's seat. He wore sunglasses and a black leather jacket. His hair coiffed, his sideburns long, Remy pulled off the Elvis Presley look quite naturally. He raised his arm, waved and whistled.

"Hurry up, man! We're on a schedule."

Eren sat in the back of the car. He leaned over and opened the door. allowing Dave to get in.

"Over here, this side."

Dave closed the door, settled into his seat, and focused his eyes squarely on the thieves. Remy looked in the rearview mirror and saw that Dave was calm, collected and unafraid.

"Eren and I are really upset about last night, Dave. We're professionals. We had no idea you were just some schmuck. The fact that you are on Zulu's list says something about you, at least. So, let me elaborate a little bit more about what we do at all these parties."

"It's really rather obvious. You steal, man. What's the connection to Zulu?" asked Dave, attempting to steer the conversation.

"That's really none of your fucking business, Dave!" Eren angrily interjected.

"Whoa, whoa! Calm down, Eren, calm down," insisted Remy. "Dave is our friend now, remember? Our *friend*. We're going to teach him how we do it tonight."

Eren was livid. Dave had been a nuisance from the start. Eren's cover was almost blown at the Kabuki affair due to Dave's interference. "It's always people who don't know what they're doing who get those that do into trouble, Dave Stevens. You nearly got me busted."

"What am I missing here?" asked Dave.

"Remember I told you about the three types of people?" said Remy. "Well, these parties are where Eren and I make our living. It's simple. We're thieves. I'm not going to sugarcoat it. I've been doing it for years, and it's always better to have a partner, or to work in a small group. We don't need people like you getting us busted."

"I'm just a *schmuck*, right? What do you want from me?"

"Well Dave, you're on the circuit, right? You've seen what I do, what we do. What I basically need from you is *trust*. I need to trust that you're not going to expose me, y'know, while I'm working," said Remy.

"I thought about turning you into the cops today. I'm pretty sure you lied about them being involved."

"Dave, you don't fuckin' listen," said Remy impatiently.

"Cops? Ha!" Eren laughed.

"I told you already, this is so much bigger than you can even imagine," Remy insisted, "that's exactly why you're here. Tonight, you're going to witness it for yourself and you're going to participate. Once you do, you'll see the whole picture. You're on my team. The cops won't help you. I know. They help themselves, little buddy. Some of them might even be on the list."

"And if I refuse, you'll kill me and maybe my family as well." said Dave, resolutely.

"Man, Dave! You got this all wrong! We don't want to hurt anybody. That makes noise and puts eyes on us. Maybe I roughed up a few nice people along the way, like we did to you last night, but the fact of the matter is we stay under the radar, like ghosts, Dave. Fucking ghosts. We just go in, do our thing, and get out of there as quickly and as safely as possible before anybody realizes they got pinched. Hopefully, we leave richer than when we walked in. I'm offering you an opportunity, Dave." Remy was growing impatient.

"We usually work on our own, just the two of us, but tonight's going to be a great opportunity to work as a squad. We saw how charming you are, so we thought it over. We believe we can use your skills here. All you must do, dear Dave, is be your dumb self," said Eren, sounding a friendlier tone.

"How?"

"It's really quite simple," said Remy, "all you need to do is go up to good-looking ladies and handsome men, introduce yourself, make small talk. You're a decoy, Dave. You're not going to steal a thing, you don't know how to pick a pocket. We'll tell you who to talk to; you keep their attention just long enough. I'm talkin' 30 seconds, more or less. We'll come around to those kind, unsuspecting victims that we've directed you to set up for us, and we're going to clean them out."

"You don't know me. We're just strangers, *right*?" said Eren.

"Yes Dave, the only mistake you made was rolling up on the wrong *someone*." said Remy. "You think, at least you used to think, that everyone is innocent like you, but you were naïve. You can't roll up on just anybody because you think you've seen them before. That's poison. You can't do that. It gets crowded at these parties. If you recognize someone, they may very well be scamming or thieving as well. You're in their way. Leave them alone. The more events you go to, the more you familiarize yourself with just about everybody who's on Zulu's list. The keys to successful party crashing are knowing why you're going, knowing what you want to get out of it, and minding your own fucking business. When everybody's having a good time, nobody's suspicious of anything, then there's a lot of bounty available. If by chance, I get to stick around for a little while, have a few drinks, a good bite, dance maybe, well that's what I love the most about what I do for a living. It's the main reason why I started on the circuit in the first place, to have a good time, just like you did, Dave. Don't fuck that up for me, Dave. Don't fuck that up."

Remy pulled off Riverside Drive and drove up 63rd Street. He parked adjacent to Thelonious Monk Circle, turned off the engine, and listened intently as Eren laid out their game plan.

"We're going to a record launch party; some band named The Seed. They're tied to a major label. The company has apparently put a lot of money behind them, so they're not just launching the record, they're showcasing the band. That means a lot of press, but it also means a lot of executives and investors. It's the perfect storm. There will be alcohol, tons of finger food, and a lot of free swag: CDs, t-shirts, bags, pins, posters".

"That's a lot of cool stuff!" said Dave, giddily.

"*Cool stuff*? What are you? A child? That's a lot of distraction, newbie. That shit keeps the crowd drunk on fun." replied

Remy. "We're not looking for souvenirs tonight, Dave. We're looking for cold, hard cash, and if we get lucky, maybe a few cell phones and some jewelry..."

"But we don't want you doing anything, Dave. *Nothing.* You don't know how to pick pockets, but you do know how to be a distraction," said Eren. "We just want you to explore the space, walk around the room, and go where *we tell you to go.* All you'll have to do is follow our eyes and play the part, Dave. It's so easy a monkey could do it."

"And if I do this tonight, I'm out? My family is safe?"

"If you don't do anything stupid tonight, we will trust you, yes," replied Remy, "and maybe, just maybe, you'll want to do it again."

Remy revealed a brand-new tuxedo jacket. It was navy and had black satin, rounded lapels, an upgrade from Dave's ruined, less-than-stylish one, the same jacket he'd worn since grad night.

"This is for you, Dave. I genuinely felt horrible about destroying your jacket and beating you senseless. What was I thinking? I should have realized. Very unprofessional of me. Apology accepted? Go ahead. Try it."

Remy tossed the jacket into the back seat. Eren helped Dave slip it on.

"Fits perfectly, man. Thank you so much," said Dave graciously, "apologies accepted. How did you know my size?"

"Eren has been sizing up guys for years," replied Remy, with a grin. "You sir, are a perfect fit for us."

"So, are you clear on everything, Dave? We can't have slip-ups." Eren was worried. Dave was more a thorn in his side than anything, adding Dave into the mix made Eren's plan slightly less than airtight.

"I guess I am," said Dave, "but I have to be honest, I'm human. I'm very, very nervous."

"Everybody's gotta start somewhere, Dave Stevens. You're going to be okay. If you blow it for us, you won't be okay. It's not complicated." Eren replied.

"Maybe I'll kill you," said Dave, half-jokingly, a hint of spaghetti-Western in his tone.

The men laughed.

Simply feeling *comfortable* after 9/11 was half of Dave's battle back to normalcy in his life. Now, the universe put him on an insane, uncontrollable rollercoaster and he didn't feel uncomfortable in the least. Dave had transformed into a regular Oliver Twist, buying into Remy's Fagin-esque scheme wholeheartedly.

Remy drove through Columbus Circle, across Central Park, then back down FDR Drive. The ride to Battery Park was a quick one. He pulled the car over and parked it a block down from a procession of cars, firetrucks, firemen, policemen and city officials. The procession seemed to be a somber parade, all those marching were in full regalia, marching slowly as they passed.

"What are we doing here?" asked Dave.

"Just got to make a stop. Pick up a friend, you wait here with Eren," said Remy.

The fire station dedication event; it was on Zulu's list, but why the stop? There was nothing there to eat or steal.

Waiting impatiently for Remy's return, Dave sat by as Eren spoke at length about his immigration process. Eren came from Chongqing, the son of a street vendor. He framed the whole tale into a real sob story but Dave ignored him, choosing to keep his eyes focused on Remy's every move.

Remy walked down the block and waited on the corner. He was then met by Trish and a man in uniform. They greeted each other warmly. Trish met up with Remy the night before outside the gallery. Dave saw them together once again and realized that Trish had a much bigger connection to everything than he initially thought. He wasn't the least bit surprised; she was the first person to tell him about the list.

Remy returned to the car, joined by the man in uniform. Remy squeezed into the back seat as the stranger took the wheel. "Move over, dead man," Remy said to Dave, "make some room. Meet my friend."

"Well, now, top o' the evening to you, fine Dr. Stevens! What puts you in the middle of this awkward kerfuffle? So terribly lovely to see you again."

It was none other than Mahone, in a very different uniform, the very same Irish gentleman who Dave met the night before at NYU, handlebar moustache et al.

"What is he doing here?" asked Dave. "I met this guy yesterday. Said he was a professor. He's in on this?"

"I told you, Dave. A lot of people get the list. Surprised? You met him out there, didn't ya? Another familiar face? Rolled up on each other, right? Mahone is our driver. It may be a party to you, but it's business, all business, for me." Remy replied.

"Monkey business for you, Dr. Stevens! My, my, sir. What a coincidence," said Mahone. He looked in the rearview mirror and saw his new mate Dave trapped and scared.

Chapter Fifteen

"In the summertime, when the weather is hot, you can stretch right up and touch the sky, when the weather's right, you got women, you got women on your mind, have a drink, have a drive, go out and see what you can find."

—*Ray Dorset*

Mahone sped up Third Avenue and burned every red light. He slowed down as he passed by one police car after another. The officers on duty peered into Mahone's car, identified him, and to a man, they either nodded or saluted, and let him go on his merry way.

Dave's mind raced from one conclusion to the next.

"Who the hell is Mahone? A fireman? A cop? A pickpocket? He knows Trish. No clean cop or firefighter with any guts would be involved with a network of petty thieves. Remy said that cops were on the list. Maybe firefighters too. I don't know what to believe."

The atmosphere in the car was tense, hot and steamy. Dave was sandwiched between Eren and Remy and he began to sweat profusely.

"Can we stop off for a bottle of water or something?" Dave pleaded. "It's awfully hot tonight." He wanted to get out and make a run for it.

"Don't get your knickers up," said Mahone, "we're just about there."

They arrived at their destination in Midtown East, a low-brow, Colombian joint with a very large neon sign out front. Half the bulbs on the sign had burned out, making it difficult to read. In its glorious past, when the neon lights shined brightly, the sign, roughly translated, read Yan's Crazy Cantina. It seemed like a tiny spot to hold such a large corporate event.

The men got out of the car and Dave panicked.

"Remy, I'm not sure if I'm on the guest list. I clicked on a ton of links and registered, but I can't remember which ones confirmed."

"That's not going to be a problem for you, Dave. In fact, that might even be a blessing. If you can't get in, then you're out, plain and simple. You can just walk away and get along with your sad, little life. You don't say shit about me and I'll burn your driver's license and forget your face. But when we get to the door and they ask you your name, you tell them the truth. You do everything you can to get in. If you do get in, there's no turning back." Remy was fair, he gave Dave an *out*.

"Now, you know specifically what to do, *right Dave?*" asked Eren.

"Yes…"

"Say it!"

"I don't know you. Just have fun. Nothing's going on," Dave repeated. "Just be my same dumb self. I'm Dave the *party crasher*, looking for food, stuff, sex, drugs, rock and roll. *Not supposed to be there.*"

"Sounds like you boys got a pip on your hands!" exclaimed Mahone.

"Yeah, well, we'll see about that," said Remy. "Okay, guys, let's go. Mahone? 9:45, right across the street."

"Cheers and best of luck to you, Stevens old boyo! I'll be around." said Mahone as he rolled up the car windows and pulled away.

"*Hola, gentleman*! Names please?" asked a sultry Latina woman. She was the gatekeeper. Her security detail was comprised of two massive men equipped with earpieces and concealed firearms.

"There must be some pretty wealthy people in there, Eren." Dave remarked.

"Fuck, Dave! I told you! Don't even acknowledge me! I don't fuckin' know you. I don't fuckin' know you!" Eren uttered under his breath, incensed that Dave was so absent-minded.

"Remy Martin."

"Yes, Mr. Martin, good evening! Have a wonderful time."

"Eren Lee."

"I'm sorry. What was that?"

"Eren. Eren Lee."

"Thank you for your patience, Mr. Lee. Have a lovely evening. And you, young man?"

"Dave. Dave Stevens."

"Hmmmm... Stevens. Stevens. Steven??"

"No. Dave Stevens. Dave Stevens."

"I don't see it here..."

Dave thought about the coin flip that nearly cost him his life. Everything is just a flip of a coin. He thought about the coin's rotations. What exactly determined the number of times it flipped, how it rolled, how it landed the way it did? Sheer luck.

"Oh, will you look at that? *Dave Stevens*. Someone wrote your name in on the last page. Dave Stevens. There it is. That's you, correct?"

"That's me. In the flesh."

"Well, I'm so sorry for the inconvenience," said the sexy gatekeeper with a smile. "Here's a pass so you can meet the band once you're in. I hope you have a really good time. Oh, hey, nice t-shirt. You're a Radiohead fan, aren't you?"

"Yeah, I saw them here a couple years ago."

Remy and Eren kept moving. Remy looked back and urged Dave to terminate his less than important conversation with the woman at the entrance.

"Oh yeah, I was there too," she replied, "just before 9/11."

"Yeah, I don't think they're really going to last. Thanks, I'm, uh, going to go in." Dave was abrupt, maybe a little rude. He saw Remy's glare; he didn't have much time to talk about music.

"How'd you get in?" asked Remy, pleasantly surprised by Dave's good fortune.

"Someone wrote my name down. It was a miracle."

"Zulu," said Eren, bluntly.

The men were sent to the rear of the cantina. Barely a dozen patrons in the place, the cantina was not the site of the record launch, merely a cached passage leading to the main venue. It was quite the cover, adding ambiance, anticipation and an aura of exclusivity to the event. A small door at the back, an emergency exit of sorts, connected the cantina to the entrance of a grand, old, once-abandoned but now-renovated, cathedral.

"Straight through here," directed the security man.

The cathedral had been dollied-up strictly for the purpose of the record launch. The ceiling was a mile high. The place was packed with hundreds of people. How this event stayed under wraps was no small feat, but rather, pure magic. The promoters had done an excellent job. Zulu's list probably had a little to do with it as well.

"Just be casual, Dave. If we need you, we'll walk up behind you, tap your shoulder or bump into you a bit, that's it. All you have to do is keep your eyes on us. Follow our instructions. You'll be perfect," said Remy.

"You don't know me, Dave. *You don't know me*," Eren repeated.

"I know. I know. I'm sorry," said Dave. He shoved Eren away.

"When we go in, we're going to scatter about. Don't do anything special. Relax. Have a good time. I'll be around soon enough," said Remy.

The promotors built a stage at the back of the room for the band, The Seed, five young fellows covered in acne, all barely old enough to drink legally. The boys performed their hit single to raucous applause. It wasn't very melodic. The bass was too heavy, the drummer missed beats, and one long guitar solo in the midst of it all was nothing less than cringeworthy. It probably took the band a minute to write the damn song and less than two to play it. Thankfully, they only performed for a short time thereafter before leaving the stage to mingle with their fans and sign autographs.

A circus theme was chosen for the band's album cover and marketing campaign. The promoters held little back. There were several easily-accessible bar stations all manned by clowns offering cotton candy and Jell-o shots.

An arena was built in the middle of the room to accommodate the main act of the evening: *Beppo and Bippo*, two massive African elephants, and their trainer, *The Amazing Tyrone*.

"Beppo and Bippo? They must be siblings," thought Dave.

The elephants were elaborately painted. They wore giant crowns on their heads and name plates around their necks. Surrounded by hundreds of unruly people and bombarded by incessant cyberpunk music, their master, the Amazing Tyrone, managed to keep them relatively calm. The elephants flopped their ears and blew their snoots from time to time as they waited in the wings for the band to end their set, but for the most part, they seemed really mellow. "Sedated. Those elephants must be sedated," said one of the guests. That was the general consensus; the gargantuan animals were pretty stoned.

Dave looked around and sized up the throng as best he knew how. "Should be here, shouldn't be here, and *us*." Glam rockers and their girlfriends, executive types in shirts and ties, hordes of fans who'd won the chance to meet The Seed, and paparazzi had all been invited to the party.

And then there were *those people,* the people Dave now easily recognized...

He walked around and wondered who Remy and Eren would choose as their victims. Dave had never lifted so much as a candy bar before he died, but now he was contemplating a life of crime as a member of Remy's crew. It was, without a doubt, exciting, but insane and unthinkable.

Remy and Eren began pointing the way, and Decoy Dave became everyone's new friend in no time at all.

While ordering a drink, Dave noticed an attractive brunette standing alone by the bar, a long-stemmed martini glass in her hand. Dave liked her. He wanted to introduce himself but the crowd around the bar was tight. Eren shuffled by and made eye contact with Dave. The brunette was Eren's target, much to Dave's dismay. Eren silently instructed Dave to sit down next to her.

She was approachable. Her purse hung over her right shoulder, so Dave had to position himself on her left side to allow Eren to do his nasty deed. The set-up was perfect.

"Great band, huh?" said Dave, casually.

"Oh yeah, I love them. My boyfriend is an assistant in the promotion department," the woman replied.

"Oh, you have a boyfriend?"

"Yes, but he's not here tonight. *I'm Sally*."

Dave saw a window of opportunity. "Oh! Cool! I'm Dave! Can I refresh your beverage?"

"Why sure, Dave!"

Sally noticed his VIP pass. "Do you work for the record company?"

"Funny you should ask," replied Dave. "I do. Yes, that's it. My pass. I do, indeed." Dave was on his game!

"*That's so cool*," she replied, excitedly. "Can I meet the band?"

"But I thought you said your boyfriend works for the company?" Dave caught her in a lie.

Her mood changed in an instant, from engaging to unsettling. She was a fan, an unrelenting groupie. *"Well, can I meet them or not?"* she asked, cannily.

Eren sat down next to poor Sally and ordered a drink. He stayed clear of Dave. He turned away, chatted with the bartender for a split second, and then he glanced back at Dave and winked. The job was done.

"Yeah, well, honey, I'm going to be getting together with the boys in the band a little later, so I can get that arranged, sure," said Dave. His convincing gab kept Sally in check.

"Oh, Dave!"

She wrapped her arms around him tightly and gave him a bear hug. Sally was there for the band, she was supposed to be there, for the CDs, the T-shirts, pins and posters. Her *gosh-awful*, cheap perfume made Dave gasp for air. Choking, he watched as Eren slithered away and then he pulled Sally's claws down gently.

"Hey, hey, no promises, no promises. I'll do what I can, but, um, I think somebody's calling me, I got to go. I'll speak to you later, *Sandy*, is it?"

"What about my drink?" Sally asked, glumly.

Dave motioned to the bartender.

"Hey, buddy! Give Sandy here another martini, okay?"

"*Sally!*" she said furiously.

"Yeah, Sally."

Dave could not care less what her name was, he was on point, able to make himself anonymous, a shadow, to disappear like Zulu. He did what he was told to do. Sally? Dave hoped he would never see her again.

The men crossed paths a half a dozen times more before their night's work was over. Dave sat back and took it all in. He had a sudden taste for adventure and it felt great. Late in the evening, the band returned to the stage for a Q&A session, but once that was over, it was time for the big show, the one everyone has been waiting for with great anticipation: the elephants!

"Ladies and gentlemen, I am your master of ceremonies, *The Amazing Tyrone*! I present to you, for your excitement and pleasure, *Beppo and Bippo!*"

The loudspeakers fired up *Entry of the Gladiators*.

"These two African siblings will amaze and astonish you!" the ringmaster declared.

The crowd applauded wildly.

The Amazing Tyrone cracked his whip and commanded the elephants to stand on their hind legs and face each other. Beppo and Bippo obeyed. He pointed his whip to the left and again, the beasts responded, giving each other high-fives. Tyrone then pointed his whip to his right, but the elephants wouldn't respond. He pointed to the right once more. Nothing.

"Hy-ah! Hy-ah!" shouted the infuriated ringmaster. He whipped Beppo's thigh savagely, but it only made the elephant angry and defiant. The mammoths began to wander aimlessly around the arena, occasionally stepping out of their boundary. The crowd became quite leery of the ringmaster's ability to stop them.

"Hy-ah! Hy-ah! Hy-ah! Hy-ah!"

Things took a turn for the worse. The Amazing Tyrone lost complete command and control of the unruly animals. The elephants stomped and trumpeted. The crowd panicked. The room grew louder by the second, becoming a cacophony, a virtual sea of frightened voices and screaming.

It didn't seem to make a difference to the elephants. Beppo mounted Bippo quite aggressively and with expected results. Beppo humped Bippo like there was no tomorrow. Bippo's snoot flailed wildly as her partner lovingly screwed her. The crowd stampeded towards the exit, creating a tremendous bottleneck at the exit door. The only way out of the riot was through the cantina.

Dave felt a familiar tap on his shoulder.

"Time to go," said Remy.

Piercing through the madding crowd with Beppo and Bippo, their tusks and all, on his tail, Remy dashed for the exit, pulled out his phone, and called Mahone.

"Success!"

Remy got through the door first and ran out of the cantina. Dave and Eren soon followed. As expected, Mahone was parked and waiting out front. Remy placed his hand on Dave's chest and felt his rapidly-beating heart.

"You stay here, Dave, we'll come get you in a few minutes. Let 'em pour out. Blend in." he insisted.

Eren, wide-eyed, delicately walked away. He nodded at Remy and then ran down the block. Remy crossed the street and got into the back of the car. Mahone hit the gas pedal, pulled over to retrieve Eren, made a hard right turn, and sped away.

Dave stood on the sidewalk, statuesque, with hordes of relieved people pouring out of the cantina behind him.

"I didn't even get a fucking T-shirt," said Sally, as she left with her pack of Seed groupies. Dave turned away so she wouldn't see him. It was a close call.

"T-shirt? At least I didn't get killed. I got a new jacket out of it, though, and now I'm free," thought Dave, but it only took a moment for his conscience to catch up with him, like a sand castle struck by a gentle wave. "Fuck. *I did it*. Well, that's that. I'm a criminal."

Dave prayed Remy and his crew wouldn't return. The parties, the list, it all seemed like fun, until it wasn't. All he set out to do in the first place was go out, feel normal again, have a good time, make new friends, and find new opportunities. Dave didn't want to squander his second chance, not now, not ever.

The list was not the answer.

He shrugged and concluded that a long walk home would help him think things through, plan, and get back to reality. "Send some CVs in the morning. *Who knows?*" he thought. "Waxman was right. I'll reach out to somebody back home. New York has been an absolute shitshow."

Dave walked only a few blocks away from the rampaging pachyderms before the dreaded sedan chock-full of bandits turned the corner and pulled up beside him. Mahone rolled down his window.

"Get your arse in the back, lad!"

"No, that's okay, I'm going to walk home…"

"No, that's not okay, lad. Get your fuckin' arse in the car!" shouted Mahone, "Don't be a frickin' baby."

Remy opened the back passenger-side door and got out.

"I told you we were going to come back and pick you up, dude. What didn't you understand? Where were you going? I thought we were all *friends* here. Get in, Dave. Don't make this hard."

There was no point in putting up a fight. Dave got in the car. His instincts told him not to, but he couldn't stop the tide.

"Good work tonight, newbie," said Eren, a man rarely complimentary.

"It was a very successful affair," Remy agreed.

"Where are we going?" asked Dave. He had a million reasons to be worried, all of them justified.

"I'm thinkin' the boys are gonna knock you off now," said Mahone.

"*Relax, Dave Stevens.* We're going to see the results of all our blood and sweat, share the spoils, if you will. Get paid for our work," said Eren slyly.

Mahone sped up. He slammed violently on his brakes and spun the car around like a top. He headed downtown, cutting across Little Italy to get to the Holland Tunnel exit.

"Hey, you guys know where I live. I'm uptown!"

Certain he knew too much, Dave thought he was going to die. Remy had every reason in the world to kill him but luckily, Remy had taken a liking to Dave.

"Not going to your place yet. We're going to our pad over in Jersey. I'm going to show you the fruits of your labor, what you did for me tonight. If everything checks out the way I think it will, you're going to be one happy camper, Dave Stevens. You won't have to worry about paying for a ride home, that's for sure. You earned your share."

After receiving Remy's assurance, Dave sat quietly for the rest of the ride. It was a lot to take in, he didn't really believe Remy. Dave watched the tunnel lights flash by, like heartbeats on a pulse oximeter, ticking off seconds of his life. Unlike the other passengers in the car, Dave had a fine appreciation for life. These petty thieves who held him hostage would, in all probability, wind up dead as doornail in an alley, a trunk of a car, or a hole in the wall somewhere, someday. This was their world; Dave was merely trapped in it.

They arrived at their destination in Jersey City, a dimly-lit tenement house. Remy had the key. There was a kitchen table, some chairs, an overhead light, and a couple of dirty mattresses on the floor inside, little else. It was the first real *safehouse* Dave had ever seen, and it was just as grimy as he imagined one would be, complete with a filthy sink and a broken toilet bowl in the bathroom.

Remy and Erin removed their jackets and sat down at the table. Mahone took off his Class A Firefighter uniform and changed back into civilian clothing. He returned with a large Fendi rucksack filled to its gills with everything the men had stolen that evening. They'd left Dave standing on the curb outside of the record launch party because they needed to get away, empty their pockets and pack up the bag. Once it was full, they went back for him. Poor Dave was hoping he'd been abandoned at the time, but he had no such luck, he was complicit in the affair.

"Dave, watch this. *You're going to love it!*" said Mahone as he gleefully emptied the contents of the bag onto the table.

"Woo-hoo!" screamed Eren.

"*Nice!*" said Remy, smoothly.

A pirates' plunder, it was quite an impressive haul. The men stole cell phones, thousands of dollars in cash, wallets, credit cards and jewelry.

"Holy shit!" exclaimed Dave. "That's everything you guys stole tonight?"

"*You guys? Us*, Dave. You participated. A regular night's work," insisted Remy, "a regular night's work. Sometimes we get twice as much. It depends on where we go. You got to think about the risks."

"Risk mitigation, very important!" said Dave, textbook words from his days studying at Wharton.

"Okay, guys, we gotta move. Let's get this split up," said Eren courtly.

Remy separated the contents and tallied up the bounty.

"Nice cash haul, boys. Okay. Phones. Nokia. Nokia. Motorola...Oh! A *BlackBerry. Nice.*"

"Hey, look at this huge engagement ring! Who got the engagement ring? asked Mahone, as he fiddled with the contraband.

"That was me," Eren said proudly, "thanks to Dave, really. I think I'm going to keep that one. I know a boy who'd like it."

"Okay. Phones? Credit cards? Canal Street. The jewelry? The Jews in the diamond district. You know how this works, boys," said Remy. "I'll sell it off, you'll get your share. Here's tonight's pay-out."

Remy made five piles of cash, one for each man and *"one as tribute to Zulu."* Every man got just short of $5000 cash and a cell phone to pawn. Remy took his bundle, along with the jewelry, credit cards, and the BlackBerry.

"Yep, this one's mine," he insisted. "Go ahead, Dave, take one. You must need a new phone. The Motorolas are good. If you don't need it, you pawn it for a couple o' hundred on Canal. I can hook you up."

"Why the BlackBerry?" asked Dave.

"Best buck for pawn," replied Remy, "for some reason, they pay me big money for BlackBerrys."

Dave hesitated.

"I did a good job. Let me have the BlackBerry."

The men laughed at him. Remy was well known for providing stolen phones to his customers on Canal Street, almost unable to supply them with new, high-tech toys fast enough.

"No! And no phone for you, then! Greedy, huh? Just cash this time, Stevens, let's not complicate things." Remy replied.

"Well, fellas, who's going to drop off Zulu's tribute?" asked Mahone.

"I'll do it," Eren insisted. "I need to see him anyways!"

"Okay, then. That settles it, our business is done for the evening," said Remy. He handed Eren two stacks of cash. Mahone took his stack and left the final one, Dave's, on the table.

"Thanks again, babes!" said Eren joyfully as he left. "Tomorrow night's gig will be a hell of a ride. I may even retire."

Remy wrapped his arm around Dave's shoulders and tried his best to make him feel welcomed. "Go ahead fellah, take your stack. It's yours. You earned it."

Dave reached for the cash but Remy slammed his hand down.

"No, no, no. Not so fast. *Comes at a price.*"

"You said it was earned."

"Yes, I did. It doesn't mean you just get it, though. You'll have to prove to me that you're not a one-trick pony. So far, your hands really aren't very dirty, are they?" Remy backed Dave into a corner.

"What more do I have to fuckin' do?" replied Dave angrily.

"You can keep the cash, Dave. I'll keep an eye on your family. Friend of mine in Pittsburgh? He's got good binoculars. You're gonna have to roll with us again tomorrow night."

"Nope. I won't. Not gonna do it." Dave didn't have a choice or say in the matter.

"Sure, you will. *One more time*. Because I need you. You get the list, right? You're using it, going out on the circuit, having your fun? Problem is, every time you go out now, you see things from a different perspective, a different lens. Your eyes are open, Dave. You now know how to behave, mind your own business, stay out of trouble. Congratulations, Mr. Stevens, you are a professional party crasher and decoy, although you don't seem like the thieving type to me. You still shake a little, huh? Look at you! You don't have it in you, Dave. Don't steal for a living, you'll get caught, it's just going to wind up messy. I'm kind of glad you get it now, though. At least you understand the seriousness of the situation. You won't take *everything* for granted. It's not free. Soft, entitled people like you? It's obvious you're not from here, Dave. I bet you've always had things easy."

VRRROOOOMMMM!!! SSSHMMMAAASHHHHH!

Dave had a meltdown.

"What the fuck do you want me to do?! Have I not done enough? What's tomorrow night?!!"

Remy was impressed with himself. Dave took the bait, he was now onboard, although reluctantly. The cash worked its magic.

"Come on, man. Cool down. Trust. *Friends*. Get home. Call up your list. Friday. Vida store opening. Put yourself on there. You might go home with a super model and a nice pair of shoes," said Remy.

"That's the Italian leather thing, right?" Dave replied. "I was going there anyway. Isn't that ironic?"

"We figured as much! You was goin' for the food, mate," said Mahone with a smile.

"No, I wasn't!" replied Dave, slightly embarrassed. Mahone was right.

"Well, now the cat's out of the bag. It ain't about the food, right?" joked Mahone.

Remy moved his hand away from Dave's cash share.

"Go ahead. You're in, Stevens. Mahone will give you a ride home. I don't suppose I'll be speaking to you until we drive back here tomorrow night after the gig. You better show up, Dave. I'll be expecting you. Same as before. Nothing changes until we're done. You do this, then we leave as friends. After that, don't get in anybody's way. We're dead to you, you're on your own. If anyone comes at you, don't expect us to help you. You rat us out? You're a dead man."

"I can't tell you how fucking crazy all this all is to me, Remy, you don't know me at all." Dave replied.

"Truth is stranger than fiction, Dave. Truth is stranger than fiction. Get your hands dirty, real dirty, before you die. Otherwise, you'll have never truly lived," replied Remy, quite philosophically.

Dave just shook his head and took his stack of cash. He folded the bills and pushed them into his pocket.

Ellery McTier's *promised one* got an A+ and $5000 on his *Party-crashing 101* entrance exam.

Chapter Sixteen

"Load up on guns, bring your friends, it's fun to lose and to pretend, she's over-bored and self-assured, oh no, I know a dirty word, hello, hello, hello, how low."

—Chris Novoselic / David Grohl / Kurt Cobain

Thursday night in the city that never slept felt particularly dreamy. It was just short of midnight. The city was unusually cold. A dense fog fell over the bridges.

"I always cut through and take 10th to get up your way," said Mahone, "best escape route."

Dave barely heard a word. He was preoccupied counting his cash. Separating it by denomination, Dave walked away with more cash money in his hands than he'd had in years. He once hit a card in Atlantic City that paid out nicely, but this windfall was at least twice that amount, if not more. He could do things. He could buy things. He could pay bills, buy cat food, the good stuff. Shawna...

"*Shawna.*"

Dave began to cry. The whole experience was overwhelming.

"Oy. Oy. Oy. Who's Shawna?? Get a hold of yourself boy, get a hold of yourself there, hey. I know it was a little bit traumatic and all, but you done good. You done good, boyo," said Mahone. He shook Dave gently.

Dave wiped the tears away from his eyes. "What was with the dress uniform?"

"I'm a volunteer fireman. I was in my best gear." Mahone replied.

"What else are you, Mahone?"

"What else are you, Dr. Stevens?"

"Don't pin that on me!" joked Dave. His sadness faded away.

"No, no. I'm serious, though. I've been a volunteer fireman for years now. Used to be full time. I lost a lot of buddies down at the Trade Center, a lot of 'em, let me tell you. Nearly lost my own life that day. Almost wish I had. We were just honoring one of the boys tonight. His kid joined the station. Brought us all to tears..."

"I was in 2," said Dave, solemnly.

"Hard to talk about it, huh?" replied Mahone. He understood Dave's experience only too well.

"Like you said, sometimes, I wish I didn't make it out."

"Yeah, I recognized that look in your eyes when I first met you. Everybody's got a story. Not everyone has *that* look," said Mahone. He pulled over and parked next to the cordoned-off bodega.

Dave got out of the car, closed the door, and shared his truth.

"I died that morning, man. Someone pulled me from the rubble. I was set to make millions working on Wall Street, but everybody I knew died and so did my career. Something brought me back, maybe God, I don't know, but I've got $5,000 in my pocket thanks to you guys, Mahone. This is a lot of money for one night's *work,* under any circumstances. If you're a firefighter, you're obviously a good person. Why are you wrapped up in this shit?"

"It's a side hustle, lad. I make good money driving. I don't prance about those parties, now, do I?" Mahone replied glibly. "Some maybe. Just the smart ones!"

"What should I do? I just wanted some free food and some free stuff until I got back on my feet. Now, I feel like I'm in over my head," Dave confessed.

"Well, you are!" Mahone laughed. "You've gotten this far, my friend. I'm sure you owe it to yourself, a little bit of excitement? Ne'er you worry, boyo, I got your back here. You'll be safe."

"Everybody seems to have my back. How come I don't feel safe at all?" Dave stepped away from the car, but he had one more question that needed a truthful answer. "Hey, that woman on the street? At the fire station. She knew you guys pretty well it seemed. She looked familiar. What's her name?"

"You fancy the lass?"

"Nah, I'm just saying, I think I might know her. Seen her out on the town."

"She's just a widow from the station, mate. Remy met her at one of our charity events. Felt bad for her. Let her go without taking a penny. I wouldn't let him." said Mahone.

"I could swear I've seen her before."

"Yeah, you make a habit of saying hello to acquaintances. Everyone ya' meet! How's that working out? Have a great day tomorrow. Don't spend all those hard-earned shillings in one place. Car will be running. Oh yeah, one more thing..."

Mahone reached into his glove compartment and pulled out Dave's driver's license.

"I think this is yours, David Stevens from West Mifflin, Pennsylvania. You're free to make your own decisions. Remy's got what he needs on ya', your family and all. Cheerio!"

The plume of smoke from the Mahone's car's exhaust pipes obscured his departure. Dave stood in the middle of the road, trapped in a gray zone of his own creation.

Creak. Creak. Creak. Creak.

Zip. Click, clack. Push. Thump.

Dave opened his apartment door gently, vainly trying to avoid Gigi's home security system. It never worked. Gigi opened her apartment door and let Chuckles out. Same as it ever was. Chuckles ran into Dave's apartment, and Gigi slammed her door in anger.

Chuckles hopped onto Dave's bed, curled herself up into a ball on his pillow, and closed her eyes. It was obvious that Gigi had overfed her. Chuckles just wanted to cuddle and snooze.

Dave walked into his bathroom and met his reliable mirror. It was time to check in with the old Dave Stevens, the Wharton grad, Ellery McTier's up-and-coming associate superstar. What would old Dave Stevens have thought of the events that had just transpired? Old Dave never showed up in the mirror for the discussion.

Dave splashed water on his face over and over again. He stared back at the mirror, unsure whether he knew the man in the mirror altogether. The one thing Dave was certain of was that he loved this new guy in the mirror, this guy was lights out, this new guy had guts and fire in his eyes.

Jettisoning his clothes to the floor, Dave took a timely shower. The drops of water trickled on his head as usual, but they no longer calmed him nor sent him back into his bank of bad memories. Normally, he'd find the warm water soothing, but he was a wickedly wound-up wreck. He could not help but think about the next heist. What about Zulu's *tribute?* Was Zulu in charge of Remy's ring? There were so many unanswered questions. There was also the matter of the $5,000 that Dave took willingly. The money said *don't ask any questions*. Remy hooked Dave into one more gig. Mahone's words were comforting, but Remy had a gun, no matter what Mahone said. Dave couldn't take Remy's threats lightly or disobey him. Remy's terms were non-negotiable.

Dave toweled off, brushed his teeth, put on a white t-shirt and his heather-grey U of Penn-Wharton sweatpants, and jumped into his bed. He desperately needed to sleep. Chuckles climbed up onto his chest and laid her head down. Dave felt her heart beat as she purred. It was a most soothing reward for his hard night's work and all the madness that came along with it.

Dave stared at the ceiling, hoping to continue that conversation with the old Dave Stevens but he dozed off. He didn't have any 9/11 nightmares that night, in fact, Dave had a fanciful dream, one of plenty and riches; he actually slept well. When he woke up, it wasn't a dream: he was flush with cash.

The hazy morning sunshine brightened up his entire apartment and turned the place into a sauna. Chuckles pawed at Dave's nose. The ceiling above was back to its normal, once optical, now eggshell white with no sign of the old Dave Stevens anywhere.

Dave sat on the edge of his bed and shook his head in disbelief. He and Chuckles stared at one another. She was a mind-reader. She wanted nothing to do with Dave in his current state, so she meowed incessantly until he got off his bed begrudgingly, marched into the kitchen and opened the window for her to leave. Chuckles was a hunter. She took off like a cannonball and flew up the fire escape to the roof, happy to leave Dave behind to stew in his misery.

The sheer excitement of places to go, people to see and money to spend, stolen money, afforded Dave a luxury he hadn't had since he lived with Mom and Dad. Gravitas.

Dave splashed his face with frighteningly cold water to wake himself up and reassure himself that everything that had happened the night before was real. The mirror confirmed it. Adrenaline took hold him. He brushed his teeth ferociously, mindlessly, until he clamped down on his tongue.

Crunch!! The sound was bone-chilling.

"*Errrghh*!!!"

Dave spat out a small chunk of his cheek and lots of blood.

Damn. It hurt.

He rinsed out his mouth and wiped the excess blood away with a wash cloth. Reaching into his cabinet, Dave took out his razor and shaving cream and was about to apply a touch of the cream to his face when he remembered he had the *dirty* money.

Assuming he'd have even more money before the night was over, perhaps enough to pack it all up and leave New York City forever, Dave went on a spending spree downtown. It was the perfect way to get rid of some cash and guilt, and the perfect time to get a proper haircut and shave. He had more than enough money to buy fresh clothes for the evening ahead and since the shops were close to the museum, it would also afford Dave the opportunity to surprise Trish by meeting up with her afterwards, conveniently, right in the heart of her neighborhood.

With his plans set, Dave left for his special day in a really good mood. He hailed a cab because, after all, he had money in his pocket, he could afford the fare. The blisters on the back of his heels were still quite painful. He had no intention of walking very much and worsening their condition. The spoils had been *earned.* Little luxuries such as cab rides, simple necessities back in Dave's McTier days, were now attainable once again.

"Bleecker and 7th, please," Dave instructed the driver.

Soho was heaven for Dave. When he first arrived in New York City, he felt an instant connection to the neighborhood. It was close to his office at MLI, and it was also the place where he made most of his memories, back in time when he had a promising career and a girlfriend named Shawna, of course.

Shawna. She was an angel who cloaked him in her wings. Dave only moved uptown because she lived there. Lester lived in Soho and had asked Dave to be his room-mate the very first day they met at MLI, but Dave knew that moving in with Lester meant nothing less than a return to fraternity life. It was time to grow up.

Walking around Soho felt like walking on a cloud, it soothed Dave. He knew of a terrific barber shop on Spring Street, a place where Lester used to chill. Dave went there and got a nice buzzcut and straight-razor shave, even treating himself to a manicure, soaking his fingers in warm lemon water.

It was then time to shop at his favorite shoe store. Shawna introduced him to the place. She took him there to buy his first pair of *cool New York shoes,* as she put it. She chose them, and he got used to them. Wanting something comfortable and expensive-looking, Dave bought a pair of Nike Shox. He'd done a bit of running over the last few nights, getaway shoes, fancy ones at that, were an absolute necessity.

His next stop was at a vintage clothing store on Broadway. Shawna bought him a thin tie there. It was his lucky tie, until, of course, it wasn't. He'd worn it the morning of 9/11, hoping to impress her later that day. He never had good luck with ties. When he arrived, Dave knew specifically what he wanted to buy there: cargo pants with plenty of deep pockets, and an Ed Hardy T-shirt. He loved Ed Hardy stuff.

He took a walk down to Canal Street, bought a black fedora, a cotton, summer one, and with that, Dave was set. The hat was his crowning glory.

His journey continued onwards, to Washington Square, back to the very spot where he'd caused all the chaos for the dog walker the night before. There were no dogs in sight, so Dave sat down next to a fountain to rest. The fiery sun beat down on his cheeks. He closed his eyes, ingested the orange and yellow hues of its rays through his eyelids, and listened to himself breathe. That, intertwined with the sounds around him, people, vehicles, airplanes, plunged Dave into a daydream, to *that* place a million miles away, the *therapy* place.

His flatline mellow shattered in the blink of an eye. It was impossible for him to forget that he was only a few hours away from danger. Growing restless and with time to kill, he called Trish. Meeting up with her for little update over coffee and scones was the plan, and it would surely help him blow off some steam.

"*Trish?*"

"Tough guy! How's my favorite party animal?" she answered, gleefully.

"I'm in Washington Square. You hungry for a scone? On me!"

"As a matter of fact, I am. You sound awfully chipper, Dave Stevens. What's up?"

"I have to say, I have learned quite a bit about the list since Monday," he replied.

"Sounds intriguing. I'm kind of proud of you, Dave. You came out of your shell. That's a good thing."

"I don't know if you could call it that, but I sure have a few things I'd like to discuss with you." Dave needed Trish to get back on the rollercoaster again, it was she who put him on it in the first place.

"Sure. Coffee? *And scones,* right?" she laughed.

"Funny. It's on me, I said. I owe you." Dave was in no mood for jocularity.

"Okay, well, it is Friday. I'll finish up early. How about I meet you in a half an hour at that coffee joint? It's kind of like *our place*," said Trish.

"Yeah. *Our place, right.* See you soon."

Dave arrived before Trish. He chose a secluded table outside, one surrounded by hedges, and placed his order. The shop had surprisingly decent iced-tea, coffee, fresh scones, delicious ice cream and free newspapers.

Trish barreled down the walkway. She was on the phone, in the midst of what seemed to be a heated discussion. Dave was quite keen on sharing everything he'd learned about Zulu's list, but he saw that she was in no mood to be interrogated. She didn't seem all too excited to see him either.

"Hey! Hey! How ya' doing, Trish? See? Scones, coffee. Even got you a nice, tall, cold glass of peach ice tea with tons of ice cubes! Not sure what you wanted to drink with your scones. It's so hot today, I thought this would be really refreshing."

"How much is this going to cost me?" she asked, wary of Dave's sudden kindness and ability to cover the tab.

"Bought and paid for, I just need a little information you may be able to provide because, let's just say, things have gotten *weird*," said Dave, with trepidation.

"Weird? I know you went out a lot this week. Anything special since we saw each other last? It's been, what? A day?"

"Yeah, what a difference a day makes. What kind of *hell* have you gotten me into? Do you have you any idea how many people get Zulu's list? Do you know what kind of people? Have you met any of them? It's not just one pickpocket here and there, Trish. There are dozens of them. This list? These free events? Nothing is as it seems, my dear," said Dave, "it's *outrageous*."

Trish was nonchalant, almost dismissive. Dave knew she was hiding something. Was she one of the thieves or just a veritable museum curator/party-beast? He saw her at the fire station ceremony, hugging Remy, chatting with Mahone.

Dave rolled the dice.

"How do you know Mahone? And Remy? Did you know that Remy pointed a loaded gun at me? How are you involved with these people?"

"*A gun? What?? Who are Mahone and Remy?*" replied Trish, hastily scrambling for an alibi.

Dave read her body language, her facial expression. He didn't need his 9/11 super senses to tell him she was lying. Still, he couldn't get her to admit to anything.

"I swear I saw you yesterday. I was downtown, and I passed by a fire station. I don't know. Seems crazy, I guess, but I thought I saw you meet up with some friends of mine there. *Imagine that*, I thought, *Trish and I know people in common*...but by the time I caught up to my friends, you, or whoever that woman was, had left. Must have been somebody else, but you have a doppelganger, Trish. She looked just you."

Trish took offense. She didn't appreciate Dave's attitude.

"I wish I had the time to *fuck around* like you do, Dave Stevens, but I work really hard, *every day*, at the museum," she growled. Trish paused to collect her thoughts.

"I'm sorry Dave, that came out wrong. I don't mean to be insensitive. I know you're trying to get your shit together. Let's talk about something else, like the *fun* you've been having instead. You've gone out every night since you got the list from Zulu. I thought Geisha Night was your style. Then you went to Trippy's? An art exhibit? Are you a regular now?"

Trish was amused by Dave's sudden enthusiasm.

"I've had a different experience every night. Last night, I went to a record launch. They had fuckin' elephants, and I mean elephants that fucked, Trish. You wouldn't believe it if I told you what happened afterwards. I still can't believe some people go to these things just to *steal* shit," he replied.

Trish showed no surprise nor any cracks in her icy exterior. If she had any direct involvement with Zulu and his list, she wasn't going to let on about it.

"Steal shit? Like you? Egg rolls, cookies, and bumper stickers?" she joked.

"No. I'm serious," Dave insisted. "I see people pickpocketing every night now. The geisha thing was nothing, a drop in the bucket." Dave didn't play it down.

"Did you call the police?"

"I'm too scared, to be honest," he replied, "I think they're involved somehow."

"Well, you could have said something to somebody, at least the first time you saw something happen at the Japanese party. Disappointed by your lack of initiative there, Dave."

"I didn't know who to speak to, what to say; it was all pretty shocking to me. My first night out, right off the bat, I witnessed a robbery, but it happens everywhere I go, at every party on Zulu's list.

"You could have said something to the people at the door. They should've have been told there were dangerous people at their party," replied Trish.

"There were *geishas* at the door," said Dave dismissively, "*geishas*! The gatekeepers at Trippy's were Elvis impersonators. *C'mon Trish!*"

She raised her eyebrows and gave Dave a flabbergasted look.

"It's pretty brave of you to go out on your own after all you've been through, but you're not some hick redneck, Dave. You know right from wrong," said Trish.

"Redneck? Nice."

"Dave, Billy and Lorena told me your life was a work in progress. I know you are overwhelmed. Zulu's list isn't just a list of places to go to get free stuff. People go out to fantasize, to be anything or anyone they want to be," she reminded him. "It's freedom. A lot of people take advantage of that."

"I've been out every night this week. Everywhere I go, I see the same people night in, night out. All week. I recognize them now. Eventually, they'll start to recognize me. The list. It's all connected. They're not supposed to be at these parties, and nor am I," admitted Dave.

"Nor am I!" said Trish with a smile. "Now you get it! Spending your life as a party crasher is no way to live, Dave. I have a job, a life. I only crash for fun. Most of those familiar faces you see don't have a life. I know who you are talking about..."

"You know more than you are telling me."

"Go back to your nerdy little world of numbers and whiz kids with great futures. Once you put yourself on the circuit, you become part of that world. The problem is, now you know too much about it, you know it's an addiction. People sleep all day to go out all night. I don't know how many people receive the list, to be honest," admitted Trish, "but I was warned about the pickpocketing going on."

She could not help but notice Dave's shopping bags.

"Upgrading the wardrobe there, handsome? It's funny how you went from complete poverty a week ago to Ed Hardy today. That is Ed Hardy, right? Nice T-shirt. You didn't become a pickpocket, did you, Dave?"

"I found some money in the couch," Dave replied. It wasn't much of a joke.

"So? It's Friday night. What are you going to do? Go out again, I assume. Anything on the list that tickles your fancy?"

Dave was acting strangely. Trish wanted to know where he was going.

"Actually, yes," Dave replied. "There's that event in Little Italy, the high-end designer thing, remember? You said you didn't know whether you'd be going. They're supposed to be giving away really expensive shoes."

"Oh yes, you were going for shoes! Looks like you just bought some," said Trish. "Yeah, probably not, but thanks. I feel like dancing, I want to go wild, but I am a little tired. Long week. It sounds like fun. I'd probably nod off though. Have a good time without me. I've been to tons of those *fashionista and garmento* things. Where do you think I got this purse?"

Trish proudly displayed a maroon-colored, Icelandic saddle bag.

"Wow. That looks expensive. Where'd you get it?"

"Zulu hosted a handbag gig for a designer from Reykjavik. He gave it to Zulu as a gift, and Zulu gave it to me."

Zulu gave it to her. It was another reason for Dave to be suspicious of Trish. The dots always seemed to connect her back to Zulu.

"Yup. Shoes. Going for shoes." Dave told a bold-faced lie. If Trish knew he was going to be Remy and Eren's decoy, she would have never let him go out that night, however, if she was somehow involved with them in any way, she wasn't letting on.

"Well, cool then. Why don't you give me a call over the weekend? I'll be around. Pretty sure it's a *no* for me tonight. I know, I know, it's Friday and all, but I feel like sitting around in my sweats and reading a book. If you're up early enough tomorrow morning, come over for some tea. I have lots; chamomile peppermint, ginger hibiscus, Earl Grey, sage..." Trish ran the gamut from cool and mysterious to matronly, all in one tea service. Dave knew they didn't have a connection, an invitation to tea usually meant a trip to the friend zone. Tea? It felt more like a trap now.

"Look, if I don't do anything stupid, like, say, getting killed, you can probably expect a call from me," said Dave, his words ringing truer than Trish could have possibly imagined.

"Can't wait to hear your next tall tale," she replied, "but it'll be hard to top the fornicating elephants!"

They finished their beverages but didn't touch the scones Dave had ordered. He called the waiter over.

"Can you wrap these up?"

"Sure. One bag or two?" replied the waiter.

"Just one," said Dave.

"Great. I'll be right back," said the waiter.

"Take them home with you, Trish. We can have them tomorrow, with tea."

"Oh, that's very thoughtful," she replied, stunned by Dave's generosity. "Don't forget, my friend, there will be a lot of beautiful people in Little Italy tonight, that's for sure. Don't fall in love with anybody too fast."

"I wouldn't know how to," said Dave melancholically, "I wouldn't know how to."

They hugged. Trish pecked him on the cheek.

The waiter returned with the bag of scones.

"Here you go."

"Just stick to your plan, Dave. Listen to your heart. Don't do anything it tells you not to do. Thanks for the scones and the coffee. You can have the iced tea. I hate peach. Hate it," said Trish.

With his hands in his pockets and a smile on his face, Dave watched as Trish walked away. She turned around and gave him a whimsical wave goodbye. Dave waved back and picked up his bags to leave.

The waiter swooped in and handed him the bill, remembering Dave all too well from their previous encounter. Dave didn't leave a tip the last time he and Trish ate there. The waiter hadn't forgotten his chintzy behavior and still felt somewhat slighted.

"That's $22.70."

Dave gave him $23.00.

"*Thanks a lot,*" said the waiter with a blank stare, "*great having you back. Here's your 30 cents change...*"

Dave looked over the bill, embarrassed that he'd given the waiter exact change and had forgotten to tip him once again. That bad habit was about to change.

"I am so sorry," Dave said apologetically, "let me make it up to you." He pulled out his cash, a stack shorter than earlier in the day, still plenty to go around. Dave handed the waiter a $100. "Today's your lucky day. Your service was great, as usual."

The waiter was pleasantly stunned to receive a $100 tip for a bill that didn't amount to much more than $23.

"*You're sure about this??*"

"As sure as that hundred has Ben Franklin on it," Dave replied.

"It's not fake??"

"No, of course not!"

"Wow! Thank you so much, sir. I wish you all the luck in the world with that girl!" said the waiter.

"Oh, she's just a friend," replied Dave, "she's just a really good friend, but thanks for the wishes. Maybe I'll use that good luck somewhere else along the line. Good karma."

"Good karma, man, good karma!" said the waiter giddily.

Dave returned to 7th Street and Bleecker and hailed a cab. With fresh clothing and money in his pocket, Dave's future looked bright. His nasty business with Remy and Eren would soon be over.

"Where are you going?" asked the driver.

"Riverside and 158th," said Dave.

"Whoa, man! All the way uptown? Not a cheap ride on a Friday afternoon, yo!" replied the less-than-enthusiastic driver.

"Just get me there in one piece, man. That's all I ask. I'm not in any rush. I'm a good tipper, I promise."

"Okay, get in, man."

Dave jumped into the back seat, tossed his bags aside, and gave the driver $100.

"I'm going to close my eyes for a while. Wake me up when we get to Kansas, okay?"

"Where?"

"Never mind."

Chapter Seventeen

"He roller coaster, he got early warning, he got muddy water, he one mojo filter, he say, one and one and one is three, got to be good looking 'cause he's so hard to see."

—*John Lennon/Paul McCartney*

Dave was exhausted, by his thoughts, his walk in the city, and his entire situation. He crashed out in the back seat of the cab in no time. When he woke up from his forty winks, he was energized. The cab pulled up in front of his building, Dave got out of the car, neatly-coiffed with shopping bags full, intent on thanking the driver.

"That's $60 even, "but you already gave me a hundred, so we good, bro," the driver insisted.

Dave gave him another $100. "No, no, man. I tied you up. Thanks for the pleasant ride, keep the change."

"Yo! Is this real, man?" asked the befuddled cabby.

"I told you I'm a good tipper. Does it have Ben Franklin on it?"

"You crazy, man!" said the driver, laughing as he pulled away.

When Dave arrived home, he found Gigi sitting on the stoop with Chuckles by her side staring at her adoringly. Gigi rarely had time on her hands, let alone to sit out front. She was always occupied with one project or another. Her presence there only further confirmed that Dave's world was, in fact, upside down.

"What's all this? You never go shopping! Dave Stevens, you are up to something." Gigi inspected him with a sisterly look - you know, the look of the sister who always tells on you.

Dave had to shake off all distractions. This was a Rubicon moment in his life. He bought the armor, had the ammunition, and more so, the confidence to embrace the moment. Gigi's interference was not part of the plan, he didn't want her involved, so the less she knew, the better.

"What makes you think that, my wonderful neighbor?" Dave replied.

"You are not right in the head," Gigi insisted. "Your hours are different. Out late every night. Chuckles acting weird. You open your window then you forget to open your window. Don't give me cock-and-bull story about what happened with my chicken. You know what it cost to raise a chicken? Soon, you probably going to bring around a strange girl. Oh, for sure you up to something, Dave." She shook her head disapprovingly.

Dave patted Gigi on her shoulder to reassure her.

"Whatever I'm doing can't be any worse than what I've been through. You know that. Things can only get better. Don't kill my buzz, Gigi."

"Things were quiet when you were a zombie, Dave. I don't need any trouble. Got enough trouble from street people near the bodega. I work so hard just to raise my chickens in peace around here. It's my heaven. *My heaven*. Mine. You know about heaven, Dave. You were there."

"Pretty much," said Dave, shrugging, "pretty much. It's just a quiet place, nothin' special."

Chuckles followed Dave into his apartment. Dave settled his bags down and went directly to his refrigerator to get something to eat. He would have eaten the scones he ordered when he was with Trish had he not been so anxious. In the caverns of his empty icebox, he found a Rolling Rock, one lonely piece of bread and some peanut butter. He made a half-sandwich, fell back on his couch, and took a bite. He sipped his beer and stared at the ceiling. It was time to conjure up old Dave Stevens.

"Hey, Dave, we're going to Little Italy tonight. Should be a lot of fun. You're going to make some cash, Dave. You're going to meet beautiful people. This event is going to be the classiest party you've been to all week," he thought aloud.

Old Dave did not respond.

"You've got the nicest clothes money can buy. You're looking good these days, Dave. Tomorrow will be the greatest day of your life. It's all going to come together. Fresh start."

Old Dave didn't have a heartbeat.

Gobbling up the remainder of his sandwich faster than a gator, Dave delved into Zulu's email as he had little time to waste. He took care of business.

"Zulu events. La, land, landing, la... Vida. La Vida store opening. That's it. That's the one. Little Italy. Mulberry. And... click. Registered! I'd bring you along for good luck, Chuckles, but you'd be too much of a chick magnet. Get it? Chick magnet! Fuck, you're funny, Chuckles. You'd just take off somewhere and I'd never see you again, you little fool. You're not coming with me."

Chuckles pawed at Dave's nose.

Dave reached into his shopping bags, pulled out his new purchases and removed the price tickets. The morning of his first important meeting at McTier, Dave wanted to make a good impression, so he showed up in a brand-new suit but forgot to remove the price tickets off his jacket's sleeve. They nicknamed him *The Price is Right,* and for a little while, it was a running office joke around the water cooler, until 9/11. He never forgot to take the tags off his clothes after that.

Dave closed his eyes and thought about the plane, Ellery, Shawna and Lester, Billy and Lorena, Trish, Remy and Eren, Gigi, her dead chicken, the dead homeless man who ran into the bodega with a shiv and a dollar; he finally came to terms with 9/11 and the fact that he'd survived. That moment of acceptance was as close to a full a recovery as Dave could expect, according to the therapist who supplied him the meds. The therapist told him that *that day* would come, and he'd *know it.*

After voraciously brushing his teeth and fine-combing his freshly cut hair, Dave did a pirouette, savoring the simplicity of putting on a new pair of pants. He tossed the Hardy T-shirt over his head, put the Shox on his feet, and adjusted his fedora. Dave was quite stylish. He took half of the stack of cash that remained, and tucked the balance of the dirty money under his mattress.

He looked at his phone. It was almost 8 p.m.

"Liftoff."

Dave opened the kitchen window. Chuckles followed him like clockwork. "Window is open. Zero grief from Gigi." He walked out his front door and put the key in the lock.

"Don't do anything stupid! It's easy for you to do stupid things," said Gigi, as she shadowed him. This time, he wasn't startled in the least. "That hat looks stupid," she remarked. She couldn't crush his spirit even though he did look silly and she was, in all probability, right on with her assessment of his outfit and behavior.

"That's not very nice! I guess you don't know much about fashion, Gigi. You ought to give me more credit," said Dave. He fumbled his keys and phone, dropped them, picked them up, and danced his way down the stairs without tripping.

"*This is my heaven, Dave,*" Gigi hollered, "*Don't ruin my heaven!*"

Dave would never walk downtown again, those days were over. He hailed a cab on Riverside Drive. The car smelled of cumin and wet dogs. The driver had a dozen pine-tree air fresheners hanging from his rearview mirror, all long expired. None of them seemed to make a difference.

"It stinks in here!" said Dave.

"Oh, I am sorry sir," said the driver apologetically, "my last customer was a dog walker. Where are you going, sir?"

"Mulberry. Little Italy?"

"Why are you going there?"

"What does it matter?" replied Dave, angrily. "None of your business."

"My friend! My friend! I am just making small talk with you. It is a long ride!" said the driver, remorsefully.

"Yeah, okay. No problem, man. Sorry for the short fuse. Just going to a party," replied Dave, calmly.

"Oh, sounds like fun. Who is there? Friends? Family? *Girls?*" asked the driver.

"Do you ask all of your customers personal questions?" replied Dave.

"No, no. I'm sorry. It's just, well, people don't want to talk to me anymore, that's all," the driver replied. "I like to talk, laugh, smile. Everyone these days is so angry."

"Are you surprised?" asked Dave.

The driver made a left turn on 125th Street and cut across town.

"Since '93, that first bomb that went off in the garage at the Trade Center? Remember that? People have always looked at me with suspicion since then. Total ignorance. Then, on 9/11, I drove people home all day and night, but now, with war everywhere, people are on edge, and man, they are just plain *racist*. I used to talk and laugh with all my customers. These days, some people see me wearing a turban and they think I'm a terrorist. They won't even get in my cab. I came here when I was a teenager, I've been wearing this turban my entire life! I was not born here, but my kids were; they're Americans. I am Sikh, from Amritsar, I'm not Taliban. Isn't the difference obvious? I love America. It's my home. Things will only get worse, I fear." cried the driver.

Dave wasn't feeling very talkative, much to his driver's chagrin. The world around them was just beginning to feel the ripple effect of 9/11. The carnage's reality was starting to settle in. Dave was trying to get beyond the ripple.

"Here you are, sir," said the driver. "Mulberry and Broome."

Dave gave him a hundred as he left the cab.

"Hey, mister, don't forget your change!" shouted the driver.

"Keep it," Dave insisted, "good karma."

Dave walked up to an atypical, nondescript, Italian coffee shop and gentlemen's club. The sounds of Tony Bennett filled the air. Vida!

At the door, he was met by two young women and a large, elderly man with a long scar on his left cheek. The women checked in guests while the man patted the guests down before allowing them entry. The man was far from the usual *security guy* Dave had grown accustomed to, but then again, it wasn't unusual to see a button-man standing out in front of a coffee shop in Little Italy.

Dave had registered in advance, but when he arrived, the women had no visible list handy. It was a smaller event than Dave had anticipated, not the huge brand launch he thought would be the case.

"Hi, are you a guest? I don't know ya'." asked one of the gatekeepers with a thick accent. She had a huge wad of gum in her mouth and was quite skilled at blowing bubbles.

"Hi. You have a guest list, right?" Dave replied, surprised by the lack of organization at the door.

"Well, who are ya'? Paulie didn't give me no list," said the brutish security guard.

The curtains rose. Dave's thespian skills were called in action. Quick, inventive thinking was now his standard procedure.

"I'm *David Stefano, fashion critic for Moda Italia New York.*" Dave's role choice was a good one. a writer, for a credible-sounding fashion magazine, no less. It pulled rank. "I'm here to look at the shoes."

"Oh, *giornalisto!* Great! Rocco, let him in. That's cray-cray. I can't believe someone sent a fashion critic! I am sooooo glad ya' hya," said the gum chewer. She was thrilled. Paparazzi. Pretty sexy. "The shoes are on the left when you get inside. You'll see them, like, right away. Make sure you eat and drink. *Mangia! Mangia!* Enjoy! Let me know if there's anything I can do for ya'."

It was Dave's easiest scam of the week.

The gentleman's club was rustic in nature. It hadn't changed since World War II. Army division banners hung from the ceiling. The walls were covered in faded photos of servicemen, *Italian-American* soldiers, who had served in America's wars.

The room had been divided into two sections. To the left stood a long wooden bar with stools for the regular clientele. A black and white, bordered, mosaic floor ran down the center of the room. A half dozen booths on the right, each equipped with salt and pepper shakers, sugar packets, a napkin holder and a jukebox, were reserved for the invitees.

The club was packed. The crowd had been bussed into the city from Long Island. They seemed to be dressed for a baptism more so than a Fashion Week event. Their voices were loud, their attire, hairdos and make-up cheap-looking, but what Dave found most interesting was that they all wore loads and loads of jewelry.

It was a private family affair that somehow managed to land on Zulu's list.

Dave cased the room, searching nervously for his partners in crime. He found them soon enough. Remy and Eren sat comfortably over by the bar, chatting with strangers. It was impossible to tell that the two men were working together. Fitting in seamlessly, they were already busy looking for targets by the time Dave got there.

Dave did as he was instructed. He set out to have a good time, eat free food, drink free booze, and meet comely people. That was his mission. Eerily, Dave didn't see any of the familiar faces he'd seen all week. Everyone on Zulu's list had bypassed the event, and for good reason: it shouldn't have been on the list altogether. Zulu's reasons for putting it there were now quite obvious.

Dave checked out the *infamous* pair of shoes, trying to justify why he had gone to the Vida party in the first place, beyond working with Remy and Eren, of course. The *brand* launch was by no means a Fashion Week event. There weren't any giveaways, no free swag, leather bags or wallets, and no free kicks for Dave, just one pair of crappy, Chinese-made, Doc Martin knockoffs with the Vida company logo printed on them.

A ponytailed man with a large gold chain around his neck and a pair of bedazzled Gucci sunglasses on his forehead stood next to the shoes on display. He was chatting with a noticeably tiny woman in a tight, red spandex dress and a cheap blonde wig. She held his complete attention. Their conversation looked rather animated, so Dave interrupted them, wanting to have a little fun for himself at their expense.

"Who's the designer of these nasty-looking shoes?" asked Dave rather rudely, ruining their moment.

"Hey! Can't you see I'm speaking to this lady?" the man angrily replied.

"I'm David Stefano, from *Moda Italia New York* magazine. If you don't mind, I'm looking for the designer."

Dave's bullshitting magic put a spell on the guests, leaving them starstruck.

"*Moda Italia New York?*" the man asked, this time in a humbler tone. He offered his hand. Dave ignored it.

"I know dat magazine," interjected the woman in the red spandex dress. "I read dat all the time. All. Da. Time. Gorgeous. Gorgeous. Da best of da best."

"*She does?*" thought Dave. He tried not to laugh.

"I'm so sorry, so sorry. I'm the designer, Paulie. Paulie Vida. Yeah, I made these combat boots and listen, they're really very, very comfortable. Didja know they're made in Italy? I guess you figured that much out and, and ..."

Paulie stuttered and then he sneezed. He'd been snorting cocaine. It was rather evident from the snow that flew out of his nostrils.

"Hiya! I'm Mary. *Nice hat!*" said the faux Blondie.

"Oh, hello Mary. You like my fedora? Bought it in Firenze. Yeah, your friend's boots are made in Italy, huh? Make sure he gives me a pair to take home before I leave tonight. I'm a size 10. You do want me to review them in *Moda*, right?"

Dave relished the moment. His act was convincing. He was looking for high marks at what amounted to be a boring affair, and his expectations sank deeper with each passing second.

Bored and wanting to go home, to Chuckles, Dave was still saddled with Remy, Eren and now unfortunately, the stupid boots and Paulie. Rather than brooding, Dave kept playing around.

"How much do these boots cost, anyway?" asked Dave smarmily.

"Oh, man I, I… once we put them in the factory, in Italy, you know, then we ship them back here, to Long Island. Y'know, it depends on how many pairs we're gonna order. So far, we're just getting to the point where we'll be ready to sell them, y'know, to people. I'll start ordering a few pairs soon, so, y'know…"

No. Dave *didn't know, y'know…*

Paulie knew absolutely nothing about the boot business. He felt that creating a brand of his own was enough of an accomplishment to merit an elaborate celebration, so Paulie threw a party for himself and his one pair of sample boots, inviting his friends and his entire family in the process, even chartering a bus to get them there.

"Mangia! Mangia, Davide! Eat something. Have a good time," Paulie insisted. "I'm really happy you are here. By the way, *who sent you?"*

Dave stared at Paulie and spoke slowly, deliberately, like Clint Eastwood.

"Who sent me? Do I *really* need to tell you?"

"No. I think I know," Paulie replied, shaken by Dave's answer. "Eat something. Have a few drinks, *Mr. Stefano*. You're an honored guest."

Dave could hardly contain himself, pleased that he could fool anyone. He kicked back and relaxed. Remy only bothered him a couple of times. It left Dave with little to worry about and even less to do. Eren stayed clear of him completely. Every time Remy called Dave in for help, Dave performed like a pro.

Late that evening, Remy was having a deep conversation with a middle-aged woman by the bar. He looked over his shoulder and nodded at Dave. Dave acted on cue and casually walked up to the woman, struck up a conversation, and got her attention.

"Hi! I'm David Stefano. Do you come here often?"

Remy did his thing and walked away, leaving the poor woman completely unaware that she'd just been violated and robbed. Dave ordered a drink from the bartender, winked at the woman, and then he, too, walked away, but he felt rather guilty, and it weighed on his conscience.

Minutes then became hours. Dave spoke with every guest there, some of them twice. He ate as much food as he could swallow: slices of processed mortadella, calabrese salami, and pieces of breaded shrimp in an extremely spicy tomato sauce that just didn't taste right. His guilt consuming him, Dave downed unholy amounts of whiskey. Every time he ordered a drink, he asked the bartender for a double dose, having now developed a habit for drowning out his sorrow.

"Hey, tarbender, just add ice to fill it up to the top."

"You're gonna kill yourself by drinking this much."

"Been dead. Overrated. Gimme another one."

Slowly but surely, the room began to spin and Dave became unruly. He had his eyes on one particular woman the entire evening. She was a unique beauty, a body double of Ronnie Spector, a vivaciously elegant black pearl amidst a sea of American Roman gladiators and cheesy, chubby, glib call girls. The woman's buttery skin glistened off a pink neon light that beamed down on her from the ceiling. Her caramel tone contrasted with the cream-colored, Seven-Year-Itch-Marilyn dress she wore so perfectly. The woman belonged on the top of a cake, a delicious chocolate cake. She was, by far, the most attractive person there. All the booze that Dave had consumed fueled his desire to talk to her.

It was a bad idea.

She sat alone, busy on a phone call, trying her best to have a bit of privacy when suddenly the booth adjacent to hers filled up with three young Middle Eastern men. The men sat down to drink espressos they'd ordered. Sure enough, Paulie Vida's ditsy little friend in the red spandex dress, Mary, tiptoed her way over to their table.

"Oh Ahmed! You showed up, and with friends too!" said Mary gleefully.

Mary seemed to know the men rather well. She bent down and giggled, displayed her charms to them, and tossed her handbag over to Dave's *wet dream,* the woman he had been fawning over the entire evening. Mary joined her in her booth soon after. They were friends, greeting one another warmly with kisses, hugs, and laughter. The women soon found a very-polluted Dave Stevens standing in front of them and staring. He imposed, sat down in their booth, and clumsily introduced himself.

"You're Mary, I know that! What, what, about you, gorgeous? What's your name?" he shouted, loud enough for the entire room to hear. "I'm Dave, Dave Stevens, Stefano, Dave…"

He was so drunk he was barely comprehensible. He closed his eyes, bent down, and kissed his dream girl's hand, but she pushed him away gently as she did not want to cause a scene. Dave wasn't exactly harmless.

"Don't mind him," said Mary, practically popping out of her red spandex dress, "he's a writer, you know, for, like, an important Italian magazine. His name is David Stefano. You remember me David, right? Mary?"

"Mary, Mary quite contrary," replied Dave.

Dave belched. His stomach had been upended by the mortadella, meat, shrimp and whiskey. His burp had a rancid, disgusting smell, so much so, it drew the attention of the three men in the booth next to him.

"*Qusamak!*" the men hollered.

Dave swung around and gave the men a daft look. One of them stared back at him irately but Dave just laughed at him; he was too drunk to care, and he was completely fixated on his vision of Venus, a woman clearly out of his league and one who wanted absolutely nothing to do with him. She had better things in mind for herself and her girlfriend, Mary.

"Who are you, goddess?" asked Dave, as he slobbered.

"I'm Dee," she replied coldly.

"Oh, Dee. That's such a nice name. D. D. DD. That's D for Dave. What's your D for?" Dave gripped on to the table corner to keep himself from falling.

Mary, the wiggy blonde, waved to the crowd by the bar.

"Let's go talk to Paulie, Dee," she said, "he loves you. He thinks you're so funny."

"Oh, Dee Dee, you're so funny, he loves you, ha!" sputtered Dave, his head swaying back and forth like a pendulum. "Seriously. What's your *Deeeeeee* stand for?"

"It's Dee, as in *disappear*, Dave. *Disappear*," she replied firmly.

"Oh, har, har, that's funny, that's so, like, hilarious," Dave babbled.

The women got up to leave. Dee pulled Dave's fedora over his eyes.

"Can you manage to watch over our handbags for a spell?" she asked, nonchalantly. "I'm just going to go over to the bar with my girl Mary for a minute or two, okay? You can do that, right? Watch over them? So nobody *steals nothin'*?"
"Dee, DD, aha-ha, ha-ha," laughed Dave, all his faculties now malfunctioning, "oh sure, sure. They...are safe...with me, oh yes. Where am I goin'? Safe! Ya' think?"

Dee miscalculated. She trusted him. Dave was hammered, so she assumed he was harmless.

Alone, intoxicated, sick, rejected, angry and depressed, Dave gazed at Dee and Mary over by the bar. They were partying with friends, smiling, happy. The women fawned over Paulie Vida as if he was royalty. Dee hadn't forgotten about the handbags she'd left behind in Dave's care, though. She looked over at him and wagged her finger, reminding him she was not too far away. Then she blew Dave a kiss, teased him, and ruffled his feathers. Dee had no interest in Dave and he knew it. Watching her enjoy herself with Paulie Vida infuriated him. Dave was drunk-jealous, the violent kind. He wanted Dee's attention, he wanted her love, but she swept him under the rug like a meaningless bug. Dave looked over at the handbags. From his mad perspective, Dee hurt his feelings, so he wanted to hurt her back. The women's handbags were low-hanging fruit, just begging to be emptied.

The moment Dee turned her eyes away from Dave, the drums rolled, the string section fiddled fiercely, the brass section blew their horns...

And Dave did it.

He rifled through their bags and stole the women's cash and credit cards. He dug deeper into one of the purses and found a phone. "BlackBerry! Score! Remy kept the BlackBerry," he remembered.

The adrenaline sobered him up slightly, but his stomach was rumbling. He placed the BlackBerry into his cargo pants pocket carefully and stuffed the cash and credit cards into his jacket pockets, leaving no room for takeout food. Of course, Dave wasn't thinking altogether. He was reckless and could have easily been caught. The Middle Eastern contingent in the booth next to him saw Dave steal everything, he did it in plain sight, but they didn't say a word or do anything to stop him.

Dumb luck? Perhaps they were there for the wrong reasons as well.

Remy swept in like a bolt of lightning.

"Time to go. Nice job, rookie."

Eren had already made his way to the exit. As Dave attempted to leave, he was impeded by Paulie Vida, his ponytail, and his Gucci sunglasses. Remy continued on as Paulie huddled Dave into a corner.

"Hey, don't forget to give me a good review, okay?" Paulie pleaded. "I'll send you the shoes. I'll send you the shoes, man, I promise. Just get me the address. Why are you leaving so soon, so quickly? Aren't you going to do an interview? Not havin' a good time?"

Good time? Dave had no time to spare. Drunk and tetchy, he was in no mood for subtleties so he pushed Paulie out of his way.

"Hey, hey there, Stefano! That's not the way you treat people around here, *do you understand?*" Paulie shouted. *"Don't you know who the fuck I am?* What? You never heard of the *Vida* family from Port Washington?"

Dave was clever, like a meat cleaver, and had enough wits about him to reply with a solid, one-handed clap. He smacked Paulie in the mouth and headed out the door with some less-than-complimentary words for him.

"I know what I think about your boots there, Mr. Vida. Better buckle up your fucking boots," Dave snapped, "they're great for walking in dog shit."

Bolting out of the club and onto Mulberry Street, Dave saw Mahone's car pull up on time, as promised. Eren and Remy got into the car, but as Dave ran towards the vehicle, spaced out and elated, he stumbled over his pigeon-toed feet and fell to the pavement, losing his fedora. Still hammered, Dave didn't feel the impact, he didn't even notice that he'd lost his hat.

Remy watched as Dave wiped out. He jumped out of the car and ran back to retrieve him. He wrapped Dave's arm around his shoulder and dragged him into the slowly moving sedan. Dave's cell phone, as well as the cash and credit cards that he'd stolen from Mary and Dee, all fell out his jacket pockets and blew away with the wind.

"My phone! My money! Remy! Stop! We've got to go back!"

"Fuck that, Dave! I'll give you a new one when we get to Jersey City! Let it go! It's nothin'! It's nothin'! Let it go!"

Remy pushed Dave into the car, slammed the door shut, and shrieked with joy. "Dave popped his cherry!! I saw him pinch somebody! Right out in the open! Fucking idiot! Coulda been caught, but he did it!! Jersey City, here we come, baby! Jersey City, here we come!"

Dave was in rough shape, on a surreal voyage, almost dead again. He drank himself into oblivion and lost complete control of his faculties. In his tipsy spin, he reached back into his bank of happy memories and he began to sing:

"I've been working on the railroad, all the live long day, I've been working on the railroad, just to pass the time away..."

The men joined in.

"Can't you hear the whistle blowin'…"

Singing as they passed through the Holland Tunnel, they carried the tune until they arrived at the safehouse.

Mahone parked the car.

"Looks can be deceiving, boys. It was a great night. Historical, baby!" Eren screamed ecstatically, "Let's get inside!"

"There wasn't much for me to do except drink and eat too much," said Dave. He was crashing, physically and mentally. "I'm going to be sick…"

"You did as you were told Dave, nothing more, nothing less. You worked like a real pro. No mistakes. Well, maybe one," said Remy, laughing heartily, "not supposed to let anyone catch you stealing, you idiot. Everyone saw you!"

"Don't make a mess and chuck yer cookies in my car, man. Get inside the house first." said Mahone. "Everything's been perfect up 'til now. Don't muck it up, Dr. Stevens, c'mon now, lad."

Chapter Eighteen

"Someone's in the kitchen with Dinah, someone's in the kitchen I know, someone's in the kitchen with Dinah, strumming on the old banjo"

—*Traditional*

"Whoa! What the… ???"

They kicked the door down. Remy was the first to be killed. They punched him in the mouth with a set of brass knuckles, then they shot him in the chest. Eren tried to shield himself by lifting up the table, but they riddled it with a hailstorm of ammo. Eren's flesh, blood and bones crashed against the back wall of the flat.

Mahone begged, but to no avail. It took only one bullet, a shot right between his eyes, to kill him.

Dave quivered and hummed uncontrollably. He shook so much, his chattering teeth cut into his lip. He prayed they wouldn't open the door and find him. Dying on 9/11 was a far nobler death than being executed next to a cold, filthy toilet bowl.

Seconds before the attack, the men had been celebrating their successful heist. They robbed a well-known Mafia family at a very private, intimate, off-the-radar party, thanks to Zulu's list.

"I done me a little valet parking while you fellows were inside," said Mahone with a smile. He placed a bundle of cash and a pair of cell phones on the table.

"I really, *really* reached my limit with those people, especially the women" said Eren. "Do you know what it takes to put on that *gay-guys-make-the-best-friends* act? We don't, okay? Fucking bitches. At least I pinched some nice ice!" Eren laughed, He added a stack of cash, four iPhones and a pair of diamond bracelets onto Mahone's pile. "One for all."

Remy beamed, unable to contain his glee.

"Now, not only do I have Mrs. Vida's personal phone number, thanks to Dave, I also have her cell phone! But please, please, let me continue, because Dave is the *real star* here."

"Where did I do, Remy?" slurred Dave, his face a ghastly, porcelain-like pale.

"Get this: I look over at Dave and let him know I need him at the bar. Knows exactly what I want him to do. I'm leaning into Mrs. V's ear. You know, for an old broad, she's really hot. So, I start telling her about my dick and she melts. I run my hand through her hair. I move it up along the back of her neck; I can feel her shiver. Clowning Dave over here orders a drink, looks at her at just the right moment, and he says *"Hi, I'm Dave Stefano, do you come here often?"* Can you believe that shit? *Do you come here often*? Like he's a fucking tourist. *I'm dying over here.* So funny. By the time she turns around to look for me, I'm gone. This little rock must be at least 10 karats, and I'm guessing that little Gucci bag Mrs. V was wearing has a lot of Benjamins in it!" Remy placed the phone, bag, and not least, Mrs. V's gaudy diamond ring on the table. "Great haul, guys. Great haul. Thank you, Dave fucking Stevens. You may be excused, schoolboy. Class is dismissed!"

"I'm *really* not feeling very well, I'm gonna puke…"

"You drank enough to kill yourself. I watched. *Echhh*," said Eren, gladly reminding Dave of his excesses.

"Did you eat anything while you were there? What? Some *Mortadelle*? *Salami*?" asked Remy. The mere mention of food made Dave gag.

"Hey, mate! Get out of here before ya' blow!" joked Mahone.

"It's not funny, Mahone! Bathroom? Where's the bathroom?" Dave pleaded.

"Over there, over there. Get it out ya', lad. We'll be here when you're done," assured Mahone as he pointed the way.

Dave ran to the bathroom and slammed the door shut. There were no lights on inside. He fell to the floor, hit his head, vomited and blacked out. The BlackBerry in his pocket buzzed repeatedly, but Dave was completely gone, he didn't even twitch. The buzzing went completely unnoticed by the jovial band of thieves in the kitchen until it finally stopped seconds before the mayhem began.

"Ok. Load up the bag. Eren's going to deliver it to Canal Street this time."

The first shot, the one that killed Remy, was as loud as a bomb. It woke Dave instantly. He heard Remy groan. He heard the assailants shout as they sprayed their machine guns all over Eren. Then, Dave heard Mahone's last words: "Dear god, for what?"

"Allahu Akbar!!!"

Dave kept still, closed his eyes, and waited for his turn to die. One of the gunmen opened the bathroom door, but before he had a chance to peer inside, he was distracted by his partner.

"There's three here, but this one with the moustache isn't Dave Stevens!"

"*What the fuck, brother??* Hurry up then! Get all the cell phones, man, just the cell phones..."

Dave was left alone in the dark, silently convulsing.

The assailants sifted through the stolen goods. They spoke some Arabic, but more than enough English for Dave to understand why they were there.

"Money? Jewelry?"

"No. No. The BlackBerry and all the cell phones! If he finds out we took anything else, I swear I blame it on you."

"Okay! Okay! *Fuck you! Ya sharmouta!*"

"You got them?"

"Yeah! But the BlackBerry isn't here, damnit!!!"

"No Stevens. No BlackBerry. Al'ama!! *Ok, we have to get the fuck out of here! Go! Go!*"

Dave waited a very long time before budging. He knew the murderers had left, but he was frightened as hell. He'd suffered a tragic death, one could even say that he was *executed* on 9/11, but he wasn't summarily executed like his three acquaintances. Their dead bodies were mangled, bullet-ridden, and Dave's fingerprints and DNA were everywhere.

The large Fendi backpack hung from Eren's broken arm. Dave peeled it away from his corpse mindfully and wiped Eren's guts off of it. He scoured his body for his wallet, an ID of some kind, but Eren had nothing on him.

He then reached into Mahone's pockets and took his wallet and car keys. "Looks like you won't be getting that grant, Dr. Mahone…" The top of Mahone's skull have been completely blown off.

Dave stood over Remy's corpse and stared down at his lifeless face. Remy's mouth still oozed blood from where he'd been punched. The brass knuckles broke his front teeth. His shirt was covered in blood and gunpowder, his chest had a massive hole in it, and his soulless eyes still gawked with surprise. Dave leaned down, pulled Remy's wallet out from the dead man's jacket pocket, and took out his driver's license.

"Thanks for the good times, Remy Martin from Paramus, New Jersey; your real frickin' name. I know where you live now. Picking your pocket was a lot easier than I thought it would be."

Dave stuffed the Fendi rucksack with the stolen cash, wallets and jewelry that the assailants had left behind. He threw it over his shoulder and backed out of the flat in haste. It was impossible to clean up the evidence he'd left behind. Dave walked through puddles of blood in a panic, completely forgetting about the repercussions of leaving a trail behind.

Weak but sober, Dave found Mahone's parked car, got in and slowly drove away. The Jersey City police were en route to the scene of the bloody massacre, Dave heard their sirens in the distance. He couldn't risk getting pulled over. The last thing he needed was a random DUI test or having to explain why he had a bloody Fendi bag full of cash, wallets and jewelry, let alone dead men's IDs in the back seat of a stolen vehicle. He drove for some time before pulling into the Newport Centre parking lot, a spot adjacent to the tunnel leading back into the city.

Dave was halfway home.

"Fuck! My phone is gone!! Think, think, think..."

Despite his clumsiness, disconnection, and subsequent vomit-induced blackout, Dave still had his wallet, keys, and the stolen goods. He was whole, minus his phone, so he thought. Nobody followed him, nobody stopped him, but he had no means of communication. He had the stolen BlackBerry but he wasn't going use it, that was for sure. It was a hot potato. Dave got away, but it didn't mean he was free.

"Just leave it all there, go home, let Gigi startle me, feed Chuckles a good can of cat food, not the cheap shit." Dave would never have to worry about paying for cat food at the bodega again. The haul in the Fendi bag was quite considerable. "That's it. Take the gear and the phone. Figure it out later. Go back home. To Gigi's *heaven*."

Singing *I've Been Working on The Railroad* once again as he sped through the Holland Tunnel, Dave was now able to sing coherently but sadly, he no longer had any chorus boys to join him in song.

Mahone's car made it to Hell's Kitchen before it ran out of gas. Dave ditched it at a Comfort Inn parking lot and dropped the car keys into a drain. He boarded the train at the station on 50th Street and Eighth Avenue, moving from car to car until he found one that was relatively empty. With the Fendi bag over his shoulder, wearing an Ed Hardy shirt covered in vomit and a hot pair of blood-soaked Nikes on his feet, Dave was nothing less than an eyesore and a glaring target, but he'd seen and done quite enough for one evening.

Nobody was going to take his can of cat food away from him.

Nobody.

Station to station, stop to stop, people came and went. Some stared at Dave intently, while others just assumed he was crazy. The A train took him to the 163rd Street station, a few blocks from his home. Dave ran out of the Amsterdam Avenue exit like a bat out of hell and made it to his apartment building safely soon thereafter.

Dave ran hastily up the stairs to his apartment, this time without stumbling. Gigi and Chuckles were nowhere to be found. His apartment door was wide open, the lock and door handle destroyed. The place had been ransacked. Dave's computer was gone. The living-room table was overturned, his couch and pillows had been slashed and scattered. His bed had been ripped up as well, its mattress flipped, Dave's hidden cash left behind. His night table had its contents junked. Dave's personal photographs of family and friends that were in its drawer had been stolen. Gone, too, were the pictures of him and Shawna taken at Chelsea Piers, the ones that were hanging on his refrigerator. His world was utterly upended, and for a change, it wasn't Chuckles' fault.

Surreal.

He needed Shawna and her calming voice to tell him he'd get through all this, but she was gone. When his nerves shattered in the past, Dave reached out to Billy, but Billy didn't know about the parties, the circuit, or their stark realities; he didn't even know *Zulu's list* existed. A casual call to Billy, out of the blue, in the middle of the night? Those calls only came at the beginning of his rehab, and only when it was an emergency, back when Dave was recuperating from his surgeries. Dave was desperate, he needed a place to hide

He considered calling Trish. She got Dave mixed up in everything, but in reality, it was Zulu's web that trapped him. Zulu never said a word to Dave about the *tribute,* all Zulu did was provide a list of places to go, people to see and things to do, for free, but surely Zulu knew people were getting robbed.

Remy, Eren and Mahone proved that, but now they were dead. Dave couldn't tie Trish or Zulu to any of it directly.

Dave then felt a buzz in his pocket. The vibrations were coming from the hot potato BlackBerry that he stole earlier that evening at the Vida affair.

"The BlackBerry!! Christ!! Dee!" Dave remembered, "That gorgeous, nasty girl. Dee. As in *disappear Dave*. Mary. Mary quite contrary. Fake blonde, tight red dress. Mary. The handbags."

The BlackBerry received a flood of messages.

First message: "Hey, boo, can you get me a McDonald's when you get home, hon? I love my McDonald's. I can't eat enough. Or maybe one of them Chinese soups, boy. You know, your girl here, she likes her Chinese soup. Anyhow boo, you get me something. You owe me, Ahmed!"

Second message: "And get some weed, boo. Get some weed. You want to taste some honey later? You get me some weed, Ahmed."

The third message was in Arabic. It was long and had several attachments, photos of Al-Qaeda warriors laughing as they surrounded a cage filled with people on fire.

The fourth message was even more frightening. It had a screenshot from Dave's computer displaying Zulu's list. The addresses of all of the previous evening's events, including the Vida affair, were written down in English below the photo.

A fifth and final message downloaded. It had a machine gun logo, contained Koranic verses, and had photo from the security camera footage from the gentleman's club showing Dave with his hands in Dee and Mary's purses.

Dave shook his head and wondered what his dad would have done with a live grenade.

Then the BlackBerry buzzed again; this time it was a call. Dave didn't want to answer it but his heart told him he had no choice.

"Hello?"

A muffled voice screamed at him in Arabic. Dave was frightened so he hung up immediately, but the BlackBerry buzzed again.

"Hello?"

"We're coming for the fucking BlackBerry, it doesn't belong to you, thief and infidel David Stevens. It belongs to me."

"Who is this?"

It all came together. The men who murdered Remy, Eren and Mahone? They weren't looking for money or jewels, they were looking for cell phones, a certain *BlackBerry* in particular. The gunmen took whatever phones they found after they murdered everyone, but they failed to come away with the one phone that mattered to them the most: the BlackBerry that Dave had stolen and had hidden in his pocket.

Once they tracked their phone down, the gunmen went to the safehouse to retrieve it, but they never found it because they never found Dave, they murdered Mahone instead. They came in hot looking for three men, one of whom was supposed be Dave, their body count was right, but they killed the wrong guy. Dave had blacked out earlier in the darkened bathroom, miraculously left to obscurity. Blacking out saved Dave's hide alright, but now, somehow, the men who were looking for the BlackBerry knew exactly who he was, where he lived, and possibly, who he loved as well.

Three men were dead. The messages Dave read on the BlackBerry amounted to something very heinous. The folks on the other end of the line knew Dave had their phone. They were at the Vida affair - the espresso drinkers. They knew Mary stole the BlackBerry from them first, and only afterwards, when they recalled seeing Dave clean out the purses, did they realize that he was the one who ultimately had it.

"I'm Dave, Dave Stevens, Stefano, Dave…" he shouted. They heard him announce his presence to the world.

They saw him leave with Remy and Eren.

Soon enough, they asked for the camera footage at the club and then they tracked their phone, following it to New Jersey.

Now, the gunmen were coming for their BlackBerry. They'd tracked it back to Dave's place in the city. Dave knew too much, they assumed, so he had to be dealt with swiftly.

So much for a good time.

Chapter Nineteen

"Uh oh, many, many, many nights go by, I sit alone at home and I cry over you, what can I do, can't help myself, 'cause baby, it's you, baby, it's you."

—*Mack David /Burt Bacharach/Barney Williams*

"Toss it away?"

Getting rid of the BlackBerry wasn't a means to an end. Dave could run down Riverside and throw it in the water, they'd track it, find it, but it wouldn't solve anything. Whoever these terrorists were, they murdered Remy's crew and had little choice but to eliminate Dave as well. They weren't going to let him go even if they got their damn phone back. It didn't work that way. They executed his *friends*, but these men were more than just killers, they planned on martyring themselves for their cause, whatever that was, and it posed greater problems for Dave.

The USA was at war. The men after Dave were just a small lesion of a bigger cancer. The administration created Homeland Security as a result of 9/11. The nation suddenly had a festering network of domestically-grown enemy combatants. The plan was to keep America safe, free of terrorism, Taliban drug lords, and Al-Qaeda suicide bombers. The war was over, over there at least, according to the President, but in reality, the war to keep everyone sane had just begun. It wasn't a light conflict, like Y2K.

"Not groovy," thought Dave. From time to time, he'd ask his father to tell him stories about the jungles of Vietnam. When the man mustered up enough strength and courage to talk about it, all he'd say to his son was: *"It wasn't groovy man, it wasn't groovy."*

Everything happened quickly. You couldn't see it coming. Whatever Dave had stumbled upon, it was bigger than he could have ever imagined. He was cornered, so he called Trish from his home phone. Her line rang five times before she finally picked up.

"Trish? It's Dave."

"It's after 2, the middle of the night, Dave! You out having fun??"

"No. I'm terrified. I need your help..."

"Oh? Not partying, Dave? I know why, *because you're in a heap of fucking trouble!!!*" Trish hollered.

"How do you know? Listen, I have a long story I got to tell you but…"

She cut him off immediately. "We don't time for long stories anymore, Dave. I have to get your stupid ass down to the museum as fast as I can!!"

"The museum?? But it's closed..."

"I'm on my way there now. I can help you. I know everything that's going on, but I need you to get to the museum safely,

Dave. There are a lot of people after you. Do you have the BlackBerry?"

"I do. I do. How do you…?"

"Shut up, Dave! Shut up! Just listen," Trish pleaded. "There are different agencies involved in this. Sorry to surprise you, Dave Stevens, I'm a detective with the NYPD. I'll tell you more when you get to the NMAI. Right now, we just have to get you there safely."

"What do you mean, *safely*?"

"The BlackBerry is tracked, Dave. It has sensitive information on it. It belongs to a cell of homegrown jihadis, terrorists. I guess you figured that much out if you opened the text messages," said Trish.

"I did."

"They want it back. It's why they're following you. They're trying to stay a step ahead of us. They know you're home now and probably thinking about running as far away as possible. If you head downtown on a train, they'll lose their signal because you're underground. They're worried you'll take the subway. Don't. Stay above ground and go uptown instead. It will confuse them. Get to Yankee Stadium, Dave. If you stay uptown, they'll think they have a chance to catch and kill you."

"Kill me?"

"Are three dead men in Jersey City not enough to convince you? Geez Dave, these are very sick, perverted, dangerous young men. They are completely brainwashed. You need to get to Yankee Stadium."

"Why Yankee Stadium?"

"Yankee Stadium is close to your place. It'll take my team the same amount of time as it will take you to get there. Gate 6, Dave. By the time you arrive, my team will be there securing the area. They'll drive you down to the museum. Getting to the stadium safely? That's on you. What did the text messages on the BlackBerry say?"

"Shit about cheeseburgers, porn, and a lot of stuff in Arabic about the list."

"Exactly," Trish confirmed. "They used the list, infiltrated the circuit, Zulu's pride and joy."

"Listen, Trish. I lost my cellphone last night. The BlackBerry is the only means I have of contacting you if I run. I'm going to use it to call you if I have to," Dave replied.

"You know the device is tracked, Dave. They'll know exactly where you are," she warned.

"I have no choice."

"There's nothing left to say other than run Dave Stevens, *run for your life!*"

Dave scurried about his apartment and changed his clothes so he wouldn't be recognized. He took off his tuxedo jacket and Ed Hardy shirt and replaced them with a hoodie and a Pittsburgh Pirates baseball cap that he'd owned since he was in little league. The cap still fit him, ironically.

His apartment was hectic mess. Dave threw his mattress back on its frame and tucked the Fendi bag underneath it for safekeeping. Chuckles reappeared, prancing her way through the kitchen window. Dave scurried out of his apartment in a frenzy, begging Chuckles not to follow him.

"C'mon girl, get out. Through the window. Go back up to the fuckin' roof and Gigi's chickens. It's not safe here."

She reluctantly turned away, jumped on the kitchen counter, meowed, and made a grandiose exit, peeved that he didn't feed her.

Dave slammed his front door but it wouldn't close properly, its hinges had been broken beyond repair. He knocked fiercely on Gigi's door hoping that maybe, just maybe, she'd answer this time. But she didn't, another bad omen.

Dave ran into the street and sprinted for about a mile before he was gassed. Out of breath, he realized that he was headed in the wrong direction. Trish told him to go uptown, but in his confusion, he ran downtown. He bent down, caught his breath, spat, lifted his head, and found a lone star in the sky.

As he was about to make a wish, Dave heard the sound of screeching truck tires barreling his way. He dove for cover and shielded himself from a storm of bullets. They hit every garbage can, wall and window on the street, but luckily, they missed Dave.

VVVVRRRROOOOMMM!!!
SSSSMMMMMAAASSSSHHH!!!!!!

"Get the fuck out of there! Now!!! Take the stairwell!!!"

Dave got up, opened his eyes, and realized it wasn't a bad dream, it was all too real. More shots rang out from the assailants' dark pickup truck. They picked up the BlackBerry's signal and knew Dave was in their immediate vicinity, but they couldn't exactly pinpoint where the signal was coming because Dave was now the run. It was a veritable cat-and-mouse game. Dave stayed as close as he could to the truck and by doing so, he had a greater chance of survival.

Dave recalled asking his dad what he and his fellow Marines did when they were surrounded by the Viet Cong in the jungle. *"Oh, trapped in a coffin?"* his father called it, *"We huddled up and prayed for deliverance, son. That's all we could do. We prayed. Worked out, huh?"*

Dave wasn't any more or less religious than the next person. He didn't believe faith had anything to do with his dad surviving Vietnam, he believed it was just the luck of the draw more than anything, but Dave's own luck seemed to be running out, so he turned to prayer.

"God Almighty, I need a little luck here. I've been good, as good as I can be. I know that's all you ask of anybody. I'm not promising I'll go to church, temple, synagogue, the mosque; you know I'm not your guy for that, but I do appreciate this second chance at life you've given me and I'm not going to squander it. Get me out of here, show me the way, shine your light on me." Dave begged.

Screeching their tires in frustration, the assassins drove down the block and turned the corner, giving Dave a chance to run away.

Suddenly, a taxi drove by and nearly ran Dave over. It parked on the side of the road to drop off a passenger. A woman got out of the car and closed the rear door, thanked the driver, tousled her hair, swung her purse over her shoulder, and walked into an adjacent brownstone. The driver turned his cab's light on and slowly drove away. He was available.

Light. It was the only thing Dave remembered about being dead. The taxi's light? It was the sign Dave was looking for. He ran down the street, screaming like a banshee, pleading for the cab to stop. It sped up, then suddenly, the driver slammed on the brakes. Dave caught up to the car, opened the back door and dove in.

"Oh, I saw you in the rearview mirror. What's the panic, sir?" said the driver.

"*You didn't hear the gunshots??* Get me to Yankee Stadium, please! But don't drive too fast."

"I'm sorry, sir, it's the middle of the night. There is no baseball game at this time."

"Please," Dave cried, "just get me to Yankee Stadium. Gate 6. I'm begging you!"

"Do you live around there, sir?" the driver asked, kindly.

"No, for God's sake, I live around here. What's it to you?" replied Dave, hysterically.

"I'm sorry, sir. I'm just being friendly. I don't want to ask too many..."

"Personal questions?"

It was the very same driver who gave Dave a ride downtown the previous day.

"Hey! It's you, the crazy, good tip guy!" said the driver joyfully.

"Yeah, well listen, my dear friend, I'm in a heap of trouble at the moment. I can't explain it, and for your sake, I'm not going to, but if you can get me to Gate 6 at Yankee Stadium safely, I'll give you the best tip you've ever had in your entire life," Dave promised.

"Gate 6, sir! Sounds like a plan! Let's do it!"

The driver took Frederick Douglass Boulevard to Harlem River Drive. The traffic was light, so he crossed the Macomb's Dam Bridge and arrived at Yankee Stadium in no time. Dave peered through the rear window of the cab to make sure they weren't followed. He pulled out the BlackBerry.

"Trish, it's Dave. I'm here! I made it! I made it!"

"Thank God." She was relieved. "Where's the money and the jewelry, Dave?"

How did Trish know about that? Dave never said a word about it. Was she trying to entrap him? The Fendi bag was under his bed. He still had a ton of cash in his pocket. Dave didn't want to elaborate about the treasure chest nor did he want to connect himself to Remy, Eren and Mahone.

"They shot at me, Trish! They shot at me! I don't know what happened. I'm calling you from the BlackBerry; it's safe, okay? I'm in a cab in front of Gate 6 but I don't see anybody else here. Where are your guys??"

Dave narrowly avoided incriminating himself. Trish wasn't his friend anymore, she was a cop. She seemed to know everything that was going on, but she'd also lied to him in the past. He was only going to surrender as much information as she needed to know and nothing more.

"Stay where you are Dave, my agents are close by. A black Suburban will turn up shortly. You can't miss it." replied Trish. "The agents will ID you. Just surrender peacefully and you'll be alright."

"Surrender?"

Dave fell back into the seat of the cab. He took a deep breath, exhaled, and gazed at his friend and savior, the cab driver. Having overheard the conversation, the driver suddenly realized the enormity of the moment.

"You are in some very deep shit, sir, aren't you?"

Dave reached into his pocket and gave the driver most of his cash, no longer having any use for that much, if any. He kept a few hundred for himself, just in case. Dave had no idea what his future held in store for him. The driver saved his life. A stranger once carried Dave out of the rubble of 2 World Trade Center, Dave was simply trying to pay the kindness forward as best he could, even if it was a little at a time. Still, this was no small change by any means, it was a lot money.

"*Sat Sri Akaal!!!*" The driver was petrified. "I can't accept this," he said, shaking his head, sputtering his words feverishly.

The large black Suburban screeched around the corner and came to a halt next to the taxi. Two agents jumped out from the side doors.

"Take it, brother," Dave insisted. "You shouldn't ask too many personal questions. I'll tell you this much, if you really want to get personal: my name is Dave Stevens, and you, sir, just saved my life. If I were you, I'd just drive away and forget that we ever met, okay?"

"But this money? These people?" asked the driver.

"No one will ever, *ever* know about it. Good karma."

Dave got out of the taxi cab. He was immediately apprehended by Trish's agents. They hustled him into the back of the truck and slammed the doors shut.

"*Bugs Bunny is in the batter's box. Bugs Bunny is in the batter's box,*" radioed the driver.

"Good evening, rather, good morning, Mr. Stevens. You sure are in the thick of it, huh?" said the smiling agent. "Patty will be happy to see you."

"Patty?" asked Dave. "Ahhh, right. Patty. Patricia. Trish."

The taxi driver stared at the Suburban as it left. Its bulletproof exterior, glistening pitch-black tinted windows, its very presence, was extremely intimidating.

He wondered why Dave had been taken away, unsure whether accepting the money that Dave had given him was the right thing to do or not.

Rather than give the whole situation too much consideration, the driver simply backed up, turned on his cab's light, and sped away.

He didn't want things to get too personal.

Chapter Twenty

"The can-can is such a pretty show, will steal your heart away, but backstage back on earth again, the dressing rooms are grey, they come on strong and it ain't too long, for they make you feel a man, but love is blind and you soon will find, you're just a boy again."

—*Ron Lane/Ronnie Wood*

"I wouldn't want to be you, Dave Stevens," said Trish, "I don't know how you survived the Trade Center disaster. I have never met anybody with such bad luck. Horror follows you everywhere you go. When this is over, forget about our *friendship*. You're a magnet for disaster."

Trish was saddened by the turn of events. She stood on the steps of the NMAI with two burly men in well-tailored suits. They seemed as eager to talk with Dave as she was. Trish's agents sat in their truck and waited for their next set of orders.

"I'll let you know what's going in a moment Dave," said Trish, "if you think things have changed quickly in the last 24 hours, they're about to be turned upside down."

"Ma'am, we're ready to roll."

"That's it for now," Trish replied. "I'm assigning you to Bugs Bunny's rabbit hole. 158th Street and Riverside. You know where you are going?"

"Mr. Stevens' apartment. 10-4 that, ma'am!"
"Correct. Station there, and wait for my call."

The Suburban turned into oncoming traffic, flashed its blue and red lights, and blared its sirens. Its destination? Uptown, Gigi's *heaven*.

"Patty?" asked Dave, beleaguered and suddenly estranged from his party-crasher *date*. "Who are you? Trish? Patty? Patricia?"

"Okey-dokey, Dave. Yes, indeed, I am Patricia Patterson, NYPD. I've been on the force for almost seven years now. This is Agent Kyle Andrews, Homeland Security, and Agent Gordon Manning, FBI," she replied, as she opened the doors to the museum. "I'm a detective. You, my friend, managed to cross wires with an investigation that spans three agencies, has been going on for close to a year now, and you may have blown it for all of us because you just couldn't mind your own business."

The group walked down a hallway and settled into an unmarked office at the rear of the building.

"You can't be serious," replied Dave, unwilling to grasp the enormity of the situation. "What have I done?"

"Oh, I am dead serious, Mr. Stevens," replied Trish, affirming the worst.

"Lorena said you worked here, at the museum."

"Well, that is partly true, I do volunteer here from time to time. I have a Master's degree in Criminology, but I did do a minor in Paleontology for fun, so I wasn't lying," Trish replied.

"So why are we here?" asked Dave.

"I don't volunteer at the museum because of my love of pre-history, Dave. The department has a shelter in the building. We've protected Presidents, dignitaries; the place was jammed on 9/11. Lorena has no clue what I really do."

FBI Agent Manning, a tall, brown-eyed, handsome man with a refined Caribbean accent, offered Dave a chair. They sat down and Manning did not mince his words.

"Patty told me you're just a civilian. You did knowingly and willingly participate in some serious felonies, Dave. I know how Remy and Eren operated. I'm pretty certain you weren't much more than a stooge. They pulled off some pretty dicey heists in the past and let me tell you, you weren't the first fool they used, just the only one who survived to talk about it. I've been tailing Remy for a few months. Every time he went over to New Jersey with stolen goods, well, those crimes became interstate felonies. Patty had him nabbed in the city on assault and attempted murder charges, that's why she befriended him. She was setting him up, Dave. Mahone and I were going to cuff him last night, but you managed to get tailed, for some god-forsaken reason, by the same bad guys that Agent Andrews and Homeland have been trying to shut down. What are the odds, Stevens? What are the frickin' odds?" said Manning.

"Mahone?" asked Dave, now numbed by the tornado spawned from his initial good intentions.

"One of our guys," replied Manning, sadly, "may he rest in peace, finally."

"Finally?"

"Mahone lost his whole crew on 9/11. He was a fireman before becoming an agent. Still volunteered, though." said Manning. "You never actually saw him steal anything, did you, Dave?"

"Well, no, come to think of it. I didn't, maybe a muffin," Dave replied. "I saw him walk away with a ton of cash, though. He said it was his share."

"It all came back to the bureau, with every fingerprint on it in the data base, yours included," replied Manning, with a frown. "Yes, Mahone. It wasn't his first rodeo, but it was going to be his last. He drove for Remy and Eren at least a dozen times. He did all the heavy lifting. He had cameras on them, managed locations. Just as we were going to go in and get them, he gets taken out by a cell of rogue, teen terrorists, and for what? A phone. Cripes."

Homeland Security Agent Andrews was a powerful-looking man. His biceps exploded out of his sleeves. Andrews did not find Dave or the party circuit very amusing. He was more concerned about dirty bombs and dead compatriots.

"You threw a fuckin' monkey wrench into my investigation, Dave," said Andrews, angrily. "Now I've got three dead guys to add to my list, one of them from Manning's team, and the terror cell I'm trying to bust knows that you have their BlackBerry, the same one I've been tracking for months. Give me the damn BlackBerry, Dave."

Dave rolled his eyes and handed him the phone.

"Why did you steal it, Dave? I thought you just wanted food, free gear, and a good time. When did you become a thief?" asked Trish.

Dave lived with his fears and his desperation every single day of his life after 9/11. Trish's sudden cooling and distance only proved that she had little empathy for him. She framed things as if Dave was the villain. She knew he was a wreck, but she still wanted him to feel a little pain.

"It's hard to explain," said Dave. "I felt inadequate. I was drunk. I got caught up in the moment. Remy threatened to kill me. You understand this, right? Manning has my back here."

"*Of course*," replied Trish, casting doubt on the depth of Dave's instability. "I went out with you, Dave. I knew the moment you got the list that you were going to use it to your advantage somehow."

"Look Trish, I just went out to have a good time, the same way you did. Don't tell me it was strictly police business. You loved the parties. Sure. I got the list, and the next thing I know, I get beaten up by a pickpocket who then waves a gun in my face and threatens to kill me and my family if I don't work for him. What am I supposed to do? He rewards me with more cash than I've seen in years. He tells me the cops are in on it. He could have just killed me, I don't why he didn't. I don't think he was a murderer at heart, but from what Manning said, he really was a cold-blooded killer, and that's pretty shocking to me because he really wasn't such a bad guy. We were so successful that first night out, Remy practically begged me to go out with them again; I had no choice, really, so I did. It just goes to show you how wrong this whole *free party* thing is, the naivete of people. You don't know what lengths people who are down on their luck will go to just to survive. Fuck them, I thought. Fuck those unsuspecting, naïve party people. Fuck everything. First night I went out with Remy and Eren? They stole a bunch of cell phones. Out of all the phones, Remy kept a BlackBerry. He said he was going to pawn it and it was worth a lot more money than the other phones. So that's what I did. I didn't give a shit. I was mad and wasted, I reached into a purse and grabbed everything I could. When I found a BlackBerry, I was psyched. I know it's just a stupid phone, but I did it, I stole it. And you know what? It wasn't any different than what I did on Wall Street. I took cash and valuables from unsuspecting people and used them, albeit briefly, for my own benefit. Those pockets were just a different commodity, I suppose. 9/11 taught me about survival of the fittest, Trish, or should I call you *Patty*? I'm a fucking survivor, Patty, a fuckin' survivor."

Andrews read the text messages on the BlackBerry. He grinned and began to laugh.

"God, I love code," he said. "Every time headquarters uses cheeseburgers in a message I crack up, I swear. Mary embedded some pretty funny intel." As he scrolled through the remaining messages, Andrews seemed satisfied. He had enough evidence to seek, capture, or destroy, his targets. "Yep, here it is. Wow. You're going to *love* this! My Arabic is pretty good. It seems my job just got a whole lot easier."

"How so?" asked Dave, hoping the news would get him off the hook somehow.

"My agent? Mary? Surely you remember Mary from your drunken haze, Dave? The blonde wig? The tight red dress? You took the BlackBerry from her, by the way, her purse." said Andrews. "We had cameras in there. Mary's been working on this gang with me for a while now. You put her operation in jeopardy, man. Her Arabic is a lot better than mine, believe me. They accused her of stealing the phone. She screamed and made a scene. She gave them a million excuses but they didn't believe her. When the phone wasn't in her purse, they had no choice but to let her go. If it would've been in her purse and they found it? Mary would been dead right now, Dave."

"So, I didn't steal it from Dee's purse?" asked Dave.

"Mary's gal pal Dee? Nope, wasn't in her purse," said Andrews. "You grabbed it from my agent, sir. Good job. Remember 9/11? Cells of terrorists. These guys I'm chasing? Bin Laden is their hero. I don't need a repeat of 9/11 happening here. They're a nasty bunch, but these guys are guppies, little homegrown fanatics. There's only the three of them. Two of them do all the shooting, they nearly put a bullet in your ass. Their leader doesn't like to get dirty. He barks a lot but he doesn't pull the trigger. Mary jerked him off and got close enough to get the BlackBerry. We've been tracking their shit online. They are totally indoctrinated. The leader, Ahmed, went to Pakistan to train. He actually has relatives there, but I know he didn't go for a wedding. They're local boys, dangerous morons from West Orange. Every message I'm reading here is begging them to *cease and desist*. Their contact with Al-Qaeda wants nothing to do with them anymore. He's begging them to stop! It says *go home to your mothers and pray*. That's a huge insult for these guys," laughed Andrews, "*your mama* jokes. These guys are hilarious."

"I grabbed it out of Mary's purse," said Dave melancholically, disappointed Dee wasn't his victim.

"An hour before you got to the Vida party, Mary was sitting at that very same table with the bad guys and her girlfriend, Dee. She put a spell on the leader of the pack. They'd been in contact through an online escort service for a while. Mary finally got close enough to get the phone off of him. He's just a kid who thinks he's a terrorist. She lured him to the Vida thing by text. He even brought his goons out to show off. She got close, gave him a hard-on, got his BlackBerry, and almost completed her mission, that is, until you snatched the friggin' thing from her. The kid had been in touch with Al-Qaeda in Afghanistan, had sent and received messages, awaited instructions, standard stuff. It seemed pretty serious in the beginning, until Homeland got noise of it a few months ago that is, when the kid came back from Peshawar. The Afghans cut these guys off suddenly, and that's when these fools started going around looking for guns and attention. We tracked the BlackBerry when it was sent from Kabul through Islamabad, the same day the kid came home from training. FedEx let it through and we followed it around thereafter. Now that they've tracked the BlackBerry to Battery Park, they think Dave has it on him and he's trying to run away. Homeland has these punks on international terrorism charges and now murder. I don't need to break up any extended network. Like I said, it's just the three of them. That's a big relief," said Andrews.

"Manning, what did you have on Remy and Eren?" asked Trish.

"Interstate conspiracy, theft, weapons, possibly murder. If Dave pressed charges? Kidnapping? Assault with intent, for sure. Doesn't matter now that our perps are dead, along with Mahone, right?" said Manning. "I'll follow up at the morgue in Jersey City. You can pin three counts of murder on those motherfuckers when you get them, Andrews, I do hope you *get 'em good...*"

"I'm so sorry about Mahone, I loved the guy," said Trish. "He was there for me, even after he lost the crew. My guy was just one of them. Mahone helped everyone heal afterwards, me, all the wives, husbands, partners, kids…"

"Hey Patty, let me remind you, your husband was a hero. He was a great fire-fighter, but he was an even better man. He won't be forgotten." Manning replied.

"I'm still in shock, to tell you the truth," said Trish, "I guess we all are, in one way or another."

"I am intrigued by this *Zulu's list*, Patterson. From everything I'm hearing about the evidence, it's quite a conspiracy. You could throw the book at that guy," said Manning.

Dave sat back in his chair, resigned to his fate. "What will to happen to me?" he asked Trish, "Do I need a lawyer?"

Andrews had plans for him. "Not if you play ball, Dave. Let me fill in the blanks. First of all, Agent Patterson has been following you since the first night you met each other."

"Is this true?"

"Yes." Trish confessed.

"Lorena and Billy? *That* first night?"

"Yes," admitted Trish. "You saw me with Mahone and Remy at the fire station as well. You knew I was lying to you. I tried to hide it. My late husband was part of Mahone's ladder company. I lost him on 9/11. You're not the only one who lost everything."

"I'm so sorry, Trish. You could have confided in me." Dave replied.

"I had a job to do, Dave. I got on Zulu's list about a year ago. NYPD was alerted to a huge uptick in theft at these free events. At first, it was pretty subtle, a missing purse here and a lost wallet there, but as Zulu's list spread, things grew violent, it wasn't just petty crimes anymore. The jobs grew larger and became more intricate. Lots of credit card stuff, hard to pin down, Canal Street…The brass downtown wanted me to put an end to it, and an end to Zulu. Remy was a real bad man who got on the list and cut a deal with Zulu. I tailed him, hoping he'd lead me to the Queen Bee. He introduced me to Zulu. There were many *Remys*, Dave. The list blossomed into something quite beautiful at first, then Zulu got greedy and put poison in his well."

"*Like me?*"

"That's what I love about you, Dave Stevens. After everything you've been through, you haven't lost that boyish charm," she replied. "You saw how much Remy and Eren were capable of stealing in one night. Zulu enabled them and many more like them, and he always received something back in return for his tips. We know about the heists, Dave. Mahone told us you took an equal share your first night out with them. Fucking elephants, huh? We're detectives, man, we're not friends on Myspace. You don't have to give back the shoes, the Ed Hardy T-shirt, or the fedora. You were an accessory, that's all. More like a car crash dummy if you ask me…"

"I lost the fedora," said Dave.

"You're better off. It's a stupid look," Trish replied with a smile.

"And Lorena?" asked Dave.

"A real friend. Met her at the museum. We get together often," Trish replied.

"You used her."

"She'll understand. She likes crazy stories."

"And me? I was followed…"

"*Of course.*"

Agent Manning shook hands with Trish and Andrews as he was leaving.

"Pleasure working with you again, Patterson. Let me know if anything else crosses any state lines. I've got a bunch of Feds chomping at the bit now that we have to bury one of our own," said Manning somberly. He then turned his attention to Dave. "Just do what they tell you to do, Stevens. Keep your nose clean. Being around you gives me the willies. I'm sure you're a nice kid and all, it just seems you're not getting the Lord's message. Get outta New York. Move somewhere far, far away, like, say, Saint Kitts and Nevis? Basseterre. My hometown. Small. Remote. Classy. Weather's always perfect. Then again, don't. Knowing your luck, the moment you ferry between those two godly islands of mine, they'll probably get hit with a Category 9 hurricane."

"I'll see you at the funeral, Manning," said Trish. "Again, I'm so sorry for your loss. It's ours, as well."

"It's what we do," replied Manning, as he left. "It's what we do. It's been Hell since September 11th, I'm sure you can relate, right, Stevens?"

Agent Andrews tossed the BlackBerry back to Dave. "Here you go! Catch!"

Dave caught the phone and looked at Andrews incredulously. "I don't want this."

"If you get any calls, Dave, you answer them. If you get a message, you reply," Andrews instructed.

"I can't do this. I can't," said Dave, mired in self-doubt.

"You prefer to go to jail? Or maybe you'd like to walk out of here and get killed, right?" said Andrews.

"I'm being tracked. They know where I am," said Dave.

"Affirmative," replied Andrews, "*exactly* where you are."

"Then I'm a sitting duck."

"No, my friend. Once again, you're a decoy. They're not going to do anything rash now that you've been out of their sights for hours. They know where you've been, they just don't know why you went to Yankee Stadium and then downtown to Battery Park. See? We confused them and bought ourselves some time. They hope you're still alone and scared, but they're on their heels at the moment and scared as well," said Andrews.

"Is that good or bad?" asked Dave, "What will they do next?"

"They're going to come for it, the BlackBerry, and they're going to try and kill you. You don't have any friends or family in the city. The only real friends you have are your landlord and those two weird lovebirds. I'm sorry, I don't mean to be insensitive, Dave. I know what you've been through. Most of my family is in the military. We've all been affected, but you have to be brave." Andrews tried the *relatable* route.

"I'm going to die again," said Dave, with resignation.

"You have to cooperate. I sent my team over to guard your apartment. When we drop you off there later, you'll be safe," Trish assured him, "but for now, we have to find Homeland's bad guys, and the only way to do that is to flush them out by letting them find you first."

"Patty's team saved your ass at Yankee Stadium. She'll have another ten squads just like them, and I'll have ten of my own, pulled up right in front of your door with an arsenal fit to kill a battalion if her forward team radios in and tells us your place is infested with those creeps. I can't wait to get that call. You just have to go home with that BlackBerry in your pocket and lay low. That's it. Go home, Dave. We'll have more agents on that block of yours than your landlord has chickens on your roof."

"My landlord? Who's my landlord? You know about Gigi's chickens, too?"

"Yeah. Gigi owns the chickens *and* the building as well, Dave. I think she also has a rabbit, definitely a cat." said Andrews.

"She owns the building??"

"Yup."

"Wow. "The cat is mine, by the way. Her name is Chuckles."

"We thought so. She goes in and out of the building through your kitchen window," replied Trish, "she's pretty cute!"

"Glad you think so," said Dave. "Where am I going from here?"

"You're getting out in front of this mess, Stevens," replied Andrews.

"You want me to be a rooster? A little, red rooster?" Dave quipped.

"He even has time for jokes, Patterson."

"Yeah, not funny, Dave. It's an NYPD operation at the moment Andrews, so I'll take the lead," said Trish. "The first thing we need to do is pay a visit to Zulu. Remy's address is on Zulu's emails, that will hold up in court. Zulu is not completely ethereal. I want to bring him in, book him, and shake him down, then I'll know where I finally stand with him. Zulu may be indirectly responsible for funding your terrorists here, Andrews. I've got him connected to Remy and Eren. He uses the code word *tribute* to collect hundreds of thousands, if not millions of dollars, in exchange for his party leads. Your jihadis may or may not have used his list, Andrews. I'm not sure if there's any proof to charge Zulu with a crime there."

"Billy said Zulu was one of your *girlfriends*. We were going to a *vernissage*. Remember that first night out? Free booze, a cool party," said Dave, reminiscing, "that's all it was supposed to be, nothing more."

Trish didn't feel like regurgitating the past.

"Are you saying I'm responsible for all this, Dave? Shut up and do what you are told to do! I'll get the cars," she replied, rather unsympathetically. "We're going to 18th and Broadway, near Warhol's Factory. Zulu lives there. Where else would you find him? Where else?" She radioed her squad. *"Joe Montana, Serpent Queen, and Bugs Bunny coming out front."*

"It felt like you and Zulu had been friends for years." said Dave.

"I'd been going to his parties for a while and yes, we grew close. I have to admit, at first, I really liked Zulu. He was always good to me and kind to so many people, really. It should help his case. I was hoping for a better outcome here," she replied, mournfully.

"I thought personal feelings don't get in the way of the law," said Dave. He understood her dilemma. Zulu's world had changed her, from Patty to Trish, and back again.

"If he gives me something here, anything, any little thing, I could then say he cooperated. At the very least, he'll have to kill the list, that is a non-starter," Trish insisted. She was delusional. Zulu's cult-like personality was hard to shake; all Trish could think about was the list.

"Once we're done talking with him, Patty and I are going to bust Zulu. We'll drop you off in the city afterwards," said Andrews, "Central Park. You're going for a walk in the park, Dave. We'll meet you over on the west side, and then we'll drive you back up to your place. Diversion."

"You're dropping me off? Just cutting me loose?" asked Dave, aghast, fearing for his safety.

"You'll be out in the open. They'd never shoot you out in the open. They'd never get close to the BlackBerry again. They know this. They'll track you down in the park soon enough, and then they'll follow you, and the phone, back to your apartment. My men are already stationed there and waiting for your arrival. We'll be with you every step of the way, Dave," Trish assured him, "like Andrews said, a walk in the park. It'll do you some good."

"*A walk in the park*," thought Dave, "*they make it seem so easy.*" He closed his eyes and drifted back to where it all began, the letter from McTier and Longley.

"You're going to New York City! You're going to New York City! Oh my God. David! It says *MLI, 2 World Trade Center, 80th floor*!" gushed Jane, his sister. "I am speechless. Oh my God... you did it, Dave! Mom! Mom!"

Chapter Twenty-One

"I'm going down, I'm going down, down, down, down, down, yes I've got my feet in the window, got my head on the ground."

—*Don Nix/Gabriel Lewis*

"Warrant secured?" asked Trish.

"Affirmative, Agent Patterson," the officer replied.

"Okay, kick that fucking door down!" she commanded.

"NYPD! WE HAVE A WARRANT! DO NOT MOVE! KEEP YOUR HANDS WHERE WE CAN SEE THEM!!"

With the force of a battering ram, Trish's team broke Zulu's front door off its mooring. A dozen men, armored and equipped, rushed in and focused their weapons' lasers on the giant.

There he laid, on a bed draped in champagne-colored silk sheets, covered in rose pedals. An extraordinary man, Zulu wasn't wearing any makeup or jewels, nor any fancy costumes to hide his enormous, fully-exposed frame. He'd been stripped of his dignity and crown. Zulu had a friend in bed with him when the police arrived, the noted Mafia-family prince, Paulie Vida. It was an odd surprise.

The task force had Zulu and Paulie surrounded. Trish and Agent Andrews stepped in. Trish had a few choice words to share with her new detainee that she'd been holding back for quite some time.

"Well, good morning to you, Teepee," said Zulu. "Thank you for not fuckin' knocking. I thought we were friends."

"*Teepee?*"

"I volunteer at the NMAI," Trish replied to her task force lead. "I don't really want to explain it to you. Don't call me Teepee. It's Agent Patterson."

"Sorry Tee, ma'am, um, Agent Patterson!" replied the officer.

"Agent Patterson? What the fuck is that? You Po-Po, Teepee? You 5-0?" asked Zulu with a deep, hearty laugh. "What you doin', Teepee?"

"Watch your mouth. That's Agent Patterson to you now. I've got a warrant to turn this place upside down Zulu, or should I say *Marty*? Martin Luther Smith. What a plain name for such a unique man. Yeah, well, your reign is over, Marty. We're going to take you in. You're going to tell us all about the list, how you got it, who's been receiving your emails..."

"You already know all that shit, bitch. I got nothing more to tell you," Zulu replied defiantly.

"Yeah, but you're going to tell it to us again, and again, and again if we ask you to, man. Our friends at the FBI had an officer killed because of that list of yours," said Andrews.

"I don't have anything to do with shit," Zulu insisted.

"Remy and your lover boy Eren are dead. We know that you emailed modified lists to different people for different reasons. You tip people off, Zulu. We planted agents at every single one of your events. That's why you and I were so close. Sure, you had good intentions, it all started out innocently enough, your little game, but you lost control, and now every free event in New York City is chock-full of thieves, pickpockets and worse. People got killed. Your friend Paulie's Mama took a pretty big hit last night, didn't she, Paulie? Robbed blind, she was. Maybe you had something to do with it, Paulie. You and Zulu. Your own family? *Really*?" said Trish.

"Hey! Keep my Mama and my family's name outta yer mouth!" Paulie cried, wrapping himself in a bed sheet.

"Arrest that *salsiccia*," said Trish. "I'm going to have a hell of a good time figuring out what to charge him with later."

"10-4," the lead officer replied. He cuffed Paulie and hustled him away.

"I don't know anything about no robberies or schemes," Zulu insisted. "I'm a promoter! I get paid to *promote*. Sometimes I charge, sometimes I don't, depends on the party. Some of them I list for free. They all get sponsored one way or another. Yo, you can seize my computer. Check my business records. Go open my safe. Clean as a whistle. Proper, like a Marine footlocker. My sugar daddy left me a lot of bread when he died. He also taught me plenty about accounting!"

Zulu's sarcasm was not appreciated.

"Cut the crap!" shouted Trish. "Let's talk about freely-distributed narcotics at your vernissage, *possibly to minors*?"
"What about them? Minors? Ha! What kind of bullshit are you trying to make up, Teepee?" replied Zulu, calmly. "Do they have you on camera doing blow with me, *Agent Patterson*?"

Andrews ran up and slugged Zulu in the mouth. "What's *tribute? Who pays you tribute?* What happens if they don't pay you??" he shouted.

"Whoa! Fuck you, man! Fuck you! Don't get handsy with me!" Zulu lunged at Andrews but he was restrained by the other officers present. "Tribute, ha! I want a lawyer!" he demanded.

"Come on, man. Relax. Don't violate his rights!" said Trish, pleading for Andrews to deescalate the situation. She pushed Andrews aside and continued to grill Zulu. "We're not stupid. Don't insult my intelligence. I know you, Zulu. I know who you know. People paid you for leads…"

"Nobody pays me shit!" insisted Zulu. "They aren't payments bitch, they're *thank yous*. I've saved more lives than you and your boys in blue ever will. People give me all kinds of things to show their appreciation for my help. Sometimes clothes, sometimes jewelry, sometimes hardcore, little Italian boy twinkie sex. I get anything I ask for, and it's free. Sometimes, it's cash money, baby. This is America. I organize shit. I move currents. People crave attention, they're naturally hedonistic. All I do is provide a roadmap to fun places where they can live out their fantasies, and you can get into to most of them for free. What a joke! People tip me off, willingly in fact. I shuffle information and put icing and sprinkles on it with a big spin. Yo, people hit me up all the time. They try and sell me on their bullshit events. They beg to be on my list. I refuse and they go wild. When they get down on their hands and knees, I put them on a list. A friggin' spam email. No big deal. They think it's special. They thank me. I throw a huge bash of my own every once in a while. They all get invited. I mysteriously show up at their events dressed out-fucking-rageously? They put me on a throne. There are hundreds of lists, but none of them get the press, the love and the attention like mine does; you know damn well, Teepee, everybody's got an angle, everybody wants something, everybody *needs* something. I just help them come out of their skin, let loose, be whoever they want to be, at least for a little while. People love a good party. You can relate, Teepee. I turned you. The record will show it. I'm sure the force approved of your often out-of-sorts behavior at my parties. Officers, she's got a real sexy little mouth on her when she's using it, right?"

Zulu mocked her, but Trish knew he had her just where he wanted her. She was compromised. The officers kept their lasers focused on Zulu as he stood up, dropped his bed sheet and revealed his shockingly large junk to them all.

"Yo, if none of you blue boys are gonna suck this, I'm getting the fuck out of here, man. Fuck this shit. You ain't got nothin' on me, Teepee."

Trish's pent-up anger came volcanically to a head. She unleashed herself on Zulu and punched him in the chest, thrusting him back down onto his bed. She then jumped on his naked body, sat on his chest, and placed her cold hands around his neck. Zulu couldn't breathe.

"Some homegrown terrorists got their hands on the fuckin' list, Zulu! They're just a few idiots from Jersey, Homeland has it under control, but they could have easily targeted a lot of innocent people! Families! Kids! For fuck's sake, Zulu!! Don't you even care??" she screamed.

Trish's officers pulled her off of Zulu. Clearly shaken by Zulu's demise, Trish put an end to a world that she loved, an underground party circuit full of music, people, food, drinks, freedom and no accountability. Trish got in way too deep, she didn't want to see it all come to an end. She couldn't forgive Zulu because sadly, tragically, people died because of his list. Zulu never did anything to stop any of it.

"Get dressed. Put on your jail suit, home-boy."

"Teepee, come on, girl. This ain't serious," said Zulu as he rose to his feet once again.

"Get the fuck down, you thug," said Trish. She slammed him to the ground, rolled him over on his stomach and pushed Zulu's face into the floor, bloodying his nose. "I don't think I'll ever be able to call you *Marty,* Zulu. The list is dead. Your parties are over. Cuff him."

"Yo! Nobody read me my Miranda! Yo! My rights, man! This shit here is unconstitutional!" said Zulu, laughing as they hauled him away.

And so, Zulu's reign as the Party King, or Queen if you will, of Manhattan, came to a nasty, bitter end. Wearing nothing more than a robe, Trish and her NYPD's finest escorted him away. As they were leaving, Zulu saw Dave sitting in the rear of a Suburban truck parked outside in front of the building.

"Yo! Trish. Will you let me have a word with my boy, Dave Stevens?" he asked. Trish was more than happy to oblige.

In chains, Zulu walked over to the truck.

"Hungry hippo," he said to Dave with a wink, "I had some serious plans for you, baby. But I'll see you again, Dave Stevens. I'll see you again."

"Zulu, thank you, man. You welcomed me into your world, you started a fire with just a spark. You reminded me how great it is to be alive. You helped me heal. I'm grateful and I promise, I won't forget you," Dave replied.

"You better not forget me, man. I told you, *starving little white boys* I keep as *amigos*," said Zulu with a mischievous smile.

Dave laughed, remembering Zulu's words quite well.

"Send me an email when you get out a jail. Like you said Zulu, *we cool, we cool*."

"Oh yeah, *we cool*, hungry hippo, *we cool*."

Chapter Twenty-Two

"I got a girl who lives up on the hill, I got a girl who lives up on the hill, talk she gonna love me, but I don't believe she will."

—*Elmore James*

Six burly, black Suburban trucks pulled up in front of the New York Athletic Club on West 59th Street facing South Central Park with great fanfare, simply to drop Dave off. It seemed rather heavy-handed to deploy such a big force, so much for subtlety; but maybe that was the point.

"You understand what *laying low* means, Dave?" asked Trish. She was less concerned for his safety than for the overall success of her operation. "You're just a small piece of the puzzle now. Stick to the plan and you'll be okay."

"The plan, huh? I feel like I'm going to die. I know that feeling all too well," Dave replied.

"Grow a pair, Dave. We didn't create this situation, you did," she replied. "We have eyes and ears on you now. The terrorists have obviously been following the signal. That's why we're dropping you off here in the park. They know you've been downtown. Now they think you're running back home because the signal is heading uptown. The perps assume you don't know where to go next. Home is where the heart is, they say. We think they're on their way back to your place. It's a game of chess Dave, not checkers. You'll walk around the park for a few hours. We'll make sure the area is clear, and if they are in Midtown, they'll follow you into the park. If they get close to you, we'll bust them."

"That's a big *if,* Trish. You don't know where they are, do you? They *might* be here in Midtown is what you are saying," said Dave, sensing he was truly vulnerable no matter what Trish promised.

"Enough, Dave! I've got boots on the ground here in the park and at your place. My team will protect you. There's no chance these guys would risk shooting you in broad daylight. I told you, walk around and breathe some fresh air, it will confuse them even more as to your whereabouts and give us enough time to set a trap so that Homeland can move in and eliminate the threat. We'll pick you up later at the entrance to the park near the Dakota. You know the place, right? Where John Lennon was shot? 72nd Street and Central Park West. It's near Strawberry Fields, I'll have an agent waiting for you there. I know you're frightened and exhausted. It'll all be over soon."

"If I catch these guys, it will be, in part, thanks to you. We'll probably save a lot of American lives today," said Andrews. "You're doing the right thing by co-operating, Dave. Serving your country. BlackBerry secured?"

"It's back in the same pocket where I put it in the first place," Dave replied.

"Like I said, the second you get a call, a text, you answer it and you contact me, copy that?" Andrews insisted. "Then we'll wait for them to make their next move."

"My guys are covering you like a blanket. Don't worry. When you get home, just stay out of their way, let them do their jobs. You're safe, Dave," Trish promised, "please trust the process."

Dave jumped out of the truck and looked across the street. There were horse-drawn carriages. They reminded him of the time he and Shawna went for a ride in one. It was the first *touristy* thing they'd ever done together, the classic carriage ride around the park. The good times they shared in Central Park were some of the only redeeming memories Dave had left of Shawna and their brief time spent as soul mates.

Trish sat in the passenger seat of the lead truck and listened to incoming dispatches while preparing her squad to proceed. She rolled down her window and offered Dave a few final words of encouragement. "Just have faith," she said. "We got you this far. You can count on us. Don't forget. The Dakota. 72nd Street and Central Park West."

"How will I know who your agent is?" asked Dave.

"He'll look at you and say, *Give peace a chance.*"

"Trish, I probably won't see you again," said Dave glumly.

"I can't say it was a pleasure to meet you," Trish replied with a frown, "take care of yourself, Dave. God made you go through all this shit for a reason. You're Teflon, bulletproof, maybe indestructible. It was fun until it wasn't. You're a decent guy, but I'll repeat myself, I sure as hell wouldn't want to be you, Dave Stevens, I wouldn't want to be you."

As the cavalcade of Suburbans pulled away, Dave crossed the street and bought an ice cream cone. "Lay low. They've got eyes on me everywhere, covering me like a blanket. Just let them do their jobs, a walk in the park."

He strolled down 59th Street onto East Drive and passed through the Central Park Zoo. It reminded him of a crazy day spent there with Shawna and Lester. All hell broke loose when Lester started feeding the lemurs hash brownies. Lester was always up for a riot. Dave and Shawna stayed back as the zookeepers chased Lester from the place.

Dave moved onward, to Sheep Meadow, where he laid down and closed his eyes. He retraced the steps and missteps that led to his current sad state of affairs. Trish was right about walking in the park; it calmed his nerves and it helped Dave focus on the good times. Good memories were all he had when he was in critical condition, but they gave him strength and the will to live, and now they gave him the courage to persevere. Dave knew he had to go back uptown and face the music, there was no avoiding it.

He continued his journey and arrived at Tavern on the Green, an infamous New York City restaurant and landmark. Dave fondly remembered the time he and Shawna attended a wedding there. That whole affair was a sham, déclassé in every way. Shawna never understood why she'd been invited to the wedding in the first place, she barely knew the bride, a girl from high school, a friend of a friend. Shawna was a bridesmaid. Why? That was perplexing.

The bride was a hippie chick, a deadhead, a psychotic vegan. She married a greaser dude, a stripped-down Mick Jagger impersonator. A couple of days after the affair, Shawna was informed that the couple's marriage had been annulled. The wedding was akin to a Woody Allen film. Dave remembered having such a great time. Shawna looked so beautiful in her bridesmaid's gown that day.

The rendezvous with the NYPD was at hand, so Dave scurried, as instructed, to Strawberry Fields. Nothing seemed real. A bus had just emptied. Dozens of tourists from China had stopped by to take pictures of a group of Krishna musicians. The Krishnas sat in a circle, equipped with their harmonium, drum and kartal cymbals. They were accompanied by a bearded busker who wore *Panto 45* glasses and played a Gibson acoustic guitar. The tourists threw change into the busker's guitar case as he belted out a version John Lennon's *Imagine*. When the ensemble finished playing the song, the crowd cheered wildly. The busker, pleased with how warmly he'd been received, offered to take requests.

"For my next number, I'd like to ask for your help. The people who come here daily, just clap your hands. And the rest of you who got off the bus, if you'd just rattle your jewelry," the busker joked. "No, seriously… any song you'd like to hear?"

"Revolution!" Dave shouted.

"That's a bit much," said the busker. "I ain't got an electric, Bobby Dylan! Gimme me some truth, an easy one, so everybody can sing along. Anyone?"

The busker looked back at Dave and winked. *"Give Peace a Chance?"*

Dave nodded approvingly.

The busker pointed toward the park exit, the one that led to Central Park West. "This one's for you, brother. War is over if you want it. Everybody now! All we are saying, is … ???"

"Give peace a chance!" the crowd replied.

Dave listened contently as the busker, the Krishnas and the crowd chanted in unison. Peace was something that had eluded Dave. It would have been nice to have some peace for a change, but Dave wasn't worried, he knew peace was coming.

The black, bulletproof Suburban truck was waiting for Dave at the exit, just as Trish promised it would be, across the street from the Dakota building, John Lennon's last home. The Dakota made Dave think about his courageous father. John Lennon was assassinated by a crazed fan in front of the place. Dave's dad loved the Beatles. Dave grew up listening to them on his dad's 8-track player. His dad told him that the Beatles' music saved him from losing his mind when he was in Vietnam. "John Lennon's murder was the greatest act of insanity in the history of modern man," he told Dave, "if you're ever there, in New York City, go up to his place and say a prayer for me there."

"Strawberry Fields. The Dakota. Look dad! Pretty groovy, huh? You know it's gonna be, alright, alright, alright. Amen."

Dave boarded the truck feeling quite mortal.

"Bugs Bunny is in the batter's box," radioed the officer. *"No sign of Yosemite Sam or Elmer Fudd."*

"Alright boys, get him home," radioed Trish. "Dave? You there?"

"Yes."

"A promise is a promise. They're going to drop you off a block down from your place," said Trish, "the forward team will take it from there."

"A promise is a promise," Dave thought. He kept his promises. The officers gave him no reason to think Trish couldn't keep hers.

Gigi had a pot of Thai shrimp prepared for Dave. She felt guilty that she had given him a hard time about his clothes and the sudden, drastic change in his social life. Perhaps it was time for her to give him a little space, but she was worried about losing her friend. In Dave's darkest moments, Gigi's food and kindness comforted him. She never asked for anything back, all she ever wanted to do was heal Dave's soul. She found a way to do that through her cooking. If she'd been a bit nasty to him in the past, a pot of shrimp usually smoothed things over.

It was late in the afternoon. Gigi was certain Dave had little to eat for dinner; she knew he never had food in his fridge. She thought she heard him come home, so she crossed the hallway with her large, steaming shrimp pot peace offering, hoping to make amends. She noticed that his door was ajar and that both the lock and the door handle had been smashed.

Chuckles stayed in Gigi's doorway and licked shrimp sauce off her whiskers.

"Dave Stevens! Dave Stevens! What happened to my door??! Hurry! Hurry! I have food for you! It's heavy and hot!" she hollered.

There was no response, so Gigi kicked the door open not-so-gently as she'd always done before and she walked in, only to gasp in fright.

She found two dead New York City police officers swimming in pools of their own blood on Dave's living room floor. A man wearing sunglasses sat on Dave's couch. He held a machine gun and was smoking a cigarette. Another man, bald and tall, stood by his side. He was armed as well, but his choice of weapon was a hand gun.

Terrified, Gigi dropped the pot of shrimp. The steamy contents fell to the floor and scattered like a breached dam.

Before she could scream for help, a third man appeared from behind the apartment door. He struck Gigi on the back of her head with the butt of his gun, knocking her unconscious.

Chapter Twenty-Three

"Police and thieves in the street, oh yeah, scaring the nation with their guns and ammunition, police and thieves in the street, oh yeah, fighting the nation with their guns and ammunition, from Genesis to Revelation, the next generation will be, hear me."

—*Lee Perry/Junior Murvin*

"*Releasing Bugs Bunny out into the wild. Team Two will check in once Bugs Bunny goes back down his rabbit hole,*" radioed the officer.

"*10-4 that, thank you.*" replied Trish. "Goodbye, Dave Stevens..."

"Goodbye, *Patricia*..."

"Funny, Dave."

Dave found himself in a familiar spot once again, standing in the middle of the road. His apartment building stood on his right side, and the bodega to his left.

The sun always set on Gigi's building, gracing it with a pinkish hue, the type of pink only seen in Petra or Jaipur. Gargoyles, magnificently-detailed demons, centaurs with lutes, and skulls, had been carved into the stones of the apartment building's entrance. As inviting as any heritage building could be, Gigi's *heaven* was a magnificent sight for

Dave's sore eyes, but the comforts of home didn't help, his senses were tingling.

Trish and Andrews were crystal clear with their instructions: go *directly* to the apartment and wait. Dave hadn't eaten a thing since he got sick in Jersey, nor had he slept in quite some time. Weak and famished, he walked into the bodega instead of sticking to the plan. Dave desperately needed a cool beverage, his favorite, peach Snapple and, of course, he had to buy cat food for Chuckles.

The tape used by the police to cordon off the bodega was long gone. It had only been a few short hours since he'd murdered the homeless man, but there he was nonetheless, Dave's stiff, cold, unfriendly Chinese adversary, back at his post behind the cash register. That's what the shopkeeper did, he murdered the man. The videotape evidence and the law didn't see it that way, but that's what it was, though, a murder.

Dave picked up a can of cat food for Chuckles. For some reason, in the midst of it all, Chuckles' cat food was Dave's biggest priority. He then took a bottle of peach Snapple iced tea out of the refrigerator, popped it open and chugged it down swiftly. The cool, flavorful beverage soothed every nerve in his body, but his relief was shattered by the shopkeeper.

"No eating! No drinking! Pay first! You pay now! You pay now or I'll call the cops!" the shopkeeper shouted. He rose up from his stool and proudly displayed a large firearm on his thigh. Why was this sadistic man still permitted to openly carry a firearm was anybody's guess.

VVVVRRRROOOOMMM!!!
SSSMMMMMAAASSSSHHH!!!!!!

Dave exploded.

"You're going to pull a gun on me?? Do you know what *this* is? It's a can of cat food. It's for my furry little friend across the street named Chuckles. *This?* This is a bottle of fuckin' Snapple! My favorite drink on earth!!! Nobody should fuckin' die for a bottle of cold ice tea!!! Me? I'm Dave! Dave Stevens! I walk in here *every fucking day*. I've paid you for every goddamn can of cat food and Snapple I've ever bought here! No credit! Not even a fuckin' nickel!! You want to kill me for that, you *sick motherfucker*??"

Dave pulled out all the cash he had left and threw it at the shopkeeper. He took a big gulp from the Snapple, finished its contents, and threw the bottle against the wall. It shattered into a million pieces. He shoved the can of cat food into the shopkeeper's face, hoping to elicit a response from the man. The shopkeeper showed no emotion.

"You cold piece of shit! Just once, *once,* you could have said *thank you, have a nice day!*" Dave shouted, "Keep the change, you fucking animal …"

Dave put the cat food in his pocket and stormed out of the bodega, leaving a trail of bills in his wake.

"*Thank you. Have a nice day*," said the shopkeeper, quite insincerely. He sat down on his stool and turned his attention back to the cowboys and Indians on his TV behind the counter, still keeping a keen eye on Dave.

The shopkeeper obviously wanted another confrontation, having clearly enjoyed killing a man. The shopkeeper was bloodthirsty and wanted to kill again. Dave was furious but he wasn't going to push it. At the end of his rope, Dave just let it go and walked away. There was no place like home.

"Just close your eyes and click your feet three times, Dave Stevens, and soon, you'll be home. There's no place like home."

Dave wasn't a fighter, a thief or murderer. He sure as hell wasn't any good at party crashing, and his pre-destined success on Wall Street never came to fruition. He was *everyman*, Dave Stevens, a nondescript guy from Pennsylvania who, like so many others before him, came to the Big Apple to live out his dream.

9/11.

Things just didn't work out.

It was time to move on.

Babe Waxman didn't tell him anything he didn't know already. Moving back to West Mifflin and tucking himself away in a small strip mall was a sound plan. It was time to return to his roots. Dave had nothing to feel ashamed about, he didn't fail in New York, New York failed him.

Dave received a text message on the BlackBerry just as Agent Andrews had predicted he would. Everything was going according to the plan.

"Give it back. We have you in our sight. Give it back now."

Andrews told Dave to contact him as soon as he received a message. Trish promised Dave he'd be safe. Her officers were stationed inside his apartment, put there to protect him. Dave was in the middle of the road again, but this time he was somewhere in between presumed safety and the scope of a gun.

The Blackberry buzzed. Another message.

This time, they sent a photo. It was a picture of Gigi. She had been abducted and was tied to Dave's living room chair. Her mouth had been covered with thick, silver industrial tape. Her clothes were bloody, her eyes gaping in fear. A man stood behind her with his gun pointed at her temple. At her feet? Two dead NYPD officers.

Dave just wanted to go home, to his coma home, the place in Scarsdale. It was his *heaven*. His daughters were there. Shawna helped him raise a flag every morning. He took a sip from the cup of coffee she'd given him. Dave picked up the morning newspaper from his doorstep, looked up at the sky, saluted the memory of his father, and walked down the driveway to move the tricycle away from the back of his Volvo. It was always the same.

Home.

Shawna was dead.

Dave's *heaven* wasn't real.

"Just close your eyes and click your feet three times, Dave Stevens, and soon, you'll be home. There's no place like home."

This wasn't Oz.

None of this would ever go away. It would follow Dave for the rest of his life. The FBI, Homeland Security, agents Manning and Andrews, Trish, Zulu, Remy, Eren, the list? They would always be a part of his story, a story that began with his death and one that would end with his desire to simply feel alive again.

If Dave didn't act immediately, Gigi would die.

It was too late to call Trish and Andrews. Their advance team was dead and their additional forces would never arrive in time to save Gigi. If and when they did arrive, things were going to get messy and innocent people were going to die in an ensuing gun battle. His loving neighbor Gigi would be the first casualty.

Collateral damage was inconsequential to Trish and Andrews, they knew the assailants weren't taking hostages. The young jihadis were on a mission of martyrdom, to destroy the infidels. This wasn't about the BlackBerry for them anymore, it was about impressing their masters and receiving 70 virgins in heaven, but they weren't going to kill anybody else until they had Dave and the phone back in their possession. What they didn't know, was that their terrorist *sugar daddies* had already disowned them and that they were going to die for nothing.

The weight on Dave's shoulders buckled him to his knees, but it didn't break him. There are times in life when the right thing is the only thing to do.

Thump! Thump! Thump! Thump! Ptoo! Ptoo!

The music.

Thump! Thump! Thump! Thump! Ptoo! Ptoo!

That first night out.

"I may seem a bit meek, Davey Boy, but I love to dance! I love to lose my shit!" screamed Trish.

Trish knew everyone.

Thump! Thump! Thump! Thump! Ptoo! Ptoo!

Fight Club.

"Oh! You are sad little pup! You're hungry, aren't you, Dave?" Trish knew full well that Dave hadn't eaten much that week.

"Yes, I am!" he shouted back unashamedly.

"Okay, you get a bite! I'll go say hello to a few friends. I'll be back!"

Trish knew Dave was weak and susceptible. She used him. He owed her nothing, but he owed Gigi everything. Gigi was his sister, mother, friend, and the purest, warmest human being he'd ever met. Trish and Andrews couldn't keep their promises. Her officers were dead, and there was no back-up in sight. The next text message that Dave received sealed the deal pretty much.

"You have 60 seconds to get up here and return the BlackBerry or we'll blow her brains out."

VVVVRRRROOOOMMM!!!
SSSSMMMMMAAASSSSHHH!!!!!!

Chapter Twenty-Four

"Sitting in the stands of the sports arena, waiting for the show to begin, red lights, green lights, strawberry wine, a good friend of mine, follow the stars, Venus and Mars are alright tonight."

—-Paul McCartney

"Can you hear me?? Can anybody hear me, man?? Jesus. Are you people even alive?? Can you walk?? Get the fuck outta there!!! Now!!! Go to the stairwell…"

It was a 12-step climb up from the vestibule to the 2nd-floor apartments. Gigi heard every step and every creak in the building when Dave tiptoed in late at night, so she knew someone was coming. The man who held her at gunpoint didn't notice a thing, nor did his cohorts. Gigi had resigned herself to the possibility that she could die at any moment, so she closed her eyes, chanted and prayed.

"*Namo Amida Buddha. Namo Amida Buddha.*"

Thump! Thump! Thump! Thump! Ptoo! Ptoo! Thump! Thump! Thump! Thump! Ptoo! Ptoo!

"Oh, Dave, I get invited to these silly things all the time. I get so many emails and invitations; I can go to a party every single night of the week if I want. I go out a lot! I meet different people. I can be anyone I want to be. Don't get out much, do you, Dave?"

"Namo Amida Buddha. Namo Amida Buddha."

*Thump! Thump! Thump! Thump! Ptoo! Ptoo!
Thump! Thump! Thump! Thump! Ptoo! Ptoo!*

Unarmed, frail, and at his rock bottom, Dave knocked on his broken apartment door and walked in slowly, with his hands up. It was his only option. He was overwhelmed by the stench of Gigi's shrimp and the dead bodies. There, he found Gigi, bound and gagged, with two armed men at her sides.

"Namo Amida Buddha. Namo Amida Buddha."

The apparent ringleader lounged on Dave's couch. He took his sunglasses off and perched them on his forehead. Casually smoking a cigarette, he looked as if he didn't have a care in the world considering he had an Uzi machine gun on his lap.

One of his henchmen cocked his gun and readied it to fire at Gigi, while the other accomplice pointed his gun at Dave. Their mastermind, the one Mary had referred to as *Ahmed*, held court and took his time, in no rush to end his final stand. His partners had already murdered Remy, Eren, Agent Mahone and two NYPD officers, so they knew their lives were possibly coming to an end as well, but their leader Ahmed intended on going out in a blaze of glory. He'd been influenced by a combination of hardcore indoctrination in Pakistan, and having watched *Scarface* and *Goodfellas* too many times back home in West Orange.

"Give me the fucking BlackBerry, infidel," Ahmed demanded, as he took a drag from his cigarette. He sat back and folded his arms behind his head. "Now!!!"

"I will," said Dave, "but you have to let her go."

The gunmen laughed at him, but then Ahmed grew quite agitated. He grabbed his Uzi, stood up, threw his cigarette to the ground and crushed it into Dave's carpet with his bootheel. He then jutted out his chin in anger and sat back down. Ahmed pulled his glasses down over his eyes and gently placed the Uzi back on his lap, caressing the machine gun like a baby. He stared at Dave like a man who existed somewhere between life and death, a place Dave knew all too well.

"Oh? You want to cut a deal? Fuck you, man. Give me back my phone," demanded Ahmed. "We're not letting anyone go. Her. You. Everyone is gonna die. America doesn't care about my people, why should I care about you? You think any Americans care when your president drops a million pounds of ordinance on the women and children of our Uma? You tell me, Dave Stevens, why is it okay to steal our oil and it is not okay for brother bin Laden's disciples to fly airplanes into the World Trade Center buildings? Were all those people in the Trade Center innocent? They were all infidels and deserved to die, as do you. Now, give me back my BlackBerry, you pickpocketing motherfucker!"

Dave kept his eyes on Gigi. He reached into his pocket and gently removed what he thought was the BlackBerry, but rather, it was the can of cat food he'd bought for Chuckles at the bodega.
"What? Are you fuckin' kidding me??!" hollered Ahmed, "Blow that bitch's brains out!! Now!!"

"No! No! Don't shoot! Don't shoot! Wrong pocket!"

Dave reached back into his jacket pocket and quickly pulled out the BlackBerry. He tossed it onto his couch knowing full well that the text messages it contained were about to change everything.

The assailants smiled, their mood shifting from anger to relief now that they had secured their device. Why they cared so much about the BlackBerry altogether was anybody's guess; it was just a phone. Youth is surely wasted on the young.

Ahmed scrolled through the messages. His complexion turned to a shade of grey and his jaw began to tremble when he read that he'd been abandoned. All that he and his stooges had done in the name of their own perverted version of Islam was for naught. As he re-read the texts a final time, Ahmed's eyes welled up with tears; he was paralyzed. He and his henchman had served no purpose on this earth other than to kill people, some innocent, some not. Their *jihad* had come to an end.

Chuckles darted through the kitchen window. She jumped off the counter and into the fray of Thai shrimp and terrorists. She startled the assailants, just as she had done to Dave so many times before.

Shaken and rattled by Chuckles' sudden appearance, Ahmed, the leader, panicked. He jumped up from his seat on the couch and his Uzi, the machine gun he had sitting grandly on his lap, fell to the floor. Dave dove to the ground, grabbed the Uzi, closed his eyes, and squeezed the damn trigger with all his might. Bullets sprayed around the apartment like they were coming out of a garden hose. Dave kept on squeezing the trigger until the machine gun's magazine was empty.

VVVVRRRRRROOOOMMM!!!!
SSSSSSMMMMMAAAASSSSSHHHHHHH!!!!!!

Dave heard every violent sound.

His body felt as if it had been pierced by a giant glass dagger once again. He had visions of Ellery, Shawna, Lester, Trish, Zulu, Remy, Erin, Mahone, Andrews, Manning, the geishas, the elephants, the safe house, the phones, the purses, the money and jewelry, his new office at McTier and Longley, the boardroom, the plane coming right for it…

VVVVRRRRRROOOOMMM!!!!
SSSSSSMMMMMAAAASSSSSHHHHHHH!!!!!!

And then, *that* silence.

Dave remembered *that* silence.

Chuckles sat on top of one of the deceased officers' chests. She nestled herself around his badge. She was eating some shrimp, content in all her glory as she suddenly had an unlimited supply of her favorite meal at her disposal.

Dave's entire apartment was riddled with bullet holes. Five men were dead, but Gigi, miraculously, was safe and anxious for her odd, but loving neighbor to release her.

Dave, uninjured, stood up slowly and took a look around at the warzone he used to call *home*. The tingling in his body and the ghosts of 9/11? They used to be his kryptonite, but now they served as his shield.

Gigi's eyes smiled as Dave gently removed the industrial tape from her mouth. He caressed her cheek and gave her a gentle kiss on her forehead. Love. True friendship. Friends are always there for one another. She never let him down. He finally came through for her.

"Are you okay?" asked Dave, crying as he untied her hands and feet.

"Dave Stevens, your apartment is a mess. When are you going to clean this place up?"

Chuckles licked her paws and whiskers and darted out the kitchen window. She was on her way up to the roof where the real party was going on.

An army of officers from the NYPD and Homeland Security soon arrived. They crashed into Dave's apartment with their hands on the triggers of their guns.

"NYPD! DON'T MOVE!! KEEP YOUR HANDS WHERE WE CAN SEE THEM!!"

"Dave, are these your new friends, the ones that I don't know, that I've never met?"

"No, Gigi. You and Chuckles are my only real friends, you know that."

Chapter Twenty-Five

"Our love was like the water, that splashes on a stone, our love is like our music, it's here, and then it's gone, so take me to the airport, and put me on a plane. I got no expectations, to pass, through here, again."

—*Mick Jagger/Keith Richards*

"Suzanne, have you seen my phone anywhere?"

"Yes, Mr. Stevens. You left it here with me at reception when your earlier appointment, Mr. Phillips, arrived. Mr. Waxman is here to see you! I can't believe it, Dave!" Suzanne replied.

"Oh. Okay. Just hold on to it for me. I can't believe Babe is here either, *for real*, not on Zoom..."

Dave was excited. It had been almost a year since the men had seen each other in the flesh. The fact that Babe was standing in the lobby of WSC Corp, a place he rarely visited anymore, was a really shocking.

"What are you doing here?" asked Dave. "You never come into the city, let alone the office anymore. This is a nice surprise."

"I know 9/11 is a tough day for you, son. The years just fly by. Can't believe it's already been decades; it seems like just yesterday. I thought, on one hand, David might be at some memorial today, but my instincts told me otherwise, and they were right. Here you are, working away. It's why I put you in charge, David," Babe replied, "Waxman, *Stevens* and Calais."

Dave had just finished interviewing a recruit in the boardroom and he felt like showing him off to his wise, old, senior partner.

"Babe, let me introduce WSC's latest draft pick, Mr. Joshua Phillips, a *Wharton* grad," said Dave proudly, elbowing the young, fresh prospect.

"That's just Jo, not Joshua. Jo. Jay. Oh. No *E*. Jo. *Jo Phillips*. It's a pleasure to meet you, Mr. Waxman. You're a legend," said the brash junior, extending his hand steadfastly.

Babe crushed the kid's hand with his grip, so much so, Jo Phillips flinched.

"Yeeooww!"

"Impressive," said Babe, "where do you come from, son?"

"Whoa, um, Cherry Hill born, sir. Grew up in Philadelphia. My father was a Wharton grad, as well. You may have heard of him? Sam Phillips? No? Not the Elvis producer, Sam Phillips. That guy is probably old enough to be my great-grandfather. No sir, my father Sam worked at Saxon and Gold before they went bankrupt in '08. His boss was Sharon Saxon? He didn't go to jail like she did, my father only lost his license for a while," said Jo.

"Saxon and Gold huh? That's rather unfortunate, son," said Babe, unimpressed by the boy's pedigree.

"My dad? He was a *top-five,* alright, but he was a No. 3. I'm a No. 1: top of my class, better than my dad."

"Oh, that is special then..." Babe smiled at Dave.

"Yeah, my dad had it rough growing up, small town and all," said Jo, still grimacing from Babe's unexpected, powerful handshake. "He tucked all his hard work away in the Caymans back in 2007. My sister and I had a proper upbringing, you know, in a *good neighborhood.* Our home is pretty luxurious, mom being an interior decorator and all. I was given all the tools I needed to succeed here at your company, sir, all I really had to do was study a little; I never had to *work*, per se. MLI will be my first and only job, once you say I'm hired. Two generations from Wharton. Just tell me where my office is, *right?*"

"City boy, huh?" Babe leered over at Dave. "Nice kid, Stevens."

"Legacy pick, Babe. Better than *top-five*; he's a #1."

Babe had enough.

"Josh..."

"Jo. Just Jo, sir. Jay. Oh. No *E.* Jo."

"Yes, well, *Jay-Oh*... Could you excuse us? Mr. Stevens and I will review your file. It's been a slice meeting you. Go to reception and see Suzanne. She'll hook you up with a bottle of *exquisite* Chinese rice wine on your way out. Don't worry, it's free," said Waxman, "our *special* clients have been enjoying it for years."

"When do I start?" asked Phillips.

Waxman ushered the recruit to the door. "Like I said son, ask Suzanne to put you down for a *call back*. She'll fix your *spelling*." He smiled at Dave, enjoying the moment as no else could.

"You know I invested a lot of energy *and* resources vetting that kid Jay-Oh, right?" joked Dave, "That Chinese rice wine…it's the kiss of death. I'm calling that boy back next week, Babe. I'm going to hire him. It's *his time*."

Dave was disappointed but not at all surprised by Babe's quick dismissal of his *top-five* candidate. Waxman had the ability to see right through most people from the moment he met them, but he could never get a clear read on Dave, and his vision wasn't what it used to be.

"Ahhh, you must see something in that kid that I don't. I trust you. Maybe it's just me making the same mistake with that kid that I made with you all those years ago. You once crawled in here. Crawled. You didn't get a prince's welcome like that pompous, rotten kid. I didn't think you were worth a dime." said Babe. "But I took a long, hard look at you and where you came from that day and I knew that if I passed on you, you'd survive, probably flourish. I couldn't figure out for the life of me what it was about you. I was scared you'd come back to bite me in the ass one day. I tried to crush you that first day we met, I tried so hard, but I couldn't do it. Looking back, I was an angry man, I was saddened by what had happened to my friends, colleagues, innocent people, the marketplace. The world has never been the same, David. After all you've been through, it's easy to see why Ellery took you under his wing. Look at us now. It's your time. This kid you brought in? He's a city boy. Soft. Can't be top-five *and* a city boy. You taught me that."

"How long are you in town?" asked Dave, so pleased to see his dear friend. A get-together with Babe had become such a rare occurrence.

"Aww, just until tonight. I'll fly back to West Palm later. The wife has an artsy-fartsy event in the Hamptons this afternoon. I'm skipping it. I hate those bullshit parties; I'd rather spend time with you."

"Let's go out for lunch, Babe. Uptown. Gigi's. Like old times. You know her Thai shrimp is still the best on earth! She hasn't seen you in years."

Suzanne, the WSC receptionist, vied for Dave's attention as he and Babe were leaving the office for the day.

"Mr. Stevens, Dee called. She left the city and will meet you back in Scarsdale tonight, *after* she picks up the girls. She told me to remind you to pass by the Volvo dealership on your way home. Your car is ready. The dents and the paint on the back bumper have all been repaired."

"Perfect, Suzanne. Call her back and leave a message; she never picks up her phone. Just tell her Babe and I went uptown for lunch. She'll know where," Dave replied. "No interruptions. Tell her I'm *disappearing*."

"Oh, and, um, Mr. Stevens? There's a *Mr. Martin Luther Smith* on the line. He's called several times. He'd like to know if you received a *list* that he sent you? A certain *Zulu* file?"

"He knows how to reach me. Tell him to send me an email and I'll take it from there. *We cool?*" said Dave, with a chuckle.

"Oh! *We cool,* Mr. Stevens. Um...*sir?*"

"Yes, Suzanne?"

"Don't forget your BlackBerry..."

Acknowledgements

This book is dedicated to people who love unconditionally, specifically the first responders and all those who perished in the course of trying to save their fellow human beings on 9/11.

I want to thank my editor, David Winch, a man who asked all the right questions and made my story better.

Many friends and family members from all over the globe buoyed my spirits as I wrote *I Love A Good Party*. Without them, it could have never evolved into the story that it is today. To you, I am eternally grateful.

Each chapter begins with a song quote. I like to incorporate a soundtrack into my stories. I encourage you to reach out and listen to the songs listed here as you read along, *gold rekkids* every one of them.

I appreciate you, dear reader. I hope you enjoyed this story.

Stick a.k.a. Johnnie Reisler

Manufactured by Amazon.ca
Bolton, ON

39276867R00188